S'WANEE

A PARANOID THRILLER

DON WINSTON

TIGERFISH

S'WANEE

A PARANOID THRILLER

Cover design: Stewart A. Williams
stewartwilliamsdesign.com
Cover photograph: © Alex S. MacLean/Landslides

ISBN: 0615770576
ISBN 13: 9780615770574

For My Parents

Author's Note

"S'wanee" is the literary doppelganger of Sewanee, the University of the South, high in the Tennessee hills. Growing up in Nashville, I was vaguely aware of it as a child. As an adult, I paid a visit to "the Domain" not so long ago, and I can only suggest you add it to your list of places to see before you die. Perhaps you'll understand why it has inspired so many poems and stories and loyalties, or why Teddy Roosevelt declared, "I believe in Sewanee with all my heart." Or why Tennessee Williams, himself a passing visitor, bequeathed his literary estate to the school.

And perhaps you'll understand why a realm this magical and spellbinding and perfect demands a doppelganger—an evil twin, if you will—just to keep the world in balance.

Although the following story is fictional, it is riddled with real-life places, histories, and happenings. I leave it to the reader to speculate which are which.

Summer

Chapter One

Seventeen-year-old high school senior Cody Marko had already sent his freshman deposit to Rutgers University when the purple and white envelope arrived, blindly, from a school called S'wanee.

Like introduction letters from other colleges (Oberlin, University of Alabama, Pomona), this one arrived with a separate letter addressed to his parent or legal guardian.

But unlike the others, this one arrived very late. In June.

"That's a slow school," his mother Marcie barked, crushing out her just-got-home cigarette on their apartment's balcony. Cody didn't let her smoke in the apartment or in the white Toyota Camry they shared. Most days, when their work schedules synced, he drove them back from the Brunswick Square Mall in East Brunswick, New Jersey—Cody at the Apple Store and Marcie at Macy's. After eight hours, she still looked immaculate in her white Clinique lab coat. She always looked immaculate. She was not yet forty.

Cody had graduated high school in May and had settled on Rutgers for a variety of reasons, mostly financial. It was cheap for New Jersey residents, they offered interest-free student loans, and he could live at home. He'd major in computer programming, schedule classes early in the day, and keep his job at the Genius Bar at the Apple store, evenings and weekends.

But mostly he couldn't leave Marcie alone. In spite of living three years in this "temporary" city and "temporary" apartment, Marcie had few friends in East Brunswick and hadn't had a steady boyfriend since the one who'd lured them here had drifted away. She'd met him in Palo Alto, California, where he was traveling on business. On the cosmetics floor at Macy's, where she worked. Shortly after, Marcie got a transfer, packed up Cody and moved them east to New Jersey. She hadn't stopped to think about whom he'd been shopping for on the cosmetics floor. Marcie rarely thought these things through.

That's how they'd ended up in Palo Alto when Cody was nine and East Brunswick when he was fifteen. That's why Cody couldn't leave her alone.

Marcie liked meeting men "on business," and she made a habit of it. "They have a job important enough to fly them around," she explained when Cody was old enough to ask about his own father. "If they're *happily* married, I steer clear. I'm not a monster. But men who buy perfume for their wives are not happily married. What an ignorant thing to buy a woman."

She'd met Cody's father on a plane from London to Sofia, when she was a flight attendant. "First class," she always reminded Cody. "Where they put the youngest and prettiest."

She'd transferred and followed him to Chicago on a temporary work visa. They never married, but she gave birth to Cody, all she needed to stay in the United States for good. She'd given him her last name. Soon after, she followed another man to Walnut Creek, outside Oakland, whom she was married to for three years. Cody vaguely recalled him.

After her divorce, she speared a boyfriend in Palo Alto, but they never married either. They got stranded in East Brunswick after the boyfriend she'd followed from the Palo Alto Macy's—"the ONE," Marcie initially claimed—had drifted away. "We'll blow this joint soon," she'd been telling Cody for two and a half years. But quality men didn't travel to East Brunswick "on business," and lacking a bead elsewhere, Marcie stayed in a restless holding pattern as Cody grew up through high school. And she neared forty.

Cody's above-average SAT score surprised him, since he'd taken it raw. He couldn't afford a prep course, and the practice tests in his school's library were outdated and marked-up. Several colleges sent him letters and brochures, but none offered scholarships, except a potential-maybe tease from the University of Alabama, seeking geographical "diversity." The others simply wanted his business. He didn't respond to any of them.

He had dreamed of NYU and living in Manhattan, but without a scholarship it wasn't doable. He didn't let himself even dream of Princeton. His scores weren't good enough, and he was "unaccomplished," at least according to the free online survey his school counselor had recommended. Cody had settled on cheap and functional and close to Marcie's apartment. It was only college, after all.

Rutgers was familiar, with its office park campus and satellite branches with thousands of students who seemed like his high school classmates—not surprising, since most of those who did go to college went there. But that wasn't a lure, since Cody had few high school friends, thanks to his late start. Friendships were set by the time he'd arrived sophomore year.

Plus, he was more than a year younger than his classmates, having just turned seventeen in January. He'd always been the youngest in his class, and Marcie couldn't remember why she'd started him early. "It didn't seem early for you," she said. "You were just very advanced, I guess." It was typical of Marcie not to think about these things, or think they mattered much.

He was a better-than-average student and ran cross-country when he could and wrote two articles for the school paper his first year, but he didn't buy a class ring or yearbook and didn't keep up with anyone on Facebook after graduation day.

His on-again, off-again girlfriend Kimberly had graduated the year before. Her parents were wealthy, and she went to Syracuse. She'd met someone else the first semester, which she informed Cody in a text. That bothered him for three long weeks, but he knew instinctively it was an unimportant pain that wouldn't matter at all once he was older. Nothing bothered Cody for very long. He got that from his mother.

Unlike Cody, however, Marcie wore her resilience on her face. She constantly beamed a dazzling and joyful smile of gratitude. "I'm an immigrant!" was her gleeful excuse. "What's the problem, kiddo?" she'd bellow whenever Cody would mope. "It's all here for you. All of it!" How could anyone complain in a country where everything was possible? America was simply a wonder to a girl from Bulgaria.

But the American Dream took money. And Marcie had to look her best—and did. "A job requirement," she'd explain in justification, loading the trunk with cheery shopping bags from all over the mall. That her Clinique lab coat uniform concealed the latest styles she claimed to "need" was conveniently lost on her, even as her closet grew ever more choked. "And it's all on sale. Every day!" from the mall's twenty-percent discount. They never discussed it, but Cody knew his mother was deeply in debt.

Cody paid almost half the rent from his wages and after the Rutgers deposit had close to four thousand dollars in his savings account. Marcie had saved nothing for her son's college education. The thought had never occurred to her.

So Cody made his peace with Rutgers. It was a fine school, as Marcie said. He sent his deposit and circled classes and entered the lottery because the good lectures were overstuffed and picked randomly, and there was always a waiting list. He would live in his mother's apartment and drive to class each morning and meet her in the mall for lunch and leave school at four and work till nine weekdays and Sundays till six. It would be like high school, but with more people around as he walked through the days. It would be over in four years.

And that's when a letter arrived, blindly, from a place called S'wanee.

• • •

"Where is it again? *Tennessee?*" Marcie asked as she breezed into the apartment one night after work, sorting mail. The pay-attention-pink bills went facedown in the stack on the kitchen counter, the blue-envelope Valpak coupons landed on the dining room table for later clipping. Cody followed behind. Marcie's mother/son dachshunds, Maisy and Max, ever desperate for attention, pinged about her legs like little clowns. "I see you, I see you," she said to them.

"Yes, Tennessee," Cody said. "Between Nashville and Chattanooga."

"Isn't Dolly Parton from Tennessee?" Marcie asked. "Did she go there?"

"I don't think so," Cody said.

"Didn't she sing a song called 'S'wanee'?" Marcie said.

"I put the letter on the coffee table. Three days ago."

Marcie picked it up. "Parent or legal guardian? Aren't you legal yet?" she asked.

"Don't worry about it," Cody said, closing the subject.

"No, no, I'll read it right now. You left it for me, it must be interesting to you. I just thought…we were done with this."

She took the letter and leashes to the door. "Back back!" she ordered the pinging dogs so the opening door wouldn't scrape their paws.

• • •

The brochure—"A Place Called S'wanee"—exploded with color. Marcie thumbed through it at the dining room table that night, as Cody had several times in the past three days. She stirred her Lean Cuisine but ate little. Food rarely passed her lips. She seemed to subsist entirely on cigarettes and Starbucks and pinot grigio over ice at night. Cody ate a regular Stouffer's lasagna.

"Hydrangeas," she said, pointing to the large flowering shrubs that popped out on nearly every page, some pink, some blue. "Big ones. It must rain a lot down there. Does it?"

Cody ate silently, not knowing hydrangeas.

"It looks expensive," she said. She pulled out a cigarette and tore off the top third, her latest gimmick at smoking less. Cody followed her onto the balcony, through the plastic vertical blinds into the sticky air.

"They might have a scholarship opening. There's a wait list," he said.

"Yes, I read that," she said. "That was in my letter, too. What exactly does that mean?" She looked out over the apartment complex pool. Across the fishbowl, two teenagers smoked while Jimi Hendrix blasted from their parents' apartment. An elderly woman in a floral housecoat sat on another balcony, staring out blankly. At least their balcony didn't face Route 18. Marcie had paid extra to face in.

"It means I can apply," Cody said.

S'wanee's letter explained that due to a handful of students who had already been offered scholarships matriculating elsewhere, there were now a small number of openings. Like most schools, S'wanee was seeking ethnic and "geographical" diversity. The letter was vague about everything else. It wasn't an offer. It was simply a statement of fact and a cordial invitation to inquire more, if interested. S'wanee wasn't begging to give away money.

"How did they get my address?" she asked. "Same as the other schools," Cody answered. "From the SATs. All the colleges buy that information." "Right," Marcie said. "The SAT knows how to milk it. Wish I'd invented it."

"I thought you liked Rutgers," Marcie said. "Don't worry about it," Cody repeated.

"No, I'll call them tomorrow. See what they're hawking." Marcie got up, her cigarette pushed into the crowded ashtray. "I have a date. Just a drink. Do you have a date? Aren't you doing laundry tonight?"

• • •

Marcie didn't leave quarters, so Cody crossed over to the gas station, bought a Gatorade, and coaxed five dollars in change from the cashier he knew. The communal washing machine was full but finished. He emptied and piled strangers' clothes in a wheeled wire bin and ran his big mixed load, editing out Marcie's bras. She hand washed her "delicates" to keep the wires strong.

In the bright, humid room, the washer hummed and squeaked. Cody opened his MacBook on his lap and piggybacked on one of the four unsecured networks that were usually running in the area. He deleted spam and launched his Safari browser.

He remembered the S'wanee web address from the letter, although it was fairly obvious.

The website needed help. At the top of the home page sat the school name, static in purple block letters. Underneath was the upended football-shaped school seal next to the Latin motto: *Ecce Quam Bonum*—untranslated. Below were twenty photographs on a plain grid, many from the brochure, but color-enhanced and brassier. Emerald-green lawns and vibrant stone paths connected matching Gothic buildings that almost looked orange. The hydrangeas appeared neon.

The only people were in archived, mostly black-and-white photos. College boys from the 1930s, '40s, and '50s. Apparently girls and color arrived together in the '60s. A few of the students wore long black gowns over their tweed jackets and ties and floral dresses. Most of the boys wore oxfords and khakis; almost all the girls wore hair bands. Everyone looked very tidy. For some reason there were three pictures of dogs. The website was a weird, intriguing mess.

There was no search box and no directory of professors, classes, or athletics. There were just two links: the admissions office and the student newspaper, the *S'wanee Purple*. It was down for the summer and only said "See You In September!" under the masthead. The admissions link had an address and phone number and nothing else.

The site had no moving parts, but it froze his browser after a few clicks. Cody force quit, relaunched, and opened a new tab.

Wikipedia listed two entries first, including "Swanee," the Al Jolson song about a Georgian river, before redirecting him to Monteagle University, the school's official name. The exclamation point flagged "multiple issues," including "needs additional references or sources for verification," "its neutrality is disputed," and "may require cleanup," which Cody remembered from other Wikipedia college entries written by overzealous students and alumni. NYU's entry in particular had tons of "issues," in a city full of opinionated loudmouths and "haters."

Monteagle College was founded in 1857 by an Episcopal diocese in Monteagle, Tennessee. In 1948, it added a science graduate program and became a university. The school was technically located in the next town called Sewanee, the place-name given by the once-native Cherokee tribe. The school's nicknames included "the Mountain" and "the Domain," but over the decades the shortened "S'wanee" became so ingrained that the school officially adopted it in the early seventies. The school sat atop the Cumberland Plateau in southeastern Tennessee. The campus was officially thirteen thousand acres, but only one thousand were developed. The rest was "scenic mountain wilderness." S'wanee had six hundred and seventy-three students from forty-three states and nine foreign countries.

Google linked only to the Wikipedia entry and the school's own underwhelming website. The town had a newspaper called the *Sewanee Gazette*, but no website. Yahoo's auto-suggest drop-down box listed "S'wanee Massacre" as a top hit, but there were no links. Perhaps an obscure Cherokee battle from the pilgrim days, or a long-defunct and quasi-forgotten student band from a faraway decade. Cool name for a band, Cody thought, wishing he played an instrument.

The dryer buzzed. It was 11:45. Cody had been looking at the school's pictures for over an hour. As he went to close his MacBook, an e-mail dinged in from S'wanee, thanking him for visiting their website and inviting him back again soon. Cody was surprised a Stone-Age website had such advanced tracking capabilities. It was an automated e-mail, not personalized, but Cody went into his browser's preferences to remove the cookie.

On second thought, he let it stay.

• • •

Thirty minutes later, Cody lay in bed, thinking. He heard Marcie return and go quietly to her room.

"How was it?" he asked through the papery wall between them.

"Eh," she said, agnostic. "Oooh, clean laundry. Thanks, kiddo."

"You'll call tomorrow?"

Marcie was silent a moment. "No, I don't think so. Why would I?"

"The school. S'wanee."

"Oh, the school. Yes. Yes, I'll call the number. Why not?"

"I can do it," Cody said.

"No, I said I'd do it," Marcie said. "Why are you still up?"

Cody could tell his mother had had one more glass of wine than usual.

"I'm not," he said. Cody needed only five hours a night and was usually up.

"Me neither. Go to sleep, kiddo."

A few moments later, Cody heard the whir of the electric toothbrush, as Marcie polished and polished.

Chapter Two

Two days later, Friday, was hot, even by eight a.m. Marcie had to be at work early for a training seminar about a new antiaging serum. "You know, they don't pay us extra for this," she complained as Cody drove them to the mall after Marcie's Starbucks pit stop. He didn't ask but knew she hadn't made the call yet.

Cody sat outside in the employee bench area behind JC-Penney. Marcie finished her wake-up cigarette and said she'd see him at lunch. Cody watched the rush-hour traffic in the distance under a peach haze. A river of cars heading to the city. He wanted to go.

By 10:15 the Genius Bar was crowded, as usual. By noon he had fixed a slow iMac by reinstalling the Firefox browser, which he wasn't supposed to do, but the customer was non-pushy and didn't talk with a Jersey accent. Like Cody, he was from someplace else. He also fixed two "fucked-up" iPods by pressing the reset buttons. He wondered if anyone read their user's manual.

He checked in an old iBook that needed more extensive service from the pro techs in the back. "It's password protected," the customer whined. "Don't you need the password?" "Don't worry about it," Cody replied to the grating voice, knowing the pro techs had password-hacking software, although he wasn't supposed to reveal that. He would think that was obvious.

At one thirty he took his sandwich from the employee refrigerator and met Marcie on the bench. The parking lot was mostly empty. Marcie was crushing out her first cigarette.

"What are you doing tonight?" she asked. "Do you have a date?"

"No," Cody answered.

"It's Friday night. I'm taking you out. Dinner and a movie. My treat. That'll be fun! We haven't done that in a while."

They hadn't done that since Christmas.

"Okay," Cody said, eating his sandwich. Marcie walked away from the bench to light her next cigarette, waving the smoke from her son who hated smoking.

• • •

Cody drove them home at six so Marcie could walk the dachshunds and "freshen up" before the movie. Stuck to their locked mailbox by the elevators was a purple and orange door tag from FedEx. For him.

"You coming up?" Marcie asked.

"I'll wait here," Cody answered.

Cody had never gotten a FedEx before. He studied the door tag. His name was handwritten in a scrawl. The package was from "TN 37383."

S'wanee had sent him a FedEx package.

It was a first delivery attempt. It had to be signed for. FedEx would attempt delivery twice more and then return the package to S'wanee. Or he could pick it up in person at the FedEx facility between five and seven today.

Cody looked up the FedEx address on his iPhone. It was twenty minutes away. It was 6:22. If he left now, he'd get there in time, even in rush hour. Cody ran up the back stairs to the street level where Marcie walked the dogs. He could take them all and bring them back, or else he'd go by himself and come back and then they'd go to the movie.

Marcie and the dogs weren't outside. He called her.

"Yes, kiddo?" Marcie said.

"Where are you?" Cody asked.

"Um. In the apartment."

"I got a FedEx package," Cody said.

"Yes. I saw that."

"I can go pick it up there before seven."

"Now?" Marcie asked. "Back back," she said, slightly annoyed at the yappy dogs.

"It's from S'wanee."

"Yes, but *now*?" Marcie was now slightly annoyed at him. "Can I *please* catch my breath?"

"I'll go and come back," Cody said.

"No!" Marcie yelled. "We'll be late for the movie."

"I don't want them to send it back," Cody said, startled by his own urgency.

"Geezus, it's a stupid *letter*. It won't self-destruct." Marcie hung up.

Cody folded the door tag in half and slid it into his back pocket, behind his wallet.

• • •

Cody couldn't concentrate on the movie, even in 3-D. On the drive to the theater next to the mall, Cody noticed FedEx trucks for the first time. In the long, snaking line for tickets, he wondered why kids wore dark hoodies with the hoods up even in the heat. He wore the same Abercrombie & Fitch moose polo he had worn to work. He'd paid full price, since there wasn't an Abercrombie at his mall.

Marcie stood out, not because she was older, but because she looked chic and sexy, like she was on a date. And she was so skinny. The girls half her age were fat and cheap-looking. Marcie really didn't belong here either.

"Do you want popcorn?" she asked as they passed the mobbed concession stand.

What had S'wanee sent him by FedEx?

There were endless commercials before the movie. Pepsi and Nike and the local Nissan. The crowd talked through them.

FedEx was expensive. And urgent. Did they send FedEx to everyone? Surely not.

Marcie nudged him. "Put on your glasses." He'd missed the previews.

And the package was sitting on a shelf, in a warehouse, twenty minutes away. Or was it already on a truck for delivery tomorrow? FedEx didn't lose packages, did they?

"Are you bored, kiddo?" Marcie whispered hoarsely, stylish in her plastic glasses, and then answered herself. "I'm bored. Let's go." The movie was loud, and Kate Beckinsale was yelling onscreen, and Marcie and Cody scooted past the zombies and walked up the aisle.

"Movies have never been worse," Marcie said in the parking garage, stamping out her cigarette. She had kept her 3-D glasses. "I paid for them."

They were at the Olive Garden in their mall. Marcie spooned her minestrone in circles. She'd eyeballed the restaurant and found the prospects wanting, happily married or not. Cody was full after half his pasta. It was rich, and the plate was big.

Tomorrow was Saturday. Cody would be at work. He'd miss the package again. Did FedEx deliver on Saturdays? Did that count as a second attempt? He had Sunday off, but he knew they wouldn't deliver then.

"Angelina Jolie is really the only movie star we have right now," Marcie said. "Her and Catherine Zeta Jones."

"I like Kristen Stewart," Cody said, filling the silence.

"She's so lazy. I feel like I'm boring her from the audience. And she doesn't know how to wear a dress. I bet she smokes a lot of pot."

Cody could call in sick tomorrow and wait for the package. But the store was busy on Saturdays, and he would lose seventy-eight dollars, after taxes.

Marcie flagged down the waiter. "Can you wrap this up? And the check, please?" She handed him her mall ID for the discount.

"Back, back!" Marcie said to the dogs at their apartment. "Can you walk them? I'm sleepy."

"Thanks for tonight," Cody said, grabbing the leashes off the counter.

"We used to have fun," Marcie said, holding her new John Irving. She was a voracious reader and bought them in hardback. "I think you need a girlfriend." She closed the door to her bedroom.

Outside, the dogs sniffed about on the grass while Cody called the 800 number from the FedEx door tag. He pressed 0 again and again until he got to an operator in India.

• • •

Cody found the FedEx warehouse on a quiet industrial street flanked by storage facilities. They were open till two on Saturdays and had held the package back from the truck. There was no parking lot, and the street was lined with cars, so he turned on his hazards.

There were three people in line. The lone attendant looked Cody's age and was in no hurry. Behind her were FedEx posters of London and Paris and Beijing. The World on Time.

She checked his driver's license and disappeared into the back. Two more people had lined up behind him.

Cody's boss had given him a full hour for lunch but asked him to hurry. The new iPads made the Genius Bar busier than usual. "Go! Go get it," Marcie told him. "I need the exercise." Marcie did speed laps around the mall's top floor during her lunch break when Cody wasn't there to eat with her.

The girl was gone forever and then passed back by the counter to the office to get her supervisor, who went to the back with her, and then the girl returned with the FedEx rectangle. She scanned and slid the envelope across, saying nothing. "Thank you," Cody said.

Cody pulled the tab across the envelope in his front seat and emptied a square cardboard sleeve onto his lap. It was white with purple lettering and said, "The Information You Requested," although he hadn't.

Even before he opened the sleeve, Cody knew what was inside.

Chapter Three

By three thirty the Genius Bar had slowed, and the next appointment was at three forty-five. Cody slipped through the back workstation, where the real geeks fixed the broken computers that had been checked in and not just reset. He took a tester MacBook with him. Nobody stopped him—everybody trusted Cody.

On the back stairs near the freight elevators, Cody slipped *The S'wanee Call* DVD into the slot. He heard the disk spin and accelerate, and the screen went black for a moment.

And then S'wanee came alive.

Clanging bells from an unseen tower and then a burst of color and energy and voices and students and professors talking to him directly, explaining this world they lived in and studied at and played in, inviting him in and asking him to stay, and he was there with them, in their beautiful world.

They were bright and casual and in between classes or on their way to practice, and some were in their ancient dorm rooms, others clustered happily on the trodden lawn, as if they'd always belonged to one another. They were articulate and excited about life and living and not embarrassed to show it to anyone who cared to look in at them. Had they always been that way?

It was a slick, fast-cutting production, an avalanche of people and places and *feelings* and longings. There was so much they wanted to show and say, to tell him all about it…

"Cody! We need you!" His boss was leaning out the metal door, down the cinder-block hallway.

• • •

"We are devoted to this thing called the S'wanee Call. The S'wanee Experience. It's life-changing, I would say."

"Because there's something about the S'wanee Call that really binds us together and that we can all say we share in."

They liked that phrase, the "S'wanee Call." It did have a ring.

"Just last weekend, a friend of mine, we were having dinner, and he said, 'You know, I just had a great S'wanee Day,' and students here really know what that means."

Maisy, the mother dachshund, nosed her way into Cody's off-limits bedroom and watched him at his computer, unafraid.

"It wouldn't be S'wanee if you weren't friends with your professors. They play more than just a teacher role; they're mentors, they're friends, they're family, I guess."

The microwave in the kitchen beeped a reminder that his Olive Garden leftovers were done and waiting.

Anne from Atlanta, English major; Ross from Boston, psychology; Maddie of Scottsdale, history; Sean from Miami, undecided; Dean Emeritus Apperson, behavioral sciences—gray, tweedy, with crisp diction and an easy smile. He sat in a tapestry chair by a crackling fireplace. Was he thin blooded, or did it get cold there? The preppy students were dressed for sunny warmth. They were white and black and Asian and Latin, although Cody suspected it was a careful sampling.

"We all live together, eat together, work together, play together, we just see all of each other all the time. It's very close-knit, very tight."

On a flowered field, an older black gentleman, nattily dressed and mustached, juggled tennis balls high as his spirited black German shepherd jumped and lunged and snatched them from the air, one-two-three. Like a circus act.

Football, basketball, soccer, swimming, track, equestrian—varsity, intramural, and club. The students were active, fit, and glowing. The girls sparkled without vanity or attitude. You could talk to them.

"The campus itself asks you to think. To think a thought."

The views from the Mountain were cinematic. The trails, trees, bluffs, and waterfalls of the Domain reminded Cody of Yosemite, or was it Yellowstone? He'd never been to either.

The music was ill matched, like the government-issue videos they showed in school. How to save a choking person and not bully gays. Cody had learned to floss his teeth to this music. S'wanee deserved a better score.

The Extra Features teased out S'wanee traditions and superstitions and ghosts—the Order of the Gownsmen honorary society, the dogs as reincarnated professors, the headless nurse who wandered by some building. The crying baby heard in the chapel when S'wanee lost a football game.

All of it fresh and trampled and pastel and threadbare and burnished and timeless and so very now. We live here together, up on the Mountain. We'll be back in the fall, just so you know.

Ecce Quam Bonum—Behold How Good.

"It's going to be hard to leave this place."

It was.

"Did they send you a *moo-vie*?" Marcie was looking over his shoulder, her eyes slightly blurry. Back early from her date, another misfire.

"You wanna see it?" said Cody, eager to share.

"How we gonna pay for it, kiddo?" Marcie asked, unplayful, leaving his room. Cody and Maisy followed.

"We can ask them," Cody said. "They've got scholarships. And loans. Just like Rutgers. They gotta have those things."

"I mean this apartment!" Marcie said, pouring her wine over ice. "So I would… what? Move? Pack up and move to a one bedroom? A studio?"

"I hadn't thought of that yet."

"I have to think about it! I thought this was settled. I thought we were done with it." Marcie thought for a moment and then kept going.

"You know," she said, "I was asking around at work, the girls at work. No one's ever heard of this."

"Heard of what?" Cody asked. "S'wanee?"

"Well, of *course* no one's heard of S'wanee. *You* haven't heard of S'wanee. What does that name mean anyway? It's so odd."

"It's a Native American name. I don't know what it means," Cody said.

"Indians? Tennessee Indians. And now it's a college," Marcie said, and then she said, "Whatever. No one's ever heard of any school trolling for students this late in the year."

"So the perfume sprayers at Macy's are now college experts?"

"Don't be ugly," Marcie scolded, and then absorbed his sting. "That was ugly."

"I mean, they don't know what they're talking about."

"One of the girls," Marcie continued, gaining steam, "actually he's a boy, and his boyfriend is a college graduate and has a very good job, and he says it's very strange."

"You have the boys at Macy's asking their *boyfriends* about this?"

"I mean, how unpopular is that place? How *desperate*?"

"Rutgers is still looking for students," Cody replied, matter-of-fact. "All years. So is every school that sent me a letter. You can check their websites. I guess they're all unpopular and desperate."

"Someone's done their homework," Marcie said, pushing back. "Someone has the same suspicions I do."

"I'm not suspicious," Cody laughed. "But enrollment is down everywhere. It's just a fact."

Marcie was out of arguments and getting louder.

"I just never thought you'd work so hard to run away from me!" she said.

"I'm not running away. It's college. People do leave home, you know. *You* did."

"My home *sucked*!"

Cody didn't respond. Marcie took a cigarette and didn't tear off the top.

"Fine," she said. "I'll call them. Right now."

She fumbled in her purse for her iPhone.

"It's almost midnight," Cody said.

"I'm sure a college this fancy has voice mail," Marcie replied.

She picked up S'wanee's letter from the coffee table and went into her room.

"No!" Cody, alarmed, followed her. "You're drunk."

Marcie rolled her eyes and continued on to her balcony. Lighting up, she squinted at the letter and dialed.

"Mom, please don't!" Cody pleaded. "Not now!"

Marcie slid the glass door between them and put her finger to her lips, listening. She blew smoke and cleared her throat.

"Yes, this is Marcie Marko," she said pleasantly, professionally. "You were kind enough to send a letter to my son Cody. About potential openings in your freshman class for this fall. I was following up to ask a few questions and...possibly start a conversation. If you could return my call at your leisure, I'd be most..."

After the call, Marcie cracked open the door for Cody. She sat on her balcony and picked a bit of tobacco from her tongue.

"Done," she said, exhaling.

"Thank you," Cody said, relieved. She'd made a better impression than he would. She usually did.

"Come sit with me, kiddo." She patted the chair and looked out over the pool.

"Do you want your wine?" he asked.

"Just come sit with me for a few minutes. It's a nice night."

• • •

Before going to bed, Cody glanced once last time at the S'wanee DVD, still animated and beautiful on his laptop. He noticed a small purple button in the bottom left corner, inviting him to visit the school's pitiful website. He was surprised they advertised that. He hit the button, which launched a new tab in his browser.

The website had grown up overnight.

Chapter Four

On Monday it rained, hard and constant. The thick air made Marcie cough on their ride to work. A single, deep hack. She'd been smoking more, and whole cigarettes. Most women her age looked defeated, almost pathetic, when they smoked, but Marcie wanded hers stylishly, with movie-star glamour. Still, she needed to stop.

Cody had stayed up late clicking through the new, improved S'wanee website. It was full-on and impressive. Not only did it include the videos off the DVD, it had full listings of classes, professors, and student organizations. The site must have been down for maintenance before. He'd merely seen the placeholder while they updated and got ready for the new school year.

At lunch, Cody took his sandwich to the food court, where they met when it was raining. Marcie was already there but stood by the ladies' room near the Panda Express, on her phone. She was listening, not talking. She was straightening her leopard-print belt around her tiny waist.

Cody caught her eye, and she held up a be-right-there finger. Then she pivoted and retreated into the ladies' room, still listening. Cody knew the look on her face and the pivoting retreat. Chastened, slightly guilty, and quietly defiant. The same look and pivot whenever bill collectors caught her at home. She always took their call—too proud to hide and confident in her fierce negotiating skills. “We bailed you guys out, you know,” she’d remind them, as leverage.

He’d seen the look just three nights ago, when her credit card company had called the apartment again. The next morning, she canceled their landline. They never used it, they were wasting money. All true, but Cody suspected the nightly calls were finally wearing down her pride. Now, apparently, they had tracked down her cell phone and followed her to work.

Cody had finished his sandwich by the time she returned and sat next to him, antsy. She rubbed her fingers and touched her stomach. She did nonsensical things with her hands whenever she was restless and thinking. She scanned the half-empty food court. Then she looked at her son and became still, as in a trance.

“You okay, Mom?” Cody asked.

Marcie blinked back to reality. “Sorry, kiddo,” she said, sucking her teeth. “Had to deal with something.”

Cody fought the urge to ask if anyone else had called. Marcie’s lunch break was already ruined.

“Are you done?” she asked, fishing into her purse. “I need a cigarette.”

“It’s raining outside,” Cody said.

“I know,” she replied, leaving the table. “I’ll catch you later.”

• • •

Marcie was late to meet him at the employee entrance that night. She was clearly still bothered by the pestering call and sat silently most of the way home.

“Stop at the Pathmark,” she said suddenly, digging into her purse for coupons.

She surprised him by making dinner. Tri-tip steak, premarinated, and rice pilaf from a box cooked in chicken broth and brussels sprouts steamed in the bag and sautéed in olive oil, soy sauce, and brown sugar. "My mother's way," she said. She also picked up a strawberry-rhubarb pie from the store's bakery. "While it's in season," she said. The dinner was an effort.

Marcie stirred her small portions and ate a few bites. She'd lit a single candle for the table. It was still raining outside.

"We should plan a trip this summer," she said. "We haven't celebrated your graduation yet."

Cody washed the dishes while Marcie took a bath and then scanned the TV channels, standing in her lavender silk robe. She settled on a *Real Housewives*, but muted the sound. She paced and peered out into the rain and decided against a smoke. She kept the cigarette between her fingers, poised.

Cody's iPhone pinged. He glanced at it and quickly went to his laptop.

S'wanee had sent him an e-mail. Addressed to him by name. It was 9:23 p.m.

It was an invitation to apply for admission. It included a link to a standardized online application service. It needed to be returned within one week.

Cody found his mother smoking on the balcony, protected by the balcony above. One arm folded and looking out.

"Did you talk to S'wanee?" he asked.

Marcie glanced over her shoulder and took a drag. "I left them a message the other night," she answered wearily.

"Yes, but did they call back?"

"It's only been two days. Plus it's a slow school." She streamed smoke outward. "I think they've made that clear."

"They sent me an application," Cody said. "They want me to apply. They're waiving the application fee."

Marcie swiveled an eye and then looked back out at the pool for a long moment. Her shoulders were so small in her robe.

“So go for it, kiddo,” she said, her back to him. “They’d be lucky to have you. You’re a good catch, you know.”

“It’s just an application,” Cody said. “It doesn’t mean anything.”

“I know what an application is.” She turned and smiled at him. “I think you should do it.”

• • •

The S’wanee/Monteagle University Application for Undergraduate Admission was fifteen pages long, straightforward, and required only moderate effort. Just the facts, please.

Name, address, birth date, Social Security number, etc. The “Family” section gave him pause. He’d long ago made peace with not knowing who his father was; he’d nothing to compare it to. But S’wanee’s inquiry made him self-conscious, almost ashamed. For the first time, he felt it unusual to have no information whatsoever. The right side of the page stayed blank.

To compensate, he included as much about Marcie as he could. Even so, half her column was empty. She had no college or graduate school. Fortunately, they didn’t ask about her high school, since he couldn’t confirm that either. His “Family” page looked sparse and mysterious. He felt like a ghost.

Things heated up on the “Academics” page. Cody had worked hard and done well in school. Marcie had encouraged that, following his report cards and checking his weekly grades and calling his teachers when she thought they’d shortchanged him. “I don’t think you read his paper *carefully* enough,” he’d heard her lecture one, blaming the teacher for Cody’s less-than-stellar grade. “Maybe you and I and the *principal* can read it over together? *Carefully*?” Cody reckoned his mother was responsible for boosting his GPA a third of a point from her strong-arm tactics. Nevertheless, he'd given her a solid foundation to build upon.

S'wanee's e-mail said not to worry about high school transcripts; they'd requested them electronically. Ditto the teacher evaluations, not necessary now. S'wanee understood teachers were hard to track down during the summer, and the admissions department was on a tight deadline anyway. Cody was relieved. He didn't trust any of his old teachers with an assignment this pivotal. He couldn't, at this moment, remember their names. They probably didn't remember his either.

Page four asked Cody to list his extracurricular activities: hours per week, honors won, offices held, letters earned. Cody withered. The application had spaces for twelve different activities. Did anybody really have that many, or did they make them up? Cody had wanted to be a joiner; he'd wanted to write full-time for the school newspaper, to letter in cross country in the fall or track in the spring, to build sets for plays, to paint spirit banners for the football games. What he did, however, was leave school at two and go work at the mall. For another school, maybe he'd lie and pad. That was common. S'wanee would never know, never check. But he couldn't. He wrote, "Technical Service Adviser—Apple Store, thirty hours/week." It was simple, accurate, and he was proud of it. S'wanee would understand. This was a scholarship application.

Disciplinary History: none. He'd never expended the necessary effort to get into trouble. He hadn't been that needy for attention. Cody knew someday he'd regret being a bore in high school, but right now he was glad.

Cody knew what was coming, any page now, and he dreaded it, and now it faced him. There was only one topic: "Indicate a person who has had significant influence on you, and describe that influence." His ex-girlfriend Kimberly had had a tutor help with her writing samples; there were classes and books on writing college essays, because this was the important part, what they read and analyzed and critiqued. How they got a feel for you.

In the empty white box, the word count blinked and would keep track up to five hundred words, which seemed so very many. He opened a blank Word page to test his thoughts, to list and organize and make sense before he put them in the application.

Now Cody wished he were more self-centered, had spent more time thinking about himself and his feelings and emotions. That came naturally to his high school classmates and other kids. There was always a cloud of babble around them—in the hallways, the lunchroom, the parking lot, the mall. Talking, texting, tweeting, sharing every detail of their days and nights. The taps were always open. It was the constant background hum in his life, like traffic or the air conditioner in his room. He had no practice of his own.

Cody zigzagged his memory for a teacher or coach who'd had any influence, much less a significant one. There was very little to mine. His mother's temporary husband had tried to exert a fatherly influence on him, but it had been fleeting and artificial, and Cody could only remember one afternoon with him in their Palo Alto apartment, when his stepfather had taught him to tie his shoes, a major victory that had eluded his mother. It was a skill he used several times a day, but it lacked the import and substance he needed here.

His grandmother Svetla in Sofia sent handwritten notes several times a year, full of advice in spotty English. She sent longer letters with the small presents for his birthday in January. Her Old World advice had once been wise and occasionally inspirational, considering they'd met in person only a handful of times. As she grew older, however, it had devolved from the vaguely practical "Never economize on your teeth" to the oddly ponderous "Eat a cooked fruit every day." In the past year, her letters had turned to warnings about girls and sex and the troubles he could get into. They were hardened and off-pitch and in old-woman handwriting, and they made him queasy.

Then there was Marcie, his good and best friend. But that wasn't influence; it was companionship. He was her sidekick and audience, but he hadn't learned from her or developed any skills or insights from their friendship. He tried to weave an essay out of their relationship, but after an hour, he hadn't finished a sentence.

It was 2:13 a.m. He laced up his Nikes, slipped out of the apartment, and went running on the streets.

He ran often to unclog his head, and he ran fast, without stretching or warming up or earphones. He just went racing through the quiet night. For the first time, he noticed his big feet slapping against the pavement, his long strides stretching farther and faster, until he was at full sprint. His mother was so petite and birdlike in her walk and mannerisms. They had very different wiring. Even their coloring was different—Marcie was olive and slightly Mediterranean; Cody had a pale, freckled face and copper-colored hair.

Cody thought and planned ahead and brooded and puzzled and got stymied and frustrated and kept it to himself. Marcie was impulsive and mercurial and loud and often sloppy. She rode life where it took her, and Cody had clutched her back, bouncing along fitfully since birth.

He was breathing harder and sprinting faster.

What had emerged in him over the past two years? Why this acute unsettledness that had nothing to do with his "temporary" city? Where did the restlessness grow from? It wasn't anger or adolescent moodiness; it felt like a natural evolution and permanent development, and he welcomed it. He wanted adventure and to go places, whatever that meant. But his mind had, recently and instinctively, started winnowing down those generalities and strained toward specifics.

This evolution pulled him farther from his mother, as much as he loved her. She'd done nothing to trigger these latent and fuzzy yearnings. They'd lain coiled in his DNA and quietly, gradually coursed their way upward to overtake his physical self, along with his deepening voice and chin stubble. It wasn't a coincidence they had all arrived together.

Cody looked at the street sign. He was very far from home. His mind was churning out thoughts disorganized and scattershot. But the tap was open.

He sprinted back, wet and winded now. It was 3:07 a.m.

He sat down at his laptop and wrote until dawn. About the father he'd never met and knew so well.

• • •

"You ready, kiddo?" Marcie called from the living room a few hours later. "Joan says there's a forty-five minute wait at the Tunnel." Marcie gauged all traffic throughout New Jersey off Joan's Lincoln Tunnel report from New York's NBC affiliate. It was usually indicative.

"Almost," Cody called back, toweling dry. He'd slept for ninety minutes and was wide-awake and alert.

He'd double- and triple-checked his answers on the application for accuracy. He'd checked the box affirming its truthfulness. He'd revised and spell-checked his writing sample.

He dressed quickly and went back to read his essay once last time, but stopped.

He'd faced as much of himself as he could for one night. He hit "submit" and then ran out the door.

• • •

By the time he'd reached his car in the parking garage, his iPhone had dinged. S'wanee had received his application.

"I finished it," he said on the drive.

"Finished what?" Marcie asked, rolling down the window.

"The application. I sent it in."

"That was fast," she replied. "We don't have time for Starbucks now. It's too hot for coffee anyway."

They rode silently, listening to the radio. Marcie looked out the window and drubbed her fingers along the armrest, nonsensically.

Chapter Five

The days creeped, and Cody relished them. His motor was running, and it felt good. He noticed the life around him with sharper senses. Inexplicably, he remembered his customers' names when they came to retrieve their fixed computers. He shared their relief when their data was intact.

"You forgot to take your break again," his boss reminded him on Tuesday afternoon.

It was mid-July, and the mall was busier than normal with summer sale shoppers. The Gap had already put up its "Back to School" window posters of beautiful, smiling people his age at an old-school college football tailgate. They were pushing vintage varsity sweaters and tartan skirts and printed khakis. In the chilly mall, the clothes looked right. He wondered how much a sweater would cost with his mall discount.

Across the country, and maybe even the world, students already set for S'wanee were shopping for the fall, too. Maybe his future classmates and friends. His roommate. Maybe his girlfriend. He wondered how many of them S'wanee had reached out to, had pursued as aggressively as him over the past few weeks. Of course, they were one step ahead; they were *in*, while Cody was in a surprisingly happy limbo.

Even on slow days, it was always showtime on the Macy's main floor. Today it bustled like a bright, cheery train station. Cody paused against the cavernous entrance and spied on his mother in her white lab coat halfway across the floor at the Clinique station. She had quarantined a customer on a high stool and was excitedly making her over, explaining each product she hoped to ring up. Even in the crowds, Marcie's dazzling smile jumped out. She was a radiant.

Seeing his mother in her element, Cody saw her fresh as more than just a friend and companion. She was a survivor. She had carried him for nine months, probably alone. She'd gone into labor and likely driven herself to the hospital in pain. There was no one to hold her hand when she gave birth to him, no one waiting outside. She'd carried him back home in the same car, stayed up countless nights for months, feeding and rocking and soothing him all by herself. His baby pictures were always of him solo, never with his mother, since there was no one else to work the camera.

She'd proudly shown off her fatherless baby and thereby instilled in him the same pride. She'd carried him into department stores and put him in their local ads, which she still saved. She'd likely have molded him into a child star had he not grown more disagreeable and less photogenic as a toddler. That dream quashed, she parlayed his stillborn modeling career into her own Macy's sales job and loved him just the same.

Other than shoe-tying, she'd taught him everything and been with him every day for seventeen years. She was fierce and relentless, this tiny doctor-looking creature hovering around yet another stranger just to make ends meet. And she was more beautiful today than ever.

Smiling, Cody turned and walked back through the mall. He didn't want to interrupt her sale. He'd catch up with her later.

• • •

Cody suspected, with guarded hopefulness, that Marcie had a new boyfriend. Or at least a promising new prospect.

Her glow was more visceral, her usual cheerfulness less a defense and more authentic. Most tellingly, she took longer walks with the dogs after work that week.

Cody knew the drill. Longer walks meant cell phone conversations Marcie didn't want him to overhear. "We can't afford walls!" she'd joke, tapping the thin, hollow partitions that divided up their apartment.

Marcie never brought her dates home, even the ones she liked. And she didn't sleep around. Only after she had a "proper boyfriend" would she even introduce him to Cody, usually in public at a restaurant. When it came to boyfriends and sex, Marcie was very "proper." That suited Cody just fine.

But if Cody were possibly-maybe-potentially going to be going away, he knew she would need a companion. He didn't want his mother to get lonely. She hadn't had a "proper" boyfriend in this town yet. He wondered where she had met this one.

On her Wednesday walk, she was gone a very long time. A good sign.

"Do you have a date?" Cody prodded when she finally returned. The dogs were exhausted.

"Aren't you nosy," she said, laughing. Her mood had brightened markedly in the past two days. Another good sign.

"When do I get to meet him?" Cody asked.

"Stop it!" She giggled, like she'd been goosed. "Don't you worry about my personal life. That's icky. I'm happily, happily single."

Cody didn't buy it.

"I'm hungry," Marcie said. "Let's go out. My treat."

Apparently she'd forgotten about the bill collector calls, too.

"We did last weekend," he said.

"That doesn't count," she said. "That was at the mall. I mean someplace fancy."

"It's only Wednesday," Cody reminded her. "We can't go out to eat every day."

She frowned and tousled his hair. Then she smiled.

"Every day is all there is, kiddo..."

• • •

Cody had Thursday off and swam in the pool. When two teenage girls came to lie out, he gathered his things and scooted off. He was uncomfortable shirtless around the girls, but he was mostly self-conscious about his feet, which he thought were ugly.

What a difference a few days made. On Monday, he felt confident and accomplished. He had momentum. By Thursday, he was anxious again. Of course, S'wanee was just now going through his application. He didn't expect an answer so fast. But he wondered who was reading it. Did they pass it around a committee? How many people were judging him, on this very day? Or maybe his application was sitting in their e-mail inbox, unopened and untouched. There was no way to know.

Friday he was back at work and even more anxious. He jumped each time his iPhone dinged. They had to be scrambling to fill those last few slots. There were only six weeks until the school year began. Students had to make plans, buy plane tickets.

"This isn't my computer," a customer at the Genius Bar told him. "This is the wrong computer."

Rutgers was having early orientation soon. Schools across the country were gearing up. Fall was coming.

"Aren't you hungry, kiddo?" Marcie asked him at lunch. "That sandwich looks yucky. Let me buy you something else."

The late-afternoon sun glared on the drive home. He never understood why traffic was worse on Fridays. He hated this time of day, especially during summer.

"Don't frown like that," Marcie said. "You'll get wrinkles."

"I'm not frowning," he said. "It's the sun."

He'd barely stepped into the apartment lobby when he saw the orange and purple FedEx door tag stuck to their mailbox.

• • •

The girl at the FedEx counter was different. Friendly and efficient. She returned in less than two minutes with a full-sized envelope she slid across to him.

"Have a nice weekend," she said.

Cody was back in his car. He had promised his mother he would wait until he got home, even as his hands ripped open the envelope and he was reading the first sentence.

S'wanee had rejected him.

Chapter Six

"Due to the extremely limited number of openings available, we regret we cannot offer you admission at this time," Marcie read aloud, already dressed for a night out. She carefully weighed each word, perplexed.

Cody could barely remember the drive to and from the FedEx office. He had no idea what time it was now.

He did remember his initial sting of suspicion that Marcie had somehow sabotaged his application. To keep him close to her. That's why she'd been so cheery all week. Now, looking at her, he felt ashamed. Marcie was quietly devastated, her maternal pride bruised. She was simmering.

"My my, that's interesting," she said, sucking her teeth. She held the letter up to the light, tilting it. "At least it's a real signature. A live hand touched this."

She drifted into the kitchen to pour a glass of wine. Cody could almost hear her ticking.

"I wonder what changed their mind," she asked herself. "They seemed so nice."

"When? You talked to them?" Cody asked.

Marcie swirled the ice in her wineglass and took a long sip.

"I called them, yes. You were there. You heard me," she said.

"But did you talk to them?"

"Yes, they called back."

Cody's stomach tensed. "When?" he asked.

"I don't know. A few days ago."

"What did you say to them?"

"I didn't say anything," Marcie replied. "I asked the usual mother questions."

"Who did you talk to?"

"The...girl who called me back. From their office. I don't know who it was."

Marcie took out a cigarette.

"Please don't smoke right now," Cody said, wanting more answers.

"I'm going outside," she said, snapping "Back back, Max!" with unusual bite. Maisy and Max retreated to the corner and put their heads down.

"What kind of mother would I be if I didn't ask questions?" Marcie went on. "I asked about the scholarship, about the financial situation. I don't know this place!"

Cody said, "Did you argue with them?" and Marcie said, "Of course not. And I didn't embarrass us. I'm your mother, and I'm allowed to ask questions about a college coming after my son!"

"It's so odd," she said, almost to herself. "They were friendly. I wonder why they changed their mind." Marcie was repeating herself. She seemed genuinely confused.

Cody saw she took this personally. It wounded her immigrant pride. He felt sorry for her.

Neither spoke until Marcie finished her cigarette and came back inside.

"Do you have a date tonight?" Cody asked.

"No," Marcie said. "Why would you think that? Why do you keep asking that?"

"You're all dressed up."

"Oh. Yes. I thought we'd go out. But...I guess not."

She turned on the television.

"I think I'll cancel the cable," she said. "There's never anything good on."

• • •

It was his writing sample. He had tried to be clever and original. Who writes about a father he's never met? The admissions department found it gimmicky and ungrateful to his mother. It was. What a stupid thing to do.

S'wanee wasn't impressed with his Apple job, didn't sympathize with his financial situation. He should have made stuff up. Why had he been so honest? No one else was.

This wasn't his mother's fault. She couldn't possibly have said anything to the school that made them turn him down. She was too polished, too sharp, and she was clearly as crushed as he was. This failure was his.

Five nights ago he sat in this room, full of expectation. That was a long time ago.

But the question that kept him awake was: Why had he let himself hope that S'wanee would accept him in the first place? Why would a college, any college that could pick its students, pick him? There was nothing special about him. He'd always known that, and S'wanee had simply agreed with him.

Cody turned his head to his alarm clock. It was 5:23 a.m.

• • •

Cody's genetic resilience came in handy over the next week. The question he had asked himself, and answered, helped him bounce back. Even faster than when his girlfriend—what was her name? Kimberly—had dumped him, since that had been a personal, targeted rejection. S'wanee was faceless, and by the middle of the week, he had more or less forgotten about it.

Rutgers e-mailed to remind him to sign up for early orientation, since even that filled up fast. He could get his books and school ID, secure a locker, and meet several hundred of his new classmates. There was a link to the Rutgers freshman class Facebook page with over ten thousand students.

"We're gonna be late, kiddo!" Marcie called, pulling him back from the Facebook death spiral.

Marcie bounced back quickly too, per usual. Things must have been heating up some with her potential new boyfriend, and that focused her mind and filled her time.

"I've got lunch plans today," she told him Monday morning as she went into the mall. That was how it began. Soon, dinner plans, and then she'd introduce Cody. Then, down the road, Marcie would be gone a couple nights a week. "Going steady." Even at her age, Marcie used coy, teenage terms.

Thursday she called in sick. "Just a summer cold," she said, still in her lavender robe. "Can you pick up some soup after work?"

Cody came home that night and smelled cigarette smoke. Just a toxic hint of it, which meant Marcie was on her balcony with the door cracked. The non-pinging dogs were already walked and fed.

"Okay, I'll leave that up to you. I'll leave that up to you," Marcie was saying, businesslike, when Cody slid open the living room balcony door. "You're the expert." The door squeaked.

"Is that you, Cody?" She peered around from her balcony, a long ash dangling.

"I've got your soup," he said.

"Thank you," she said, and then she said brightly into the phone, "Yes, he's here. I'll talk to you later."

“Thanks for the soup,” she said, whisking into the kitchen. She was dressed for a night out. “I’m much better. Just allergies. Weird things bloom in this state. Did you get the mail?”

“Who was that?” Cody asked.

Marcie sorted through the mail. She put the bills on the dining room table, faceup, unafraid.

“Yes yes yes,” she said, confessing. “There is someone...”

She giggled, her hands darting nonsensically about her stomach. “But…it’s complicated,” she finished.

It usually was.

“You going out with him tonight?” Cody asked.

“Not ready for that. You’ll meet him. It’s complicated.”

“Is he married or something?” Cody asked.

“Something like that,” she said quickly. “Let’s go out to dinner. I’ve been holed up in here all day.”

Marcie was very chatty at the restaurant. Life was back to normal. She picked up the check without a second thought.

She must have met a rich one.

• • •

Rutgers was prettier than Cody had remembered. The girls were prettier, too.

He sat in a colossal auditorium with several hundred others while older students talked about intramurals and fraternities and community outreach programs. Habitat for Humanity was already signing up incoming freshman for a building project weekend.

Cody saw several faces he recognized from high school. He vowed to introduce himself and learn their names.

The program ended with the co-ed cheerleading squad doing a *Glee*-esque routine, trying to whip the crowd into a frenzy. It was cheesy and fun. Afterward, they passed out surprisingly cool, vintage-looking, faded red ringer T's with "Rutgers" printed across the chest. A girl flashed Cody a winning smile and said, "Go Knights!"

The students were herded into color-coded groups of one hundred for a campus tour. Cody awkwardly met a few in his group, but mostly kept to himself. His tour started with the library and then the student center, and they were heading toward the main gym.

And then his iPhone rang. From a 617 area code.

"Cody?" a male voice said tentatively.

"Yes?" Cody answered, quietly, in the middle of the crowd.

"Hello? Is this Cody Marko?" The voice was louder.

Cody stopped walking as the crowd migrated around him. A flabby girl in a tank top stood behind him, stupidly. Finally, annoyed, she pivoted around him and kept up with the group.

"Yes, who is this?" Cody said, still hushed.

"Did I catch you at a bad time, Cody?" the voice asked brightly.

"Who is this?" Cody repeated.

"Oh, my bad." The voice laughed. "It's Ross. Ross Marling. From S'wanee."

• • •

"You still there?" Ross said.

"Yes. Yes, I'm here," Cody said. He was standing under a tree by the sidewalk. His tour group had gone into the gym, not missing him.

"Yes, this is Ross. I'm a junior at S'wanee. I mean, I'll be a junior this fall."

Cody's phone hand was trembling slightly.

"Hi, Ross."

"Cody, this is embarrassing. I'm embarrassed."

"Okay," was all Cody could say. S'wanee had a voice.

"Did you get a letter from school? Last week or sometime?"

"From school?"

"From S'wanee. It was probably a FedEx."

"Yes," Cody said. "They sent me a FedEx."

"Okay. I have to apologize. Can you talk right now? Is this a bad time?"

The next tour group was herding past him, toward the gym. Slowly. The student tour guide talked through a portable intercom to reach the back of the crowd.

"I can talk right now," Cody said. "It's not a bad time at all."

"They fucked up," Ross said. "I'm embarrassed."

"Okay," Cody repeated. The elbow of his phone arm felt wobbly.

"I'm in Boston. I'm from Boston," Ross said. "You ever been here?"

"No."

"Where are you right now, Cody?" Ross asked. "Are you in New Jersey?"

"I'm at Rutgers."

"Rutgers University? Have they started already?"

"It's early orientation."

"Oh God," Ross said with a pause. "You like it there?"

"It's okay," Cody said. "It's big."

"But you haven't started classes?"

"No."

"Whew!" Ross laughed again. "So. You got a minute?"

• • •

Ross explained he was a student rep on S'wanee's admissions committee. He had personally suggested Cody to the committee in the spring, when scholarship openings had become available.

"I cover the Northeast," he said. "We need more Yankees down there."

He had lists from the College Board, based on SAT scores and geography. He'd made his recommendations and then left on summer break. The admissions department did the rest, including automatically, and mistakenly, rejecting Cody's application.

"S'wanee dropped the ball, I guess," he apologized. "They're a little slow down there in the summer." Marcie would agree, year-round.

Ross had followed up that week and learned of S'wanee's error.

It was all very confusing. Cody didn't push it.

"Long story short," Ross said. "We want you at S'wanee."

Cody was silent.

"You there?" Ross asked.

"Yes, I'm here." Cody could barely hold the phone.

"It's a full scholarship. I mean, with the normal strings. Good grades, campus job, work/study stuff. It's what I do, too. I'm on the same scholarship. Cody, it's a free ride."

"I…well. Thank you," Cody stammered.

"Hey bud, just think about it. I know it's last minute. I'm embarrassed. So is S'wanee."

"No, it's cool." Cody was forming sentences again. "It's just…I've already got my locker. I paid my deposit. To Rutgers."

"S'wanee can get that back, I'm sure. These schools talk to each other."

"Okay."

"S'wanee can also talk to your parents."

"My mother," Cody said.

"Whoever. S'wanee can call her. I'm sure she has questions."

"I think they already talked to her. Once."

"S'wanee's gonna send you a new-student packet. That okay? Just look it over."

"Okay," Cody said, and then he said, "They can send through the mail. Doesn't have to be FedEx."

"Good deal." Ross laughed again. "I'll tell them that."

"Just 'cause sometimes I miss the FedEx guy."

"S'wanee's a great place, Cody," Ross said. "It's really the greatest place in the world."

Cody remembered.

"I'll call back in a couple days, cool?" Ross said.

"Sure, that's cool, Ross. Thanks, man."

"Greatest place in the world, Cody." Ross hung up.

Cody sat on a bench under the tree and watched the next group lumber past. An enormous mass. There wasn't a single pretty girl.

• • •

That night, Marcie was unusually chatty. The Clinique rep had come to roll out new products, and Macy's computer system had gone down for an hour, which meant writing up sales by hand and inputting later. That added an extra hour to her day, but they paid her for it. And she was convinced her coworker June, whom she liked a lot, was pregnant because she took unexpected breaks from the floor and hadn't gone with her for drinks at Ruby Tuesday for three weeks now.

"That boyfriend better marry her," Marcie said, *tsk*ing.

"S'wanee called today," Cody said, interrupting her.

Marcie took a breath and said, "Yes, I know. They called me, too."

She sat at the dining table and rested her chin on tented fingers, with sparkling eyes. She'd been waiting for this.

"Who called you?" Cody asked.

"Dean Somebody." Marcie shrugged. His move.

"What did he say?"

"They screwed up." She shrugged again.

She reached across the table and took his hand firmly.

"Cody. Is this what you want?"

Cody assembled his thoughts.

"I've been selfish." Marcie went on. "I've been scared. This is all new to me. I've never been alone."

She was calm and focused.

"But it's not so far away," she continued. "It's a great opportunity. And a great honor. God knows, I went far from home to pursue my dream. I remember. I get it."

"I want to go," Cody said simply, and for the first time. Even to himself.

Marcie beamed brightly and bolted up. "Goodbye, Rutgers! Hello, S'wanee!" she said, giggling. "God, that name makes me laugh!"

"It's just a two-hour flight," Cody said, standing up.

"If that!" Marcie corrected. "I've done my homework." And then she said, "Believe me, I gave them the third degree."

"You can come visit."

"Oh, I will," she said in mock warning. "I'll shake things up down there. Bring'em up to speed."

"I'll call them tomorrow."

"Let's call them now!" Marcie said, grabbing her phone. "Before I change my mind."

"I love you, Mom." Cody said, halting. He hadn't said that in a long time.

"I love you too, Cody," Marcie said, and then she said, "What have I always told you? It's all here for you!"

She opened her arms to the world.
"All of it, kiddo!"

Chapter Seven

S'wanee sent separate packets to Cody and Marcie, through regular mail. Cody's was larger—new-student information in a big purple and white folder that read "Yea, S'wanee's Right!" in school-spirit lettering.

Travel information, lodging options (for parents and visitors), academic schedule with breaks and holidays, a pamphlet called "Rights, Rules, and Responsibilities" with a postcard he had to sign and return, pledging he had read and would comply. Typical college rules on drinking, drugs, and sexual harassment. The Honor Code, the cornerstone of "the S'wanee Experience," was a separate document he would sign in person at a special ceremony during orientation week.

"Scholarship Guidelines" listed Cody's part of the deal: maintaining a GPA of 3.0 or above, twenty hours of work/study per week (an on-campus job TBD), and, of course, strict compliance with the school's general rules. In exchange, he would receive free tuition, room and board, book and supplies allowance, and a five-hundred-dollar stipend per semester in on-campus "Tiger Bucks". Plus two round-trip coach tickets per academic year, his choice when and where. His scholarship status would come up for review at the end of each semester. Another form to sign.

Tucked in the folder pocket was an accordion pamphlet that said "S'wanee Freshman Map." It folded out to a full-size poster with a cartoon aerial view of the campus. It reminded Cody of the ride map from Six Flags Great Adventure.

Cody taped the poster to his wall and learned it: All Saints Chapel, Shapard Tower, Breslin Tower, Rebel's Rest (residence hall), McClurg Student Center, Convocation Hall, DuPont Library, Gailor Hall (literature), Spencer Hall (sciences), Bishop's Common (student union), Fowler Sport and Fitness Center, and the Klondyke Book and Supply Store. There were dozens of other buildings strewn across the map, but apparently S'wanee thought that was all the freshmen needed to know for now.

The highlight of the orientation packet was a glossy paperback picture book called *S'wanee Places*, a self-described A-Z primer of all things "S'waneeana." The history, traditions, legends and lore of the college since its birth. It was thick and beautiful, and Cody sank deeply into every page.

"Cody, we'll miss the next train!" Marcie bellowed, breaking the spell.

She was taking him into the city, to Macy's flagship in Herald Square. "Better stuff," she explained. "Same discount."

Cody took his new book in his backpack and studied on the train. H for "Honor Code" and Q for "Quadrangle." The "S'wanee Curse" entry piqued his interest, but it simply said "See S'wanee Streaker." Flipping forward, that entry taunted him back to "S'wanee Curse," an endless, playful cycle of mystery and concealment. *Wascally Wabbits.*

As the train tunneled under the river, Cody flipped through the "Notable Alumni" section. There was a secretary of state from the 1890s and several congressmen and a few senators over the decades. A serious-looking general from World War II and a captain from the Korean War. Ambassadors, a CIA associate director, a doctor who was an early pioneer of heart and kidney transplants, a lawyer in the *Abrams v. United States* case, and a few US District Court judges.

There was a writer of a Broadway play he'd never heard of, a conductor of the LA Philharmonic, the former head of NBC Radio (who lived out his final days at the S'wanee Inn), one of the original actors on the soap opera *As the World Turns*, and the current editor-in-chief of *Newsweek* magazine.

It was a long, impressive list, his fellow S'waneeans.

People stood and shuffled to the doors as the train slowed.

Marcie breezed through the crowded blocks around Penn Station in her swinging floral dress. She dazzled on her way to Herald Square.

"Steamy in the city!" she said to no one, as Cody hustled to keep up.

An MTA bus was already advertising the Rockettes Christmas show, which seemed odd in the extreme heat. Another roared past with a Broadway show called *Bloody Bloody Andrew Jackson*. Cody liked the title.

"My boy's a freshman," Marcie told the Jamaican saleswoman at the Macy's Ralph Lauren shop, where she insisted they start. "S'wanee. Heard of it?"

"I haven't," the woman replied, sorting mediums and thirty-inch waists for Cody.

"It's a fine school," Marcie said matter-of-factly. "Very classic."

Marcie picked chinos in khaki, navy, and "college gray."

"Flat front," she insisted, knowing her styles. She showed him how to cinch the waist with a belt. "Paper bag style," she schooled.

She picked lambs-wool sweaters—crew neck and V-neck—in navy, heather gray, and moss.

"Any without the pony?" she asked.

The saleswoman trailed them up to the home floor, where Marcie picked out prepackaged twin sheet sets: white and blue-striped, two hundred thread count. "You need two sets," she told Cody. "And one blanket."

At the cash register, Marcie whipped out her Macy's discount ID, and the saleswoman watched her commission evaporate.

"Transfer to the East Brunswick store, please?" Marcie said, filling out a familiar form. "No sales tax, right?"

Marcie didn't let Cody see the bill. "My treat," she insisted. She bought nothing for herself.

Afterward they took the F train down to Washington Square Park, their usual custom, so Marcie could walk through the West Village. It reminded her of her childhood in Sofia.

Cody eyed the NYU summer students cutting through the park and felt their equal, if not better.

Marcie sipped pinot grigio and Cody a root beer at a sidewalk café off Christopher Street. Here, the bus stop ads were gay-oriented: 2xist Underwear and ads calling for volunteers for a six-month HIV vaccine trial. Cody thought it scary to be a human guinea pig, no matter the cause. How did an HIV trial work, anyway?

"I've loved this day," Marcie said, finishing her wine. "I'm going to miss coming to the city with you."

"I'm not going to Mars," Cody said. "We'll do it again."

"Yep," she said, flagging the waiter. "Let's beat rush hour."

They barely got a seat on the Trenton local. Marcie scoured the commuters with little interest. Cody flipped to the O's in his book: Order of the Gownsmen.

He read that section again. And again.

They were home in no time.

• • •

The last few weeks of summer were a blur.

Rutgers promptly returned Cody's deposit with a check and a letter expressing regret and wishing him the best in his future endeavors. He could keep the T-shirt.

"I knew your deposit wouldn't be a problem," Ross said when he called, as he did every few days, overcompensating for S'wanee's rejection screwup.

Cody offered the deposit to his mother to help cover rent. She refused. "You made it; you keep it," she said. "I'll be fine."

"You getting excited?" Ross asked on another call. "If you have any questions, just call or shoot me an e-mail. Anytime."

"Is there a Facebook page for the freshmen?" Cody asked.

"Hmm," Ross replied. "That's a great idea. I'll suggest it. S'wanee's a little slow on the tech stuff. They just updated their website, though. They're trying."

"Is there, like, cell phone reception there?" Cody asked, wondering how ass-backward the place was.

"Oh yeah. Oh definitely," Ross assured him. "There's a new tower and everything. Wi-Fi, All-G, the school's got all the network stuff." Ross laughed. "S'wanee was slow to join the digital revolution, but they finally caved a while back."

"Okay, cool," Cody said.

"I got a network booster, though," Ross said. "In case I'm working on my laptop down by the waterfalls or something."

Cody didn't know what waterfalls he meant but made a mental note to get a booster before he lost his Apple discount.

"You know S'wanee doesn't let freshmen bring cars, right?" Ross asked.

"Yeah, I read that," Cody said. "I wasn't going to anyway." He didn't add that he and his mother shared one.

"Apparently it's a common rule at Southern colleges," Ross explained. "Another old-school thing. But you won't need one. I can pick you up at the airport."

"Thanks, Ross. That'd be cool," Cody said.

"I think they're making me your mentor anyway. It's like a big brother thing. Every freshman gets one." And then, out of the blue, "Hey, are you really seventeen?"

"I'll be seventeen and a half when school starts," Cody said, momentarily concerned. "Is that cool?"

"Sure, that's very cool," Ross said. "I'm actually old for my class. I took a year off before freshman year. Did you skip a grade? You a prodigy or something?"

"Nah," Cody said. "My mom started me young. Must be a Bulgarian thing."

"Ha." Ross laughed. "You're funny, Cody. I'll check back in a couple days, cool?"

Marcie walked around with a printout from the *Huffington Post*: "Preparing for the College Drop-Off," although she'd only be dropping him off at the airport on the big day. S'wanee paid for one ticket, and Marcie had used up her vacation anyway. She checked off the list as she worked her way through it daily. "I should expect a 'complicated cocktail of emotions,'" she mused, reading from the page. "Good times. This website cracks me up." But she scoured it every day.

She ordered a dozen cardboard boxes from a moving company. Cody needed only one.

"I can always use more boxes," Marcie said, dragging the bundle into her room.

Cody worked out almost every day in the building's gymlet. He ran less because his mind didn't need clearing, and he wanted to bulk up more. He thought about going to the tanning salon in the strip mall down the street, but there were always girls around the front desk. And, being from Jersey, he didn't want to show up at S'wanee looking Snooki-Orange.

He went one last time to his silver-haired barber Gino, who was surprised to hear Cody's news and peppered him with questions.

"S'wanee? Never heard of it. Where is it?" and "I thought you was going to Rutgers. Why'd you change your mind?" and "You leaving your mother?" and "Rutgers is a fine school. What's wrong with it?" and "Who's gonna cut your hair there?" And then he asked again, "Where is this S'wanee? Is that a real school?" Gino's questions were increasingly skeptical and pointed, as if Cody were betraying the state of New Jersey by leaving it.

"I hope you know what you're doing," Gino said uncertainly, dusting Cody's neck with talcum. "Be careful with college girls. They want an MRS degree." At Cody's confusion, Gino clarified, with vigor: "They're looking for husbands." Like his barbershop, Gino was stuck in a bygone era.

"I'll see you at Christmas," Cody said, shaking his hand.

"Just be careful," Gino warned one last time, watching him leave.

Cody gave two weeks' notice at the Apple Store. His boss wished him well and said he could come back to the Genius Bar next summer or anytime.

"Hey, get me an iPod before you quit," Marcie said, since Cody's discount was larger there. "The big one. I'll pay you back. Do they still make it in pink?"

Cody bought the pink iPod and a digital network booster called the Troller—the fancy kind with the frequency monitor. He liked the idea of working on his laptop by S'wanee's "waterfalls," wherever they were.

• • •

Cody was packing his box, scrutinizing his high school wardrobe for the first time and newly grateful for Marcie's shopping spree a few weeks before. She might be a loose cannon plunging deeper in debt, but she had a good eye. He'd save up and buy her something nice for Christmas.

The Troller worked like a charm, picking up wireless networks he'd never seen before. The onscreen frequency monitor gauged the strength of each with a zigzagging wave. A tech from the Apple Store gave Cody the password decoder they used to unlock computers, since they trusted him with it. He could now piggyback, harmlessly, on any network he picked up.

His laptop dinged a new e-mail. S'wanee's housing department wanted information so they could place him in the right dorm with the right roommate.

The e-mail linked him to a personalized page with dozens of questions and circles to dot-in answers. Did he smoke (no), was he an early riser or a night owl (both), taste in music (rock) and movies (action and horror), windows open or closed at night (not sure), any allergies or medications for chronic conditions (not applicable). Did he intend to study in his room or someplace else (not sure). They snuck in a question at the bottom of the page about his sexual orientation. Cody was tempted to dot "not applicable" to be jerky but decided a scholarship student should respect the (free) housing department and chose "straight," the truth. No one had ever asked him that question before.

The questions on the second page were to be ranked 1 (strongly disagree) up to 5 (strongly agree) with 3 being neutral. "I want a roommate I can be friends with" or "I prefer to keep to myself" (3 on each). "I get lonely easily" (2), "I don't understand the way people behave nowadays" (3), "I don't want what most people seem to want" (4), "I wish people would be a lot kinder than they are" (4), "It seems that right and wrong are pretty ambivalent these days" (4), "I feel confused about the world a lot" (4), "It often seems that it's the nice people who lose" (5). "Life has become less and less meaningful to me." Cody left that blank, but the page called him on it, and he put in "1" before it let him move on.

Cody noticed the Troller's frequency monitor zigging wildly. Apparently he was piggybacking on a very strong network.

The third page had two rows of color blocks. They weren't normal colors Cody recognized, like blue or red or yellow, but they were variations in shades he couldn't name. He was supposed to click on each one in the order in which they "appealed" to him at this moment, instinctively, without thinking. One by one they disappeared as he clicked away, followed by a "Please

Wait," as a timer ticked backward from ten. The same color blocks appeared again, in the same order, and he was asked to repeat the process. This happened three times.

Next up were blocks of psychedelic patterns in bright colors: polka dots, stripes, paisleys. Same deal. This was fun, trippy stuff.

Strangely familiar music piped in on the next page. It reminded Cody of some ancient arcade game (Pac-Man? Donkey Kong?). It was repetitive and silly and made him smile. The blocks were in vibrant, geometric black-and-white patterns that seemed to move if you stared at them, like an optical illusion. They made him dizzy. He was to drag his favorite ten patterns into the box at the bottom. Then drag his favorite five from those. Down to two. The Pac-Man music withered and stopped.

The frequency monitor zigged wild and red.

An elaborate maze popped up to fill the screen, with a blinking mouse in the center. Cody used his keypad to navigate through the maze, and the instructions told him to take all the time he needed. It was intricate, and he backtracked from several dead ends, making little progress. Just as he started to suspect the maze was shape-shifting to trap him forever, the screen went white, as if it sensed his suspicion and didn't want to play anymore. The page said simply, "Thank you. Yea, S'wanee's Right!"

Then the page automatically closed out his browser. The Troller's frequency monitor dropped to a calm, yellow wave.

Cody blinked at the screen for a moment. The vibrant patterns had given him a slight headache. That was a funny questionnaire. He wondered what kind of roommate it would pair him with, as he went to take a short nap.

• • •

The Apple Store gave Cody a small going-away party in the back with red velvet cupcakes and sugar-free Red Bull. He reset his final iPod and promised to visit at Christmas. He took his packed box to Macy's, where Marcie had arranged for it to be shipped UPS Ground with their special rates.

"So we're supposed to have this talk," Marcie said that night, slipping on her reading glasses. She held a printout from the *Huffington Post*. They had ordered in Chinese, and Marcie sat on the sofa in her lavender robe with her wine.

"Arianna Huffington had this talk with her daughter before she went to college," Marcie continued, scanning the page like a checklist. "She calls it a 'teachable moment.'"

Marcie added, "Arianna's an immigrant, too," which apparently made her advice endlessly relevant. "An extremely successful one."

"She married a rich gay guy and took half his money," Cody reminded her, as usual.

"Whatever works," Marcie replied, on cue.

"So, yeah," she continued, uncomfortable with words of wisdom. "You're probably gonna drink. But don't drink too much. It's probably just beer anyway. You'll have to learn your limits."

Check.

"But Cody, don't do drugs. Even pot. Don't get started with that stuff."

Next?

"Get enough sleep. You can't stay up all night and be at your best."

Okay.

"But get out and meet people. Meet your classmates. Get to know your professors. Get out of your room."

Thanks, Arianna.

"Let's see." Marcie continued onto the next page. "Roommates. Nah, you're not gonna have one…"

"What?" Cody stopped her. "How do you know that?"

"Oh." Marcie looked up. "I don't know that." She sipped her wine, teething the ice, and went back to the page. "Respect their boundaries and ask the same in return."

Arianna Huffington sounded like a real bore.

"And girls…"

Please God, not sex.

"Well, you'll figure that out, won't you?"

Whew.

"Yes, Mom," Cody said, grateful.

"Or boys?" Marcie said, glancing up from the page. "We don't judge."

"No." He shrugged. "Not boys."

"I didn't think so." Marcie shrugged back. "But we don't judge. Just be safe, no matter what. They taught you all that in school, right?"

Marcie put down the tip sheet and removed her glasses.

"Cody, here's the deal. Here's how it works in this country. Anything is possible. The opportunities are there. You go out and you grab them and you put them in your basket. That's how you make your fortune here. You don't worry about what others think of you, and you don't look back."

"Okay," Cody said, unsure if she was talking to him or to herself.

"That's how immigrants make it here. Always have. That's how we do it."

She burrowed back into the sofa.

"Just don't hurt anybody."

"I won't," Cody said, laughing.

Marcie seemed troubled, her mood shifting. "Come give your mother a hug."

Cody leaned against Marcie, and she put her arm around him, stroking his hair.

"I'm going to miss you, Cody."

"I'll miss you too, Mom. But I'll be back."

"It won't be the same. You'll be different. I'll miss you the way you are now."

"I'll be the same, Mom."

Marcie didn't respond. She just held him tighter as they stared at the blank television in silence.

Chapter Eight

It poured rain on the big day.

"We should give ourselves extra time!" Marcie bellowed from the kitchen. "Joan says traffic's a bitch today."

Cody struggled to close his black Samsonite roller, praying the zipper wouldn't break. He checked the flight one more time before shutting down his laptop and slipping it into the travel case for his orange backpack. Marcie had bought him one with extra padding for protection. He had changed shirts three times and settled on his favorite faded navy polo from Abercrombie with a red windbreaker on top.

He took one last look around his room to make sure he hadn't forgotten anything. It didn't feel like leaving home; he was walking out of a room at an apartment building.

Maisy and Max, who had sensed change over the past few weeks, sat at attention in the living room, their heads cocked quizzically in unison. The change was here and now. Cody kneeled to stroke their heads, and they raised their noses for one last sniff to remember him by.

"Let's go, kiddo!" Marcie called, already out the door. "Ticket? ID?"

Marcie refused to drop him off at the curb and pulled into the expensive short-term parking at Newark Liberty International.

She was usually a nervous, jerky driver, but today she was focused and sure, even in the rain.

The tired, concrete, *Jetsons*-esque Newark terminals looked even gloomier in the downpour, and the late-summer travel crowds were massive, steamy, and testy.

Cody helped a Hasidic man with a polite, quiet family work the self-service kiosk and then took his own luggage to the counter when called. Marcie stared mournfully at the Hasidic mother's wig and whispered in Cody's ear, "I would never shave my head for a man. Especially that one."

The security line started at the bottom of the escalators across from Nathan's Famous. Cody turned to hug his mother.

"What are you doing?" she barked, stopping the embrace. "I'm coming to the gate."

"You can't without a ticket," Cody explained.

Marcie rolled her eyes and pulled a piece of paper from her Coach bag. "I know how it works," she said. "I bought this last week. Full fare."

"You're coming with me?" Cody asked in momentary panic.

"To the *gate*, yes," she said, shepherding him toward the security line. "I'm taking my son to the *gate* on his way to *college.* I'm not dropping him off at security."

She slipped off her Burberry trench, revealing her white Clinique lab coat underneath. "I'll refund the ticket on the way out. Have you never heard of this, Mr. Genius Bar?"

"You'll be late for work," Cody said.

"Let 'em fire me." She shrugged, inching through the line in her stocking feet. "Get out your ID."

She locked her arm in his, strutting proudly down the long windowed corridor toward the gates, beaming her megawatt smile. She ignored a well-dressed executive at the shoe shine. Outside the weather was drearier, and all the jets were parked.

Her mood started to darken once they reached the massive flying saucer gate area and saw his flight was delayed like all the others.

"Mom, you don't need to stay," Cody assured her an hour later. "I'm fine."

"I'm not leaving until you do," Marcie snapped, oblivious to the crowds around them. She was rubbing her hands nervously. "I thought this would be quick and painless. This isn't easy, Cody. It's not easy letting you go."

Thirty minutes later, she said, "This is a bad idea. You shouldn't fly today. Let's go home."

"The weather's clearing," Cody replied, pointing toward the city.

Marcie abruptly bolted up. "I can't sit here." She paced the flying saucer until a table opened up by the cappuccino stand in the center. Cody sat next to her.

"You can't smoke in here," he said as she pulled her American Spirits from her bag.

"I can hold it, can't I?" Marcie said, rubbing the back of her neck. "I know airports, Cody. I spent years in them."

One of the flights started to board. A couple tried to join them at their table. "These are taken," she said, pulling the chairs closer. The couple left.

Another flight boarded. The flying saucer was rumbling to life.

"I'll call as soon as I land," Cody said, trying to calm his mother.

"And from the car, too," she said. "And when you get to this place."

Marcie took a used napkin off the table and dabbed her neck. She still clutched her unlit cigarette.

Cody's flight was called for preboarding.

Marcie suddenly gasped for breath. Unable to catch one, she clutched her throat, drowning.

Marcie was hyperventilating.

"Mom, what's wrong?" Cody asked, alarmed.

Marcie didn't answer, shaking her head, desperate.

"Mom!"

"I'm so scared!" she burst out, still gasping. "I'm just so scared!" She gulped loudly, trying to swallow. People were starting to notice.

"Mom, do you need a doctor?"

"Why did I agree to this?" Marcie grabbed his arm. "I don't know this place. I don't know where you're going. And I'm so scared for you!"

Her face was red, her eyes wild.

"I don't know what's happening to me. It's so dark in here!"

She was heaving now, spastically. She clutched the edge of the table with both hands. She swooped her head down close to the surface. She focused her eyes.

"It's a panic attack, Cody," she said. "I've read about them. I'm panicking."

Marcie breathed deeply, normalizing. A complicated cocktail of emotions.

People were crowding to board Cody's flight. The line was long. Cody soothed his mother.

"I don't have to go," he said. "I won't go."

"No no no," Marcie replied, forcing an I'm-okay smile to onlookers. "This is stupid. This is silly. I'm going to miss you, kiddo. I'm going to miss you so much."

She sat up straight. Her hands darted about her neck and stomach nonsensically. A good sign.

"I can't leave you like this," Cody said. "You can't drive like this."

Marcie stood up.

"Get in line," she barked. "Get on the plane."

• • •

"Good morning, sir." The gate attendant smiled, feeding Cody's boarding pass into the machine. It beeped three times.

"You've been upgraded, Mr. Marko," she said. "Just a moment, please. Your new boarding pass is printing."

• • •

Cody scooted past an older, professional woman on her BlackBerry to his wide, upholstered armchair by the window. The pretty, young flight attendant offered to hang his windbreaker.

He peered out and saw his mother at the airport window, scanning the back length of the plane, not knowing he'd been moved to the front. She stood at attention in her white lab coat, like a tiny doctor. Cody smiled and waved at her, but she didn't see him.

"Champagne, orange juice, water?" The flight attendant lowered a tray.

"How much is it?" Cody asked, feeling stupid as he said it.

"It's complimentary, sir."

He took an orange juice, and the older, professional woman took a water. He started to put the glass on the armrest. The professional woman smiled and pivoted a little perch out from the middle and set her glass on it. Cody found his and did the same.

"You live in Nashville?" the woman asked pleasantly as she turned off her BlackBerry.

"No, ma'am," Cody answered. "I'm going to college there." Then he said quickly, "I mean, I'll be a freshman there."

He looked back out at his mother. Was it the rain dripping down the window, or was she crying?

"Vanderbilt?" the woman asked.

"S'wanee," Cody replied, still staring at his mother.

Marcie looked directly at his window, and Cody waved as fast as he could. She didn't see him and returned to scanning the back of the plane.

After a moment, the woman said, "S'wanee. Is that in Nashville?"

"Near Chattanooga. I think."

The gangway pulled away. The jet backed up from the gate.

"S'wanee," the woman said again, musing. "I know I've heard of it. I've definitely heard of it. A long time ago, I think."

The jet rolled off, and Cody watched his mother watching his plane until she disappeared and was gone.

"Well, congratulations," the woman said, as the safety video played. "You must be excited."

"Yes," Cody said.

"You're going all by yourself?"

"Yes, ma'am." It dawned on him that yes, he was all by himself. Marcie was gone, and it suddenly felt strange.

"That's very brave." She chuckled. "I held my daughter's hand all the way to the dorm. I thought she'd never let go." And then she said, "But that changed fast. You grow up fast at college. Too fast."

Cody pulled his S'wanee picture book from his bag and picked up where he had left off: "S'wanee Fog—a typical fall and winter atmospheric condition of the Domain; sometimes used also to refer to the mind-set of certain students." He loved this book.

"S'wanee," the woman repeated again, as the jet thundered and rattled loudly down the runway, accelerating. "Why does that name ring a bell? It actually gave me a little chill when you first said it. Isn't that funny? Something happened there. It was in the news when I was in high school. So long ago…"

Cody looked down as New Jersey got smaller below him. He felt weightless and strong. He was in first class and on his way to S'wanee. They wanted him so bad they had paid for an upgrade, to welcome him.

He couldn't see his mall, or his high school, had no clue where to look for them, and he already felt a world apart from both. S'wanee had plucked him out and was whisking him far away, because they saw something in him that no one, including himself, ever had. S'wanee knew him better than he knew himself.

It seemed funny to him now that he'd ever considered Rutgers in the first place. Not that he was better or smarter, although maybe he was, but why did he always limit himself to whatever was comfortable and nonthreatening? S'wanee had already taught him a lesson, and he hadn't even gotten there yet.

Now he understood why he'd been so restless in high school, detached from his classmates, not included and not bothered by it. Why he'd so easily shrugged off his girlfriend's rejection (what was her name? Kimberly!). And why he didn't care that no other girls at school had paid him much attention at all.

There had been a fleeting moment toward the end of his senior year, as his classmates bonded closer and he felt increasingly alienated, when he feared he might really be an outcast. A social misfit. A permanent condition. He would have skipped his graduation if Marcie had let him.

But now, just a few months later, he realized he was simply different from the others, and that was nobody's fault. He was innately smarter, more talented, and more ambitious than the students he'd been thrown together with by chance. Now he was rising above them, not with arrogance, but with a humble understanding.

Everything in his life started now, on this very day.

His book had fanned open to the back. A glorious picture of where he was going, and a simple poem written about it.

A towered city set within a wood,
Far from the world, upon a mountain's crest;
Where the storms of life burst not, nor cares intrude.
There Learning dwells, and Peace is Wisdom's guest.

"Hot towel, Mr. Marko?" The flight attendant smiled, holding a tong with a small white terry cloth. It was steaming. Cody took the hot towel and, watching the still-thinking woman next to him, wiped his face and hands.

Fall

Chapter One

Cody had never felt his ears pop like this.

He was in Ross's shiny black Jeep Wrangler with black tinted windows. A rolling black box, climbing steadily to higher elevations through the thick green hills. The AC was blasting.

Cody had instantly recognized Ross through the glass wall of the waiting lounge in the Nashville airport. He'd been prominently featured in the S'wanee DVD. It was like meeting a movie star. Today he wore a madras shirt, ripped khaki shorts, flip-flops, and a wide smile.

"Mr. Marko! You made it!" He grinned, shoulder-clapping Cody. "Great to finally put a face with your face! How was your flight, bud?"

Ross laughed when Cody thanked him for the upgrade. "Don't get used to that. That was S'wanee's apology for their screwup. A one-off." He had a bright, warm voice that carried.

"Have you been waiting here the whole time?" Cody asked, checking his watch.

"Not at all, bud. We knew your flight was late. We were tracking you. I left when you did."

They walked past the Spirit of Nashville gift shop with "Team Swift" T-shirts and guitar ashtrays and boxes of candy called

GooGoo Clusters. "You want any souvenirs?" Ross asked. "It's mostly crap." The airport smelled like new carpet.

There was a singer with a guitar in a lavender bar called Tootsie's Orchid Lounge. Cody had never seen live performers at an airport before. It was festive here.

"Chattanooga's actually closer to school," Ross said as they descended the escalator in the newly carpeted, light-filled terminal. "But you gotta connect through Charlotte or Raleigh. Pain in the ass." A country music version of a song Cody vaguely recognized played over the loudspeaker . By the time they reached the bottom, he had pinpointed it: Sting's "Every Breath You Take." Country-style elevator Muzak.

"Slowest baggage claim on the planet," Ross said as they loitered around the idle carousel. Ross had one foot up on the edge, rocking back and forth. Outside, it looked bright and blistering. Carrie Underwood welcomed them to Nashville over the loudspeaker. A few minutes later, someone named Vince Gill reminded everyone to use the recycling bins.

Ross had a crisp, restless energy that stood out in the languid crowd. Clearly Yankee.

"My mom," Cody said suddenly, turning on his iPhone. "I gotta call her." He momentarily felt silly about that.

"Take your time." Ross nodded, rocking deeper against the carousel. "We got plenty of it." Cody moved to the chairs by the window.

"First class!" Marcie squealed when Cody told her. "I remember it well."

"I couldn't find my tray." Cody laughed, one eye on the still dead carousel. "It was in the armrest. I felt like an idiot." Ross kept rocking but glanced in Cody's direction before turning back.

"Did they give you lunch?" she asked, and then she said to someone else, "Can you ring that up for me? My boy just got to college."

"Yeah, it was chicken. It had something inside it."

"Probably Chicken Kiev. Did it squirt?"

"A little when I cut into it."

"Chicken Kiev. That's standard. Warm nuts, too?"

"Yeah, they gave us that first."

"Yeah, that's a domestic thing. We didn't do that. We had real appetizers." And then she said quickly, "But that's very exciting, Cody. Such a treat for you."

"Ross said don't get used to it. To first class, I mean."

"Is Ross nice?" Marcie asked.

"He's very cool. He's from Boston. They have singers here at the airport. Country music singers."

"I was thinking about you. Every minute."

"Are you doing better, Mom?" he asked.

"Tell Ross to drive safely. In fact, put him on the phone for a second."

The carousel buzzed an alarm and jolted to life.

"Hey Mom, I gotta go. My bag is coming out."

"Put Ross on the phone for a second."

"I'll call from the car, okay?"

A guitar in a black case was the first out. A young guy in a cowboy hat and tight jeans snatched it up.

Ross scooted briskly through the genteel, "after you" crowd, pulling Cody's luggage.

"You need the john?" Ross asked abruptly, smiling.

"I'm good, man," Cody answered, since Ross seemed in a hurry.

They whisked out the sliding door into the bright heat, as Reese Witherspoon on the loudspeaker welcomed them to Music City, USA.

• • •

Cody's ears kept popping as they climbed higher into the lush, green hills. They had been clogged when he landed and now were getting worse.

Ross had spirited them from the airport, checking traffic on the radio (the local "U-Turn Laverne" sounded very different from Joan) before switching to XM Alternative.

"Roadie?" Ross handed Cody a Rolling Rock from a cooler in the backseat.

"Thanks man," Cody said. "Can I drink this in here?" The Jeep looked and smelled brand-new.

"Sure. That's why I brought them," Ross said. "To get the party started."

Cody twisted the cap easily without the usual fizz. He'd never had a beer in a moving car before.

Nashville was busier than Cody expected, with traffic snarls on the highway—Ross called it the "interstate"—and a surprisingly dense downtown skyline in the distance. One skyscraper looked like Batman's cowl with pointy ears. "They call it the Batman Building." Ross shrugged. "I think it's AT&T."

He merged onto another highway leading out. "It's a pretty cool town," he said. "We come in for concerts or Broadway shows. S'wanee does field trips and picks up the tab." He impatiently sped around a Ford Taurus and gunned ahead. "The drivers are a little stupid, though."

"Is that all you packed?" Ross asked, tipping his head back.

"I mailed a box, too," Cody answered.

"Oh, right," Ross said. "From Macy's. It's in your room."

Cody couldn't wait to see both.

"Seriously, if you have any questions about the place, you can always come to me," Ross said. "That's what I'm here for. You're my 'project.'" Ross laughed at that, and so did Cody.

"That's cool, man," Cody said, looking over at him, since his popping ears made it hard to hear. In the blazing afternoon sun, Ross looked older, more grown-up. Definitely an upperclassman.

They were far outside the city now, and traffic was light. Ross was speeding. There were long stretches with no houses or buildings, just rolling fields and dilapidated barns and billboards for outlet malls.

"Like they say: Once you leave Nashville, you're in Tennessee." Ross laughed. He laughed a lot. Cody was on his second beer. They were cold, but a little flat.

They passed a white split-rail fence that stretched for miles. Beyond were vast rolling green meadows dotted with stationary black cows grazing.

There were lots of billboards for fireworks, with cherry bombs getting star billing on most. They must be extra explosive, the top of the pyrotechnic food chain. There were billboards for Rock City, Ruby Falls, the Chattanooga Choo Choo, which rang a bell from somewhere. It was freezing in the Jeep.

"I've been reading the S'wanee book," Cody said, tilting the side blower outward. "The encyclopedia one."

"Yeah…that's…cool…one," Ross seemed to say, but with the loud alternative music, the roar of the AC, and the hum of the Jeep, Cody's clogged ears didn't catch it all. "You…know… more? …Ask."

"What about the Order of the Gownsmen?" Cody asked of his favorite section, hearing his own voice through his head.

"Yeah? What about it?"

"Are you in it?"

"Nah, not yet," Ross said, and Cody forced a yawn, straining to hear him. "They induct new members at the end of their junior year, for those who get in." Cody's ears popped through their fog, and it was clearer now.

"How do they pick it?" Cody asked.

"Well, lots of things," Ross said. "GPA mostly, but it's more than that. You gotta do a special project for your major. You write a thesis or do a big science project. It all depends."

Moments later, Ross said, "I mean, it's kinda a big deal. But not critical. It's just a S'wanee thing." He shrugged, downplaying its importance.

"But yeah, it's very old-school," he continued after a beat. "Like Oxford/Cambridge old-school. That's where they got it. They give you those Harry Potter gowns, and people pass them down through the generations, with their initials embroidered."

Finally, he said, "Okay, since I'm your mentor, I'll tell you: It's a very big deal." He laughed loudly. "Every junior is obsessed with it. They just play it cool, like I am now."

"What's your major?" Cody asked, his ears clouding again.

"Psychology," Ross said, shifting lanes around a green and yellow eighteen-wheeler that said "Palamino" on the back. Ross was going over eighty.

"Are you doing a special project?"

"Yeah. Been…almost…year…now…"

"What kind of project?" Cody asked.

"…eh…dull psych…rats…maze…"

Cody made a joke about the e-mail rat's maze the housing department had trapped him in, which fell flat because Ross didn't get it. Cody's attempts to clarify only made it fall flatter, so he reverted to more questions about Ross's Gownsmen project. "... routine...testing…" Ross sputtered, seemingly dismissive."... we'll see."

Cody nodded and looked ahead, not hearing. He'd ask more when his ears were working.

They cruised past a brown highway sign that read "Lynchburg, TN—Home of Jack Daniel's Distillery." Ross pointed at it and said something that amused him, although Cody caught only the words "…dry county…"

"…*yo*?" Ross said louder, a few minutes later, looking over.

"Sorry, what?" Cody said, pointing at his ears.

Ross laughed and took an exit toward a small collection of gas stations and diners in the middle of nowhere.

"I said," he continued loudly, "I gotta use the john. You?"

Cody nodded, holding up his near-empty beer.

Stuckey's was part restaurant and part gift shop of strange things. The bathrooms were very clean. Ross waited for Cody and then tossed him a white squishy log wrapped in plastic as they left.

"That, Cody, is a pecan roll," he said. "It's a Stuckey's rite of passage. Hell, Stuckey's *itself* is a rite of passage. The white stuff is called *nougat*." He mouthed the word like caviar.

"Thanks, Ross," Cody said, playfully buzzed. "Want some?"

"Fuck no. It's all yours."

On the way out, they passed a morbidly obese, humorless couple with wiry hair. They could be spouses or siblings. They stared down Ross and Cody like alien invaders.

"Remember, Cody: Once you leave Nashville…" Ross said under his breath.

"You're in Tennessee," Cody chimed in, sharing the joke. As Ross tossed something into the back, Cody unwrapped and took a small bite of the chalky, chewy candy. It was odd and surprisingly good.

• • •

They were at a very high elevation, and the scenery was stunning. Cody sensed they were getting close but didn't ask. The highway snaked one tight curve after another through the massive limestone bluffs, and Ross handled them expertly. Even taller mountains loomed ahead. Static increasingly swarmed the satellite music.

The altitude and a third beer made Cody light-headed and giddy. He was on a fun ride.

A green road sign said Monteagle was one mile ahead. Ross took the exit and sped down a near empty road dotted with no-name gas stations and diners and a Salvation Army store. He sailed past a fast-food drive-in called Sonic, which stood out, brand-new and gleaming. It was crowded with cars as Ross raced by.

"Whoops," Ross said, and then Cody saw the flashing police lights on their tail. "Hold your beer down." Cody hid the half-full bottle in his door pocket as Ross pulled over.

"You know how fast you were going, sir?" The cop was typically humorless, with a thick, country twang. "License and registration." Ross dug into the glove compartment and pulled out his wallet.

The cop looked through the window over at Cody. "Is that an open container in the car?" he asked. "How old are you?"

"It's litter," Ross answered, handing over his license along with his S'wanee school ID. The cop studied the ID and seemed trumped.

"I'll have to call this in," the cop said.

"I understand, sir," Ross replied, and rolled up the window as the cop walked back to his car. "I shouldn't be going that fast," he added but didn't seem concerned.

Cody had gotten a ticket once in New Jersey. It had bothered him for months. He was always terrified of getting in trouble. Now, with Ross, he felt relaxed, even though he'd just been caught drinking underage by a stern, itching-to-lock-someone-up cop in a small Tennessee town. He felt almost high.

The cop knocked on the window, and Ross rolled it down, smiling. "You still can't be going so fast," the cop said, handing back the license and ID. "You still can't be drinking in the car. I'm reporting this."

"I understand, sir, and you're right," Ross said.

"We have laws in this town. You gotta follow them."

"Can I have your name, Officer? I'd like to recommend you."

"You don't need my name," the cop said as he walked off. "Just obey the laws while you're here."

Ross drove away carefully, ticketless. They were outside the little town and passed a string of small beige brick houses. They were sad and lifeless, with old pickup trucks in the front yards and clothes hung on wires and a sign to reelect the county commissioner. An old woman in a housecoat sat in a folding chair on her front porch, fanning herself as she watched them pass.

Now they were going deeper into a wooded stretch. Cody had never seen such lush trees and grass. They were approaching two tall stone pillars on either side of the road. Suddenly, Ross pulled over and grabbed his BlackBerry.

"I gotta send a text before we go in," he said. "You gotta text anyone?"

"I was gonna call my Mom when I got there," Cody said.

"Well, do it now," Ross instructed. "That's another little S'wanee quirk. They don't like cell phones. I mean, it's not against the rules or anything. It's like a peer pressure thing. To keep the community engaged with each other and not always buried in their phones."

"I get it," Cody said.

"You'll hear someone say, 'Save S'wanee,' whenever anybody's using their phone. It's a playful reminder. You'll get used to it."

"Save S'wanee," Cody repeated, still feeling buzzed.

"S'wanee has lots of quirks." Ross laughed. "But I like this one. Just gotta wean myself off my CrackBerry after the summer." And then he said, "You won't get a strong enough signal here to call. But you can take a picture of the gates and send it to her, so she knows you're here." Ross pointed straight ahead. "The gates to the Domain."

Cody wandered up to the ancient pillars. On one side was a shiny copper plaque that read "S'WANEE" in thick letters. On the other side, a plaque said "THE DOMAIN" in matching font. Both plaques looked brand-new and regal. The school clearly kept them sparkling clean.

Cody took a picture of each on his iPhone. He attached them to an e-mail to his mother with the subject line: "Save S'wanee." He smiled, knowing his mother wouldn't understand, as he hit the "send" button.

"I'm all set, champ!" Ross was leaning out the Jeep window. "Are you set?"

As Ross drove through the gates, he tapped the Jeep's ceiling and smiled at Cody when he looked up quizzically. "I'm just giving her back," Ross said.

"Who? What?" Cody asked. How buzzed was he?

"My S'wanee Angel," Ross schooled. "Another tradition. You tap your ceiling to pick her up when you leave the Domain. She watches over you in the big, bad world. Then you release her when you return, so someone else can take her."

"Do I get one, too?" Cody asked, loving these quirks.

"Sure, when you leave again someday. But you don't need protection when you're inside the Domain." Ross turned to Cody and grinned.

"Nobody does."

• • •

It was a long drive from the gates through the quaint little town of S'wanee. After ten minutes, Ross took a right past a rustic bar and restaurant called Shenanigans, with picnic tables on the porch and neon beer signs in the window, past a small car mechanic, past an antiques shop with chairs and a sofa sitting outside on display.

He pulled up to a small stone kiosk and stopped. A portly security guard in a gray uniform came out and peered into the window.

“A little trouble on the way, Ross?” the guard asked, smiling.

“Sorry, Bob,” Ross replied. “I forget about that Sonic speed trap. Thanks for working it out.”

Ross turned to Cody. “Cody, this is Proctor Bob. He keeps out the bad guys.”

“Nice to meet you, sir,” Cody said.

“Yep, yep,” Proctor Bob said, backing away and slapping the Jeep’s roof twice. “Have at it, boys.”

Ross drove past the kiosk. Up a winding road called University Avenue: freshly paved asphalt, flanked by towering weeping willows that seemed to wave hello in the breeze.

The road straightened out, and then suddenly, just like that, Cody was there.

Chapter Two

Cody's pulse ticked faster. It was even more beautiful than he'd expected.

It was a storybook village, a collection of magic castles. They matched one another in identical stone—not orange or pink or brown, but a wondrous meld of all three, glowing in the rich, complex afternoon sun.

He had seen the Statue of Liberty, the Empire State Building, the Golden Gate Bridge—all more glorious in person than in pictures. He felt the same awe now.

In the distance, bells and chimes riddled the air to welcome him. They came from those two majestic stone towers he knew well from his book: Breslin Tower—darker, ancient, comparatively squat; and Shapard Tower—younger, taller, more robust. The father/son towers seemed to compete for Cody's attention with their merry greetings.

Ross drove slowly down University Avenue, as if letting Cody drink it all in. He rolled down the tinted windows, and the hot, thick air flooded the freezing Jeep. It was fragrant with freshly cut grass and a sharply sweet smell Cody didn't recognize. Perhaps it came from the hundreds of blooming wildflowers or the thick vines snaking up the castles. Cody immediately remembered the hydrangeas from the brochure. They were in huge bushes clustered everywhere, with large, globelike blooms of pink and blue. The colors were softer in person. They reminded him of Marcie, and he made a mental note to call her.

They passed the Klondyke Book and Supply Store, where a few students chatted out front. They stopped their conversation and watched them roll by. Ross's Jeep was the only car on the street, and it attracted a lot of attention.

"Whaddup?" Ross shouted at his friends and gave them the finger. They returned the gesture but were mostly interested in Cody, since he was new. Ross rolled on.

"Klondyke, McClurg," Ross listed as they inched past the stone buildings. "Remember any of these? From the pictures?"

"I think so," Cody said, peering past the buildings along the street to the groups of small castles beyond, wondering what they were, since they weren't named on his cartoon map.

Outside McClurg Student Center, near the bike rack, sat three dogs staring at the front door, panting and waiting. McClurg was clearly a newer building, more architecturally modern, albeit built with the same warm, stone bricks. Through the tall windows, Cody saw only a handful of people at tables, as it was too late for lunch and too early for dinner. They were adults, not students. Parents? Professors?

"Hello, Fletcher!" Ross yelled across Cody, through his window. The same older black gentleman from the DVD was leaving McClurg with a plastic doggy bag. Fletcher was nattily dressed as before and waved back as he approached the Jeep. Cody felt like he already knew these people. The young German shepherd mix followed him, leaping and lunging for the bag. The same circus act, although more aggressive in person.

"Fine afternoon, Mr. Ross," Fletcher said in his easy, resonant voice, leaning into Cody's window. "Where you coming from?"

"Just bringing in the last of my charges. Cody, Fletcher. He runs the place."

"That's right, I do." Fletcher chuckled. "Kept it clean and going for the past forty-seven years. Don't you go making a mess for me now." He chuckled again, although Cody could tell he meant it.

"I won't, sir," Cody said, extending his hand. "Nice to meet you."

The black German shepherd lunged up at Cody's window with a threatening bark. Cody jumped back as Fletcher grabbed the collar and snapped the dog back.

"Down, Nesta!" Fletcher ordered, and Nesta looked away and around, not listening or caring.

"When'd you get this one?" Ross asked. Nesta started barking again, wildly, at nothing.

"Aw, the school gave her to me in June, after little Trixie passed on," Fletcher said, scarcely audible through Nesta's incessant barks. "They found her somewhere. She needs some training." Nesta was lunging again for Fletcher's doggy bag, which he held over his head. Fletcher's hands were wrinkled and worn, like a lifetime laborer.

"Good luck with that." Ross laughed, although Cody didn't see the humor. This dog was a little nuts.

"Carry on," Fletcher said, crossing University Avenue as Ross drove off. In the rearview mirror, Cody saw Nesta leap toward Fletcher's neck, desperate for the bag and deaf to Fletcher's orders. Very different from Maisy's and Max's pinging. He hoped Nesta had had her shots.

Just ahead, a bright, gleaming banner with purple letters hung high above University Avenue, billowing in the breeze: "Welcome Home! Yea, S'wanee's Right!"

On the left, tucked off on a field in front of another unnamed building, dozens of students grouped about, holding red plastic cups. They were dressed in moving-in clothes, although their work seemed done. The girls were mostly in shorts and tank tops and flip-flops. In the center, several boys played a pickup game of shirts-and-skins touch football. Even at a distance, they looked incredibly athletic—ripped and buff, almost freakishly so. They were all barefoot, and their broad, cut chests glistened with sweat. The girls were watching the boys, and Cody realized he would have to work out more. Until then, he'd play on the shirts team.

In the crowd, one girl poked another, then another, and soon the whole group was watching the Jeep. The boys stopped the game to watch, too. Ross kept driving, and the group disappeared behind a tree.

"The Quad," Ross pointed out across Cody, who already knew. The centerpiece of the campus, up close and in person. All Saints Chapel and the two glorious towers looming right above him, still ringing. Cody had to remember to swallow.

"You there, kid?" Ross asked.

"Yeah, I'm just…looking," Cody said, watching students crisscross the Quad. They were watching him, too. "It's…just awesome."

Ross laughed. "Yeah, I remember," he said. "It's overwhelming at first. You never quite get used to it." Ross slowed down even more. "And it's your home now. For now."

Cody looked ahead, down University Avenue, canopied with trees. What else was down there? There was so much more.

Ross took a slow left into a pink gravel driveway that led to a two-story log cabin gingerbread house with a red tile roof and bright white lacy trim that looked like icing. Blanketing the front, cascading down on all sides, draped hundreds of bright purple flower pendulums that sprang from thick, ancient vines.

"Actually, *this* is your home," Ross said, turning off the Jeep. "Rebel's Rest, aka Purple Haze. Oldest dorm on campus."

It didn't look like a dorm. It was, in fact, a home.

"You coming?" Ross called from outside the Jeep. He already had Cody's luggage from the back.

Cody's legs felt wobbly. He was still buzzed and overwhelmed by it all. Rebel's Rest stood magical and silent in front of him.

"Here? I live here?" he wanted to ask, but didn't.

S'wanee divided the freshman class into five sections of thirty students each, like a high school homeroom. These sections lived, ate, and took classes together. Freshmen all studied the same core curriculum, preordained by the university. It was an old-school system that most colleges had abandoned, but S'wanee stood firm in what worked. Only in sophomore year did students branch out with classes they chose and friends they picked, as they pursued a major and an ongoing college life.

Cody knew all this. But all he could think about was the magical log cabin in front of him. It would be, he decided, the first real home he ever knew. S'wanee could pick his friends and classes and control his whole life, as long as they let him stay here.

"Where is everybody?" Cody asked, wondering if he was early, or late, or, unlikely, had the whole place to himself. He had trouble focusing his mind to ask the right questions.

"Oh, they're around," Ross said from the front porch, waiting for Cody. "Most frosh got in yesterday, or this morning. I'm sure some are still trickling in, or with their parents for the last time. Or whatever." Ross shrugged and looked around. "They're probably out exploring." And then he said, "Upperclassmen get back this weekend. Except those stalking new prey at Freshman Week."

Cody laughed, but Ross put his finger to his lips, shushing him. "Listen," he said. Inside Rebel's Rest, someone was playing an a cappella Aretha Franklin gospel song. It was a beautiful, strange thing to hear in a college dorm. Ross quietly cracked the front door open and motioned Cody to follow.

The foyer felt refreshingly cool and looked warm, rich, and inviting. It smelled exactly like Cody thought a log cabin would. The wooden, wide-planked hallway ran straight toward the back underneath a threadbare Persian runner. An antique grandfather clock with Roman numerals ticked patiently along the side.

Off either side of the foyer were living rooms with fireplaces and tufted leather sink-down sofas and overstuffed club chairs and more well-trod rugs. There were shelves of leather books and a round table flanked by wooden desk chairs. Crackled oil portraits of serious and long-dead people hung on the walls from ornate, gold frames. In one corner was a wicker basket stacked with board games: Scrabble, Monopoly, and Clue. Next to the front door sat a blue and white porcelain stand full of purple and white striped college umbrellas for the taking. Next to that sat a picnic basket brimming with flashlights.

It took a moment to register that the beautiful singing coming from the back was a live person. At the same time, Cody first noticed the delicious smells of cooking bacon and freshly baked cookies. The singing abruptly stopped and then a husky muttering: "I declare, Pearl, where *did* you hide the Clabber Girl?"

"Don't stop on our account, Pearl!" Ross hollered toward the back.

There was a brief, confused silence, and then the woman hollered back, "Ross? You here? Wait, wait!" There was a kitchen clattering and a shuffling, and then Pearl was in the hallway barreling toward them with open arms.

She was big and black and beautiful. Her hair was perfectly coiffed in an old-school globe style. She wore a plain navy dress under her khaki, flour-dusted apron. She shuffled at them in pink bedroom slippers with flowers embroidered on the arch. She wiped her hands on her apron and threw her arms around Cody.

"Cody's here! Now we're all full!" she squealed through laughter. Unlike his own mother's bony and brittle embrace, Pearl's was lush and enveloping. It was a *hug*.

"Look at this handsome boy," she said, pulling back to inspect him with a wide smile. Her age was unguessable, but her sparkling, knowing eyes put her somewhere in her fifties. "All my kids are so good-looking this year. Really fine-looking."

She reached over and swatted Ross on the arm. "You were supposed to call before you got here," she scolded him. "I don't have my shoes on!"

"I texted," Ross said, and Pearl raspberried her lips. "Text, my foot," she dismissed. "Baby, we don't text." She turned to Cody and repeated through a low, guttural laugh, "Baby, we don't text. Pearl doesn't have a mo-*bile* phone."

On a dime, Pearl got down to business.

"Let's get you settled in," she said. "You hungry? The cookies are still cooling."

"I'm okay, thanks," Cody replied politely, although he wanted one.

"I got him a Stuckey's pecan log," Ross added.

"Yuck. Let's get you to your room."

"Upstairs, right? 2B?" Ross asked, pointing back to the foyer staircase.

"Follow me," Pearl ordered as she shuffled down the long hall toward the back. This was a log mansion. She stopped in the huge dining room, which was clearly a newer addition. Fresh flowers adorned each of the three round tables. Beyond the full-length windows with tartan drapes was a stone back porch and a contained grassy field encircled by several smaller log cabins, like a campground.

"Where is everybody?" Pearl asked herself, and then she called out toward the open back door, "Banjo! Come show your classmate to his room!"

"What, I'm the houseboy now?" shouted back a playfully grumpy voice.

A light-skinned black dude rose from a wicker rocking chair on the back porch. Curiously, he was wearing a safety-orange construction hard hat. He was also strumming a banjo.

"That's right; you're my houseboy." Pearl didn't skip a beat. "Help Cody with his luggage."

Banjo padded inside in a plaid shirt, olive shorts, and yellow flips. And the look-at-me orange hard hat.

"You pick the man of color to carry the luggage?" he asked. Up close, Cody saw the freckles fanned across his light-brown face under sharp hazel eyes. Maybe he wasn't black after all.

“Honey, you don’t got much color,” Pearl chortled, and headed back toward the kitchen. “Ross, come reach the baking soda for me, would ya? It’s up high.”

Banjo grabbed Cody’s bag without looking at him.

“Follow me, paleface,” he said on his way to the stairs.

• • •

“Hell no, it’s not my real name,” Banjo said, sprawled across Cody’s twin bed like he owned it. “My real name’s Arthur.” His voice sounded a perpetual yodel.

Cody was surprised to have a single room, front and center upstairs, overlooking the Quad. From here, he could see the hub of campus activity. Were it not for the very old and very tall evergreen tree right across University Avenue, he’d have a perfect view of All Saints Chapel. The spires of the attached Shapard Tower peeked out over the top of the tree, which was almost perfectly centered in Cody’s window. The old tree was cordoned off with spikes and ropes to keep students from trampling on the fresh sod that surrounded it. It reminded Cody of the Rockefeller Center Christmas tree.

“But the names at this school are whack,” Banjo continued, foraging through Cody’s freshman orientation folder, which had been on his pillow. “Paxton, Emerson, Vail, Bishop…I forget the others. All these blue-blood legacy names! But not just legacies: At the Klondyke, I met an Asian dude named Dollar. *Dollar!* His parents didn’t go here, and I *know* they didn’t name him that. So fuck it, I made up a new name for myself, too.”

Banjo Frisbeed the round, preprinted name tag from Cody’s packet. On his own, which he wore on his belt loop, Banjo had marked out his real name and written in his newly adopted one. "Who you gonna be?" he asked.

"I'll be Cody," Cody said, ducking from the slanted ceiling. His room was small but charmingly decorated. There were freshly painted moldings and wainscoting underneath new-looking yellow-and-red plaid wallpaper. Another small Persian rug covered the worn wooden floor that creaked. In addition to the twin bed, there was an antique desk, a chair, and a chest of drawers. His box from home sat on his desk next to a lamp of burnished brass. A purple and white S'wanee pennant hung on the wall, and a cube dorm refrigerator nestled in the corner. The little room was like a cozy cocoon. And it was all his.

"When did you meet all these people?" Cody asked. "When'd you get here?"

"My dad dropped me off yesterday," Banjo replied. "He went back to Memphis. He had to work today. You scholarship, too?"

Cody paused for an instant and then said, "Yeah. I'm scholarship, too."

"They put the scholarship kids up here, in the Big House. So Pearl can put us to work, probably. They give you a campus job yet?"

"Not yet."

"I'm working at the gym. The equipment desk. Handing towels out to the rich white kids." Banjo's racial chip on the shoulder had a harmless, comical tinge.

"I gotta give you a new name," Banjo continued. "Twinkle Eyes, maybe. You've been all twinkly since you got here."

"Arthur, you still got my shampoo?" At the door, a skinny kid in a towel stood nervously tapping his bare foot. He was tall and plain and so scrawny that Cody immediately felt more confident in his own physique. He had dark bird's-nest hair and seemed slightly on edge. He looked at the floor and not at Cody.

"Elliott, I told you my name is Banjo."

"Banjo, you got my shampoo? It's not in the shower." Elliott yawned forcefully.

"Your *Suave* is in my caddy. Help yourself."

"Leave it in the shower next time. Better yet, get your own."

"Twinkle, this is Elliott. Aka Mr. Sunshine. We're the three floor servants up here." Banjo and Elliott already shared an ease and familiar banter with each other. They had a day on him.

Cody extended his hand, and Elliott shook it quickly, barely making eye contact.

"Hey, Elliott."

"Hey, Cody." Elliott yawned again. It was less a sleepy yawn and more a nervous tick. Cody wondered if he even knew he was doing it.

Downstairs, from the back, came a ringing triangle. Banjo scanned the printed schedule from Cody's packet and checked his watch.

"Better get dolled up fast," Banjo said. "It's time to mix and mingle."

• • •

Banjo was right: These names were goofy.

Cody had taken a quick shower, after Elliott, in the upstairs bathroom the three of them shared. It reminded Cody of the Restoration Hardware from his old mall. There was a white claw-foot tub with an exposed shower/hand shower contraption of daunting complexity. Water sprayed everywhere as Cody struggled with knobs and valves to tame the beast. He'd learn.

He hurriedly unpacked and picked out a green moose polo to go with his Levi's. He wadded and tossed his sweaty travel clothes into the corner, making a mental note to get a hamper, and mussed up his hair with pomade. He followed Banjo's lead by pinning his name tag through his belt loop.

"Light a fire, Jersey," Banjo yodeled from the hallway, testing a new nickname. "They've tapped the keg."

The Rebel's Rest "shrimp boil" mixer was in full swing. The sun was gone, but the sky was still light. Around the backyard fire pit mulled the rest of his name-tagged section mates, seemingly materialized from just an hour ago. They stopped and turned when Cody, hatless Banjo, and Elliott—the scholarship trio—stepped out the back door, instinctively huddled together for security.

There was no need, and the trio easily folded into the crowd. Everyone seemed eager to meet everyone else, although a few clearly knew one another from some common past. Cody pegged these as the lucky "legacies"—children of alumni—who had likely grown up together, on special occasions, at this very place. Now they belonged in their own right.

Caleb was chatting with Emerson and Sinkler about the Philadelphia Eagles' upcoming season, and Paxton was laughing with Huger about how bloated Vince Vaughn looked in his latest comedy that Cody had skipped, and Bishop was flirting with Vail, earnestly interested in her summer escapades at her parents' place on St. Simons Island and lamenting how crowded it was with tourists in August. Skit, perky and bold, taunted Cody and Banjo for wearing their name tags on their waist. "You want people to look down south to know who you are?"

They were dressed casually and almost uniformly: guys in polos or plaid shirts over wife beaters and khaki, olive, or navy cargo shorts with frayed legs; girls in floral or pastel tops and slimming pants or very short shorts. Everybody wore flip-flops in a rainbow of colors. Cody felt overdressed in jeans and wrongly dressed with his moose. Everyone else had whales. Apparently, the moose was out. What did a whale shirt cost?

"How's your room, Tiger?" Ross beamed, handing Cody a fresh beer in a purple plastic cup. Cody was eager to recharge his buzz.

The other students were mostly white with a few Latinos and a couple of Asians. Banjo was the only black kid—if he was, in fact, black. Everyone was incredibly fit and athletic-looking. According to their name tags, they were from Atlanta and Cleveland and Seattle and Miami, and at least two were from San Diego. There was one international student—a waifish girl from Germany, although she sounded American. "My father's stationed there," Cody overheard her say. All the boys were clean-shaven. It appeared everyone had gotten a haircut right before they'd arrived.

"It's my real name," said a stunning Asian girl named Sin, cornered by the name-police Banjo. "It's Asian. Where the hell did you get yours, *Banjo*?"

Pearl was a gracious, multitasking hostess. She alternated between overseeing the catering staff as they boiled kettles of shrimp on a portable kerosene cooker to the setup on the picnic benches covered in red-and-white checked tablecloths to seamlessly introducing Archer to Buzz and pulling Elliott from the shadows to talk with a bubbly blonde named Houston, who was clearly a few beers in. In between gentle pairings, she'd stand to the side, hands on hips, and peer out over her brood, mother-hen-like.

"Fletcher! Bring yourself over here for some shrimp and grits, ya hear?" she bellowed across Abbo's Alley—the wild, vast field of oaks and daffodils and sweet clover that abutted Rebel's Rest and connected the campus to the staff housing in the dark wilderness beyond. Fletcher was walking home with his beast Nesta who seemed almost bipolar—one minute calmly snooping and then suddenly lunging into the air at her master. Nesta was a handful.

"I don't like that dog," Banjo muttered.

Fletcher begged off, claiming he had more work to do before the start of the school year, "As soon as I go lock this rascal up!" Fletcher looked worn out. He was too old for a dog so spirited.

Caleb was the natural leader of the section. He was tall and blond with a bright, wide smile and perfect teeth. Cody had watched him work the crowd, meeting everyone with ease, and was a little wary of anyone so outgoing. From a distance, he seemed like a tool. All that changed when it was Cody's turn in Caleb's spotlight.

"New Jersey gets a bum rap, but I think it's beautiful," Caleb from DC said, focused on Cody like he was the only one at the party. "I really trust Jersey people. They say what they think." It was like meeting an Olympian. It was impossible not to like him. Within minutes, he knew almost everything about Cody's life and seemed genuinely curious and interested. "Dude, you've grown up in some awesome cities. I'm jealous." Caleb spoke about himself only if it were needed to keep the conversation going. Not surprisingly, he was a S'wanee legacy. Cody wondered if he might be a future US president. "Hey bud, you need a refill?" Caleb asked, taking Cody's empty cup back to the keg.

"Cody, get some food in your stomach," Pearl ordered, bringing him a plate of shrimp and biscuits and cole slaw and yellow porridge. "I don't want you wobbly."

"Thank you, Pearl," Cody replied, wondering if he seemed drunk. The porridge was gritty and cheesy and good.

By now it was dark, and the warm air was dotted with blinking fireflies, which Banjo called lightning bugs. The freestanding speakers piped in an eclectic mix of acoustic, rock, and alternative, none of which Cody recognized. The crowd was liquored up and increasingly animated. A few were bumming cigarettes and smoking. Skit and Sin rhythmically weave-danced with each other off to the side.

"That Sin's a little tigress," Banjo slurred in Cody's ear. "I could get into a little Ching Chong with that…"

Ross silenced the music for his impromptu welcome speech by the crackling fire pit. Lit from below, Ross looked even older. Apparently college turned kids into adults quickly. He urged the newbies to conserve their energy for the busy week ahead, prompting the expected dismissive laughter. He and Pearl lived on-site at Rebel's Rest and were there for any questions, concerns, or general counseling, all through freshman year. It was their job. They were all one big family this first year.

Girls clustered around Ross after the music returned. He was instantly the center of female attention. Upperclass authority clearly had its privileges. Even the Adonis Caleb ranked lower and was forgotten for the moment.

Cody's iPhone jolted him. He already knew who it was.

"It's almost midnight!" Marcie snapped. "What the hell is going on down there?" Ross was right about S'wanee's cell phone reception: It was so crystal clear, he could hear Marcie drag on her cigarette.

"I forgot to call," Cody whispered from the porch, his back to the party. "It's been so busy here."

"I *know* you forgot to call, kiddo. Why are you whispering? What's that music?"

"It's just a party, Mom. With my classmates."

"And you're drinking, aren't you?" Cody was amused by Marcie's newfound maternal concern. She must already be lonely. It seemed like days since he'd last seen her.

"A little. Arianna Huffington said it was okay." Cody peeked around to make sure no one saw him talking on his cell.

From the back of the party, near the keg, Emerson grinned and shouted, "Save S'wanee!" *Caught.* Houston joined in, and then Huger and Caleb and even Banjo, good-naturedly chanting in unison, policing their own. "Save S'wanee!"

"Mom, I gotta jet," Cody said, covering his other ear.

"'Save S'wanee'? Is that *code* for something?" Marcie demanded. "Who are those idiots?"

The crowd was upon him, encircling him.

"I'll call tomorrow. I promise!" Cody said, and Skit poured her full beer on his head. Huger followed. And Sin. Even Elliott joined in.

"It sounds like a damn *cult*..." Marcie started as Cody cut her off and submitted to the drenching assault. It felt good in the hot night, and he had never laughed so hard.

• • •

P!nk and Heath Ledger were hosting the lighting of the Rockefeller Center Christmas tree, which had been moved this year to the S'wanee Quad, right across from Cody's bedroom window. They had built an ice rink in front of All Saints Chapel, around the huge evergreen tree. Disney on Ice sent Rapunzel and the Seven Dwarves to perform for the show, and they were rehearsing on skates.

Fletcher and Ross oversaw the decorating of the tree. Two workers on hydraulic lifts replaced several of the branches while Ross buried the electrical cables in the sod so nobody would trip. An older gentleman with silver hair and an iPad was really in charge and seemed to give Ross a hard time. Soon after Shapard Tower struck four o'clock, there was a loud, cracking pop that startled everyone and extinguished the thousands of fireflies. The cast of *Survivor* crowded around Cody's window to watch and urged him to go back to bed, which he did.

Chapter Three

"Put your shoes on before you come to my dining room!" Pearl ordered Huger, who had stumbled in barefoot from his cabin out back. "I've told you before."

The breakfast buffet steamed with scrambled eggs and thick slab bacon and homemade buttermilk biscuits with a creamy sausage gravy Pearl called "sawmill." Cody poured a mug of coffee, which was unusual for him, but he needed a jolt. He loaded it up with cream and sugar, since he hated the taste. "That's some faggy coffee," Banjo sniffed.

The conversations were muted all around. "What time did you crash?" and "I think Paxton booted," and "I can't find my hair band; did you borrow it?" and "The beds are better here." The dining room was simultaneously chatty and hushed: groggy mutterings punctuated by clinking forks and plates, as Rebel's Rest recharged for the busy day ahead. A bed-headed Bishop and Vail came in together, and Cody wondered if they'd hooked up.

On the low-volume wall TV, CNN's morning show reported on the Brazilian president's trip to the White House and how the weak economy was swelling the ranks of army recruitment and the latest theories behind the mysterious deaths of birds, cows, fish, and whales washing ashore worldwide. There was a rumor a famous sitcom star was adopting a child.

“Banjo, turn that off during meals,” Pearl said.

“Yes’m.” Banjo bowed and clicked it off.

Ross bounded in, freshly showered, and lifted the room’s energy. “Rally, Tigers!” He cheered like a den leader. “We got a ten o’clock!”

S’wanee had a packed Freshman Week schedule, some events optional, most mandatory. As the Rebel’s Rest section migrated across University Avenue, the scholarship trio fell back in together, slightly separated from the group. Without alcohol to embolden their mingling, this seemed to be their natural state. Banjo had his hard hat on again, like a beacon.

Shapard Tower was belling out a song to wake up the campus. Cody listened carefully to decipher it.

“Are they playing ‘Poker Face’?” he asked.

“Probably,” Banjo grumbled. “Yesterday they were playing ‘Yellow Submarine.’ Dude up there must be on some serious herb.”

New student check-in was organized in Burwell Garden, near the center of campus, in rotating shifts by section. Upperclass volunteers with iPads ran the show, and it was efficient and surprisingly high-tech.

“Welcome to S’wanee, Cody.” Perky sophomore Lauren in school T-shirt and name tag smiled as she checked off his name. From a rolling plastic cart, she located and handed him an iPad, his name labeled on the back cover. “Yours for the year, hooked into the school’s network. All your reading assignments, problem sets, and correspondence are delivered here automatically. We’re paperless. Please take good care of it.”

“I’ve seen you,” Cody said, unable to resist. “You were on the DVD.”

“What DVD?” Lauren was puzzled.

“From the school. The one they sent.” Cody had studied every frame.

"Oh, right." Lauren laughed, moving on to the next freshman. "I didn't think anybody saw that. Yep, my big debut. Have a great S'wanee Day!"

"An inch to the left. No, your other left," junior Clifton guided, digital camera in hand. "Big smile now." He snapped Cody's awkward grin in front of the Burwell Garden fountain, and moments later his S'wanee ID card spat from a dispenser at the next table.

"It's an all-in-one," junior Meade schooled him. "Library, McClurg Student Center, sporting events, movies, whatever. It's loaded up with your Tiger Bucks. Please keep it with you at all times." Cody looked goofy on the card but didn't ask for a do over, since others were waiting. "You're all set, Cody. Have a great S'wanee…Oh wait…" Meade checked something on her iPad.

"Cody Marko? The infirmary needs to see you. This morning."

Cody checked his printed schedule and stammered, "I…have to meet my academic adviser."

"That can wait." Meade shrugged. "Do you know where the infirmary is?"

"I'll show him," Banjo said. "I had to go yesterday."

• • •

"You had your MMR as an infant, but I don't see the measles booster in your records," Dr. Nagle told him. The school infirmary looked like another little stone house from the outside, but inside was sterile-looking and cliniclike. Dr. Nagle was dressed in an open-collar shirt and khakis, like he hadn't planned to work that day, although he didn't seem to mind. Cody sat on the padded table covered in white paper, his feet dangling.

"Most teens have the booster for extra protection," Dr. Nagle continued. "The FDA recommends it. Do you remember if you had one?"

"I don't remember," Cody said. "I haven't had a shot in a long time."

"I called your mother. She didn't remember either. She said maybe she forgot to get you one."

That wasn't surprising.

"It's odd your high school didn't follow up. Measles is so contagious that one case at a school is considered an epidemic." Cody wasn't surprised his high school had dropped the ball either. They scarcely knew his name.

"No matter." Dr. Nagle stood up in the turquoise and white examination room. "We can give you another. S'wanee requires that booster."

"Okay." Cody shrugged.

"You're not afraid of needles, are you?"

"No. I mean, it's what it is."

"How about your flu shot? It's a bit early in the season, but might as well give you both, since you're here. One needle instead of two."

"Sure," said Cody.

Dr. Nagle returned a few minutes later with a handheld contraption that looked like a weapon.

"You ever had the vaccine gun?" Dr. Nagle asked.

"I don't think so," Cody said, not liking the look or sound of it.

"This might fall on deaf ears"—the doctor smiled—"but you shouldn't drink for twenty-four hours."

Cody first smelled and then felt the cold antiseptic swabbed on his upper arm. He was looking the other way.

"Just a slight pinch and sting." The doctor whistled in through his teeth, and an instant later, a spring unloaded with a *thwack*.

It hurt like hell: a sharp, searing jolt that seemed to blow his shoulder muscles apart and penetrate deep into the bone. He'd never felt anything like it. Were shots always this painful?

"Piece of cake," Dr. Nagle said, taping a cotton swab across his arm and covering it all with a Band-Aid. Cody still hadn't looked; his arm felt heavy and stiff and violated. He wondered if the quack had broken off the needle inside him.

"It might be sore for a day or so," Dr. Nagle advised. "It's a live vaccine. But if it gets inflamed or you feel feverish, let us know immediately, won't you?"

"You never had the gun before?" Banjo asked when he and Elliott picked Cody up outside the infirmary. "It's a bitch, right? I'd rather catch the fucking flu."

• • •

The student activity fair, called Tiger Tracks, was in full swing on the front lawn of the DuPont Library, each group vying to lure freshmen into their clutches. There was the bimonthly campus newspaper, the *S'wanee Purple*, the S'wanee Model UN, the *Mountain Goat* arts magazine.

"'Mountain Goat' is S'wanee-ese for 'closet queer,'" Banjo schooled him. "Figures."

From his book, Cody remembered that Mountain Goat was originally the name of the steam train that used to connect the mile-high campus to the real world below. "'Riding the Mountain Goat' clearly has a different meaning these days," Banjo huffed, not particularly interested in Cody's history lesson. Elliott didn't get the joke. He was too busy casing the other students furtively, eyes flicking up and down, hands in pockets. He was like a coiled, stuck spring. At least he wasn't yawning.

For the first time, Cody saw a large cross section of his fellow students milling about. He couldn't tell the new from the returning; they all seemed equally comfortable in this place. The trio stuck together, booth to booth, although Banjo's screaming hat attracted plenty of attention to all three.

There were College Republicans and Democrats, the Arcadians—student tour guides—and something called Ducks Unlimited, which seemed like an environmental group. The ubiquitous Habitat for Humanity was signing up volunteers to build an elementary school extension down from the Mountain. The university orchestra's string quartet played on the side, and across the way singers from the S'wanee Cadence stood in a semicircle and smiled and crooned in harmony at one another. It was awkward watching them.

On the edge of the fair, outside the largest building Cody had yet seen, stood a cluster of parents watching the student activities. They were dorkily dressed fathers—starched short-sleeve shirts tucked into pressed khakis—and Cody was once again glad Marcie hadn't come, since she would have had nothing in common with them, or likely their wives either. She was young and hip and unguarded; these stragglers were older and proper and, frankly, embarrassing—milling about and staring. They, too, had discovered Banjo's fluorescent hat and, one by one, locked on to the trio.

Ross came out of the large, gleaming building and welcomed the parents. The building looked brand-new, with tall windows and electric sliding doors, but made of the same dusty-pink sandstone blocks that blended in with the rest of the ancient architecture. One of the fathers whispered to Ross, and Ross turned and looked out at the fair, by chance catching Cody's eye. He smiled and winked at Cody and then nodded at the father. As Ross herded the parents inside, Cody saw the name engraved in the concrete slab above the portico: Spencer Hall. Cody was increasingly in awe of Ross's magnetism; even the parents treated him like a rock star.

The school radio station WUTS—"WUTS in Your Ear?"—had freestanding speakers blaring an eclectic mix that reminded Cody of last night's mixer. Their members weren't so much recruiting as passively grooving in a stoned stupor. Their booth was comically sandwiched between the Young Life Christian Group and the Bacchus "responsible drinking" Society, which also handed out condoms in a rainbow of colors. "*Why don't we get drunk and screw*?" Banjo sang as he passed.

Over near the S'wanee Natural History Society, Bishop and Vail were socializing with a group Cody hadn't seen before. Not surprisingly, Caleb was glad-handing another gang by the Student Government Assembly. Either they were all more adept at intermingling than Cody was, or else they knew one another from before. Clearly, the freshman class was crawling with legacies.

There was a canoe team, crew team, men's and women's rugby clubs, cycling team, climbing club, martial arts club, and fencing, all staffed with incredibly fit athletes who seemed to own the school. There was also table tennis and paintball, which partially piqued Elliott's interest. Cody himself sniffed closer to the ultimate Frisbee club. "Look, but don't touch," Banjo warned him. "These clubs are for the full-fare kids. We won't have time." Although friendly and welcoming, nobody actively recruited the trio, as if they could smell their scholarship status and its constraints.

Nevertheless, Cody loaded up with flyers and Frisbees and water bottles and key chain bottle openers, which he stuffed into his orange L.L.Bean backpack. A sudden sharp pain flashed through his arm. The vaccine still felt thick in his shoulder, like it was clogged there. He instinctively flicked his hand back and forth fanlike, and the pain eased a bit. When he looked up and around, he locked eyes with a most unusual girl, who was staring at him from across the fair.

Or at least he thought she was staring from behind black catlike sunglasses. Her hair matched her glasses and hung just below her ears, cut straight and severe, like a boy. In fact, her angular, curveless body could pass for a boy's. But her milky, flawless skin, fitted black tank top, and shock of red lipstick instantly cleared up any confusion. Over her shoulder slung a zebra-print purse with her freshman name tag pinned on the strap, too far away to read.

She was with a small group of girls, all blond and bubbling, over by the S'wanee Peace Coalition. As strikingly unique as she was, she folded effortlessly into the group. Like his own trio, her first friends at S'wanee were preordained by geography. She patiently nodded at their gigglings and appeared to add a comment of no importance. Then she removed her black cat-eye sunglasses and leveled an even gaze right at Cody.

He had seen her somewhere before; she looked so familiar. Not in person, but onscreen, in a passing, fleeting way. For a brief moment, he thought maybe on the S'wanee DVD, and he scrolled through it in his mind, but that wasn't possible, since she was new here, too. No, it was from somewhere else. A television show, a commercial, maybe even a movie. S'wanee had its share of famous actors in the past. She sorta looked like Sara Bareilles and had a similar style as Gwen Stefani, but she was neither. Maybe she was a model, or just looked like one. She caught him staring back at her, and Cody quickly looked away.

Cody felt a slight chill of fever, even in the hot sun. That damn vaccine was making him sweat, and his face and scalp felt clammy with drip. He wiped it away with his good hand. Now her group had migrated, along with her, to the crew team booth with its tall, bronzed gods, a few of whom had stripped off their shirts both to soak up the sun and to show off the sport's effects on their ripped physiques. Their scheme was working, and their booth was crowded.

But The Girl kept glancing Cody's way, eyeing him like a pet in a cage. He wanted to get closer, to see the color of her eyes, to nail down the mystery. But his face felt hot and chilled almost simultaneously. Was he breaking out, or was he blotchy with rash? Is that why The Girl was staring? He needed a mirror.

"Dude, does my face look weird?" he asked Banjo.

"*Dood*, of course your face looks weird," Banjo replied automatically, not looking at him, eyeing the Tiger Girls in the center dancing a routine. "You're just now figuring this out?" He shot Cody a puzzled look and kept going.

"'Cause that chick keeps staring." Cody subtly nodded in her direction, and Banjo sized her up.

"Probably wants to feast on your blood," he mumbled, giving a thumbs-down. "She shouldn't be out in the daylight. The werewolves might get her."

Then, just like that, The Girl and her preselected friends collected themselves and wandered off from the fair, giggling and chatting. The Girl didn't look back and was gone.

"Dude, let's bolt." Banjo corralled the trio. "There's a taco bar outside McClurg."

As they passed Spencer Hall, the parents watched stupidly from behind the lobby's glass doors and windows. Didn't they know the school now belonged to the kids? Wasn't it time to let go?

• • •

The afternoon's campus tour—technically optional but mandatory in Cody's mind—left him feeling shortchanged. The tour compactly covered just the main buildings that Cody had already seen. The campus stretched out much farther, but their student tour guide—a flat-faced, wiry-haired chick from the Arcadian booth—urged them to explore the rest on their own.

"It's the besth way," she said with a sporadic speech impediment that was tough to diagnose. "Just get out and lose yourthelf in the Domain. You'll find your way back." She repeated many of the legends and ghost stories from Cody's book ("Beware the Headlezz Gownsman. He studied so hard hizz head fell off.") and talked about the S'wanee Fog ("I hear it's crazy. I mean, I *know* it ith.") As they passed All Saints Chapel, she warned them about the S'wanee Curse.

"There's a college seal on the floor in the narthex," she lectured, pointing at the front door. "You must never step on it. Never. It unleashes the S'wanee Curse." And Cody asked, "What's that do?" He'd never heard of a narthex and wondered if it was just another word the girl was mangling. She was an odd choice for tour guide.

"You'll never graduate," the guide said earnestly. "It will wreak havoc on your life, and you'll never graduate." She smiled, relishing the legend's threat. "Of course, there are ways to reverth it, but they bring their own perils." She peered devilishly at Cody, hoping for more questions.

"We won't step on it," Banjo grumbled, bored, and the girl soon ended the tour and withed them luck. "Exit Hammerface," Banjo said as soon as she left.

Banjo led them down University Avenue to the Fowler Sport and Fitness Center to show off his "cotton field," a joke he had to explain to Cody and Elliott. "Where the slaves slaved." He pointed to the gleaming counter where he'd be handing out towels. "Slaves worked here?" Elliott asked, still confused, and Banjo dropped it. Cody wondered what his own campus job would be.

The school's fitness center was more like a plush country club—clean and newly renovated with an indoor Olympic pool, indoor/outdoor tennis, high-tech cardio and weight rooms, all backed against a meticulously manicured golf course that stretched out forever. It was mostly peopled with professors and staff, no doubt enjoying the calm before the imminent onslaught of returning students. The wood-paneled lobby showcased S'wanee's athletic heritage with dozens of engraved and tarnished silver trophies, cups, plaques, and framed and faded glory photos of long-ago teams. S'wanee apparently had lost its athletic edge, since all the awards were decades old.

The rest of the afternoon's schedule was packed with optional lectures and presentations. "S'wanee Stories" in Guerry Auditorium, "Living and Learning" in Blackwell, "Embracing Change and Moving Forward" in Convocation Hall.

"Snooze-a-roni," Banjo decreed, blowing them off. "We gotta track down some action for tonight." He led the trio back to Rebel's Rest, where Pearl served homemade peach ice cream and sweet tea on the back porch, while Banjo strummed bluegrass tunes from his rocking chair. In the downstairs parlor, Sin played classical music on the baby grand, superbly. Cody wondered why he'd never learned to play an instrument.

That night, after a delicious but messy picnic supper of fried chicken and waffles, there was an outdoor screening of *Beyond the Valley of the Dolls* on the Quad, which Banjo judged "craptastic." From his bag of too-salty popcorn, Cody scoured the dozens of flickering faces on the lawn, faces he was starting to recognize and remember. But he didn't see The Girl. The movie was an old, scratchy reel-to-reel; it was a weird, druggy, and surprisingly graphic flick, and after the film broke for the third time, in the middle of a group sex scene, Banjo had had enough.

"Let's troll," he ordered the trio, furtively checking a text. "I got a bead on the action."

Instead of a Greek system, S'wanee had its own collection of not-so-secret secret societies. There was the Black Ribbon, the Sphinx, the Silver Spoon, and the Anchovies. But the big two, and the only ones with houses, were the Highlanders and the Wellingtons.

Banjo easily navigated the dense woods of the pitch-black Manigault Park, following the music and yellow front porch light to the Wellington Lodge tucked toward the back. He turned the knob of the "secret" house, the name clearly visible in leprechaun font, and they waltzed right in. Cody's first college party was at full boil.

There were sofas and chairs and a pool table, and the air was smoky and stale, and it was packed and hot and loud, and the beer flowed behind the massive oak bar. "Belly up!" hollered an upperclassman manning the tap when he saw the trio. Cody briefly considered Dr. Quack's warning about booze, but his arm felt better, just a little stiff now, and he grabbed the overflowing cup and took a long gulp.

The Highlanders and Wellingtons were famous for wearing kilts on special occasions, and apparently tonight qualified. Any kilt would do, and nobody matched. They wore them with blue or pink oxford button-downs or faded polos—the damn whale again—and mostly flips or slides. A few shuffled in unlaced Wallabees. Their hair was longer, and they were boisterous, rowdy, and welcoming. There were dozens of girls flitting about, but not The Girl.

"Where you from?" and "Welcome, Tiger!" and "Purple Haze? Great fucking house. I lived there freshman year," and Cody was on his third beer, and four boys were kneeling around the Ping-Pong table, blowing the plastic ball back from the edge and trying to huff it to their opponents' side. Each time the ball fell off led to cheers and a chug. They crushed the ball and grabbed a fresh one from a box and started all over. The music was loud, and everyone dripped with sweat and nobody cared.

"So what's your prank?" a Wellington asked the trio, dealing cards around a table near the back deck. "What prank?" Cody asked, and the Wellington said, "Freshmen gotta pull a prank before classes start to make their mark." Another Wellington said, "You just got one day left."

"What kind of prank?" Elliott asked, drinking heavily and surprisingly social. "We'll pull a prank," Banjo assured them, sorting his cards. "Any suggestions?"

"Not the clapper," Ross warned them, pulling up a chair, apparently a member. "Stay away from the clapper, seriously." Ross seemed to be everywhere always, and effortlessly took charge wherever he went. Cody was proud his big brother was also the big man on campus. He felt cool and accepted just being near him.

"Freshmen used to steal the clapper from the Shapard Tower bell, so it wouldn't ring and classes wouldn't start," Ross explained, as a Wellington poured Cody another beer from the pitcher. "Back in the early seventies, a couple dunderheads fell and got killed. That definitely canceled classes, but the school threatened to replace the bells with a tape-recorded speaker if anyone tried it again." The Wellingtons booed in unison.

"Pranks are fine, but stay away from the tower," Ross finished. "Save the bells." And everyone in the room chanted "Save the bells!" and "Save S'wanee!" and Cody drank deep from his beer and wondered why Ross's fingers looked dirty and soiled, like he'd been digging. Ross slapped Cody on the back and went off to talk to some girls who were waiting for him.

"Now *that's* what I'm talking about!" Banjo shouted as a Wellington slammed a fresh bottle on the table. "You a bourbon boy, Cody?"

"Dunno," Cody slurred, as shots were poured all around. His arm felt good as new, and it was hotter and louder in here, and it was very smoky but he didn't mind, and he raised his shot glass with everyone as a group of Kilts by the bar counted to three.

• • •

Brad Pitt and Fergie came to do a live performance of *Mr. and Mrs. Smith* outside in Burwell Garden, but it was poorly rehearsed and awkward, and they soon gave up to chat with the students. Brad Pitt flirted with the freshman girls, which was creepy since he could be their father. Fergie wore the same black dress with the slit up the leg from the poster and was archly beautiful. She looked Cody straight in the eye, and he told her how much he liked "Salt." She smiled and rubbed his arm and went to get in the fountain. He ran to warn her that the fish might bite, but she slipped down the drain and disappeared.

• • •

A warm, wet nose woke Cody to Nesta with concern in her big brown eyes.

"What you find, girl?" Fletcher asked nearby. Cody was lying curled in the middle of Abbo's Alley in last night's clothes. It was still dark on the edge of daybreak, and the ground was only slightly damp. Nesta licked his face and backed away, tail wagging, proud of herself. Fletcher saw Cody, nodded and smiled, and kept walking, jangling a zookeeper-size ring of keys.

"Heh-heh." Fletcher continued across the field toward University Avenue. "Haven't seen *that* in a while!" He stopped to watch Cody stagger to his feet, silent in his confusion, leaving a shadow of crushed daffodils and sweet clover. "Why, good *morning*, son." Fletcher bowed, almost a taunt. Cody's legs and feet were sore, like he'd been sprinting without stretching, or maybe like he'd been sleeping on the ground all night. His mouth was thick and tasted like smoke.

"You'd best be getting home," Fletcher called back as he ambled on. "It's going to be a beautiful day! C'mon, Nesta! C'mon, girl!" He slapped his thigh, and Nesta bounded happily toward him. She was playful and obedient this morning, a dog transformed who heeled at her master's side.

Cody walked unsteadily toward Rebel's Rest, silent in the predawn darkness. Across University Avenue, Nesta abruptly halted on the edge of the Quad and backed away from Shapard Tower, even as Fletcher unlocked the doors. He called and slapped his thigh and finally walked toward her, but Nesta, hearing or smelling or sensing something the way dogs mysteriously do, froze and wouldn't budge. She wasn't going there.

Chapter Four

"So what's her name? Who'd you deal with?" Banjo badgered him again, and again Cody answered, "I didn't hook up with anybody." The trio crowded the bathroom, showering, shaving, teeth-brushing.

"So what's up with your French exit, dude?" Banjo pulled his razor upward, against the grain. He was meticulous. "You just disappeared."

"I don't know. I don't remember."

"Dude, you were gone," Elliott dogged, toweling off from the shower beast. He and Banjo both seemed proud of their loose-cannon hall mate. "I looked over and your eyes clicked off. Like a zombie. How much bourbon did you drink?"

"Whatever you guys did," Cody answered, although he didn't feel hung-over. Maybe Dr. Quack was right about the vaccine and drinking. He rinsed with Listerine to nuke the foul, smoky taste from his mouth, and his spit was thick and dangly.

"You don't remember anything?" Banjo asked in earnest, following Cody to his room. Outside his window, dozens of bees gently shopped the purple blooms that crawled up and over Rebel's Rest. "What time did you get back?"

"This morning sometime." Cody shrugged, not giving them more ammo with his waking up in Abbo's Alley. He was already getting enough flack. There was a slight ringing in his ears because last night's music was loud and he'd been sitting near the speakers.

"Dude, you missed out," Banjo continued. "We planned our prank. It's all set."

"What's the prank?" Cody asked, distracted, putting all his weight on one foot to head off the charley horse that threatened his calf. At least his arm was back to normal, except for a slight dull throb.

"You'll have to see for yourself," Banjo said. "It's not that big a deal, but the Wellingtons thought it was good. They helped us."

From downstairs, Pearl bellowed, "Who's been tracking mud through this house?" She muttered something to herself, and then she bellowed again: "Please leave all muddy shoes outside on the front porch!"

Cody changed into khakis and a button-down shirt and his one pair of loafers. He snuck his wet and muddy Nikes downstairs and put them outside the front door. He'd knock them clean once the mud had dried. There was no rain, and the ground was dry, and Cody hurried because he was running late.

• • •

At least he now knew what an alcohol-induced blackout was like: just a magical gap in time, missing hours gone for good and never to be recalled. It was, in a way, sorta cool and ultimately harmless.

Now he also knew what déjà vu was like, because he had been here, in this very living room, looking at the same man with the same golden retriever in front of the now dormant fireplace.

Cody might as well be the cameraman for the S'wanee DVD, framing this identical shot.

"I trust you're getting settled into this wonderful place," the silver-haired man in the tapestry chair said with a warm, confident smile.

By chance or apparent luck of the lottery, Ivan Apperson, the dean of students, had been assigned as Cody's academic adviser. He was the Big Dog, the man who ran it all, and his official residence was a large, richly appointed sandstone mansion just around the corner from Rebel's Rest. The floors creaked, and it smelled like fresh flowers, and it was the lushest showplace on campus. It was called Cravens Hall.

"Yes, I am, sir," Cody said, sitting up straight. "I'm sorry I missed yesterday. They sent me over to the..." Dean Apperson smiled with his lips closed and waved him off.

"Rules, rules," he said with a husky, resonant voice that carried far with apparently little effort. His eyes were ice blue and almost childlike, and his face looked younger than his hair, and he had smile wrinkles around his mouth and eyes. He was probably in his early sixties but had the curious, eager air of a young boy. He looked and sounded like he used to smoke, a lot.

"We try to have as few rules here as possible," Dean Apperson continued. "Few limitations, few constraints, and almost no barriers. Our only requirement, which is more of a request, is that you explore, experiment, and expand." He was impeccably dressed in a subtle, multicolored plaid summer tweed jacket, a very thin blue-striped dress shirt, and what must have been the official S'wanee tie: purple and embroidered with dozens of repeating school crests. He wore light-gray heather trousers and brown leather shoes with brass side buckles, no laces. There was something both rugged and dandy about him. He sipped tea from a china cup and seemed genuinely delighted to spend time with his young advisee.

"My door is always open to you, Cody, and I hope you'll use it. Come to me with any questions, concerns, complaints, or even just for a glass of sherry, or whatever your poison. I probably have it." He smiled and indicated his very well-stocked bar by the window. "Any hour of the day or night, but preferably before eleven p.m., as I'm an early riser. As you can imagine, it's a rigorous, challenging, and rewarding job I have here." He had the polished air of a politician, as well as the habit, in speech, of repeating and subtly expanding his points with synonyms, to drive them home. It was slightly hypnotic.

"I will personally monitor your academic and personal progress, which I hope will be swift, steady, and ever upward. If you hit a snag along your journey here, we'll work through it together. I'll be watching." Beneath his warm smile lay a benevolent warning.

"Yes, sir," Cody said, wary of his own teacup, since it looked so delicate, and he thought his hand might tremble.

"Please. Ivan. Or Dean Apperson, if you prefer. But not 'sir.' Makes me feel old, decrepit, irrelevant." He abruptly stood up, and his golden retriever took notice. At that moment, Ross came into the living room from the hallway, carrying a leather saddlebag.

"Good morning, Ross," Dean Apperson said brightly. "I was just getting acquainted with our charge, our project."

"He's doing just fine." Ross beamed his megawatt smile. "Apparently had an adventurous night last night." Cody tensed in embarrassment, but Dean Apperson diffused it immediately.

"Well, I should hope so." He laughed. "Boys will be boys. Or at least they should be while they can." He took the leather saddlebag that Ross held, assistantlike. "Okay. So much to do." As he donned the black Harry Potter gown slung over his chair, his old retriever struggled to her feet and sniffed at Cody, wagging her tail expectantly.

"Meet our new friend, Beverly," Dean Apperson said to the dog, and then he said to Cody, "Beverly likes you. She doesn't stand up for just anybody. She *can't*."

"Good girl, Beverly." Cody stroked her happy head, savvy enough to befriend the Big Dog's dog. "You could teach Nesta a thing or two; couldn't you, girl?"

"What's wrong with Nesta?" Dean Apperson perked, his deep-set blues twinkling. "You mean Fletcher's dog?"

"She's just young," Cody backtracked, and thought, "*And mentally ill.*"

"Those rescues." Dean Apperson shook his head, slinging the saddlebag over his gowned arm. "You never know what they've been through. They gravitate here from all over the town, fleeing their negligent, sometimes abusive owners. We hate to destroy them." He took one last sip of his tea and cradled the cup in its saucer. "But if anyone can tame the savage beast, it's Dog Whisperer Fletcher. Nesta will be docile and civilized and quoting Thoreau in no time." Ross laughed, and then Cody laughed, even though he couldn't pinpoint the joke.

"We'll see you at the Signing?" Dean Apperson asked rhetorically, holding the front door open. "Have a great S'wanee Day!" He chuckled at his own use of the silly phrase and then shrugged amiably, like it hit the spot anyway.

"Exceptionally fine day," Cody heard him declare as he marched off past a magnolia tree. "Even finer than yesterday…"

• • •

"I envy each one of you, for the adventure, the journey, the *odyssey* you are about to begin," Dean Apperson orated from the podium, gown flowing. "I once sat in those very seats, at this very ceremony, in this God-favored spot, and what I would give to experience it all again, fresh and new and innocent. Well, maybe not *so* innocent."

Hundreds laughed appreciatively, in unison. Cody laughed with them, again struggling to isolate the punch line.

All Saints Chapel was glorious, glowing, and packed. It was the jewel in S'wanee's ornate crown, and today it was burnished and polished for maximum sparkle. Sunlight electrified the stained-glass windows that surrounded all sides and traced S'wanee's history from the laying of the cornerstone, through various wars and expansions, to tributes to many of the school's long-dead luminaries. The windows literally wrapped the audience in the rich heritage of the Domain.

This was the moment: the focal point of the week and official gateway to his S'wanee life. The chapel overflowed with freshmen in blazers and ties and floral dresses, grouped together by section, Rebel's Rest right up front on the left. Across the aisle sat two rows of black-gowned professors, some holding purple folders. In his section, Cody sat between a yawn-stifling Elliott and a solemn-looking Banjo.

"But for all the wondrous gifts that S'wanee will bestow during your time here, we make a few demands in return." Dean Apperson continued, bracing his hands on the podium, as if for balance. Behind him, a white-haired organist, likely the same goofball who played Top 40 up in the tower, sat at the ready, *Phantom of the Opera*–style. "We demand your curiosity, your willingness to expand and experiment, your constant growth and personal evolution. And, most of all, we demand your honor."

Movement caught Cody's eye, and he looked over to the stoic Banjo, mock wanking himself in boredom. Just beyond, Cody noticed how unusual the towering stained-glass window was. It was a scene of a campus building on fire and students running in all directions through the snow, and there were purple-spotted Alice-in-Wonderland mushrooms scattered about and a red Volkswagen Bug sitting upside down on the altar of All Saints. Rebel's Rest sat smack in the window center, serene, purple pendulums and all, right above the numerals "MCMLXXI." The window looked both panicked and gleeful, and it was hard to tell if it commemorated a tragic event, or just a very wild party.

Another movement caught his eye, and Cody looked behind to Pearl a few rows back, dressed splendidly in a flowered hat and sitting among the other housemothers. She winked and pointed to his outfit and gave him an "A-OK." That morning, Cody had realized, in panic, that he'd forgotten to pack a coat and tie. "I'm sure I can find you something," Pearl said, whisking out a too-big navy blazer and whale-embroidered tie. The labels said "Vineyard Vines," and now Cody looked as spiffy as the others. The Signing demanded everyone's finest.

"By signing your name to our ancient register," the Big Dog went on, his voice rising, "you agree, without hesitation, to our codes, our traditions, our history. Make no mistake—the S'wanee Registry is a pact, an official contract, affirming your permanent and lifelong commitment to our values, our goals, and our heritage. Consider it carefully, for once you sign, there is no turning back."

Dean Apperson looked over the crowd in pointed silence. The door in the back creaked loudly, and Cody turned. The Girl hurried in, late and unapologetic. She wore, amazingly, a navy pinstripe man's suit, tightly fit. She wore a white dress shirt and a silver necktie. From her breast pocket flowed a gauzy pink silk square like a puff of magic smoke. She was stunning, and her cross-dressing finest put all the other girls to shame. Her clicking high heels echoed through the silent chapel as she sought out her section midway down the aisle and slipped in.

His spell broken, Dean Apperson stared her down and seemed tempted to scold, but came up short. The Girl confounded even him. Instead, he resumed his rhythm and added a crescendo.

"To the newest ladies and gentlemen of the Domain, it is my proudest honor and greatest privilege to invite you now to add your name to the enduring history of S'wanee." He nodded to the Phantom of the Opera, and everyone stood, as the first chord blasted.

Instantly, from the huge organ pipes, hundreds of Ping-Pong balls fired like bullets. They rained down across the audience and bounced off heads, chairs and walls, and bounced against the stained-glass windows and against one another, and kept bouncing in all directions. The audience erupted in laughter, and so did Cody, finally understanding a joke. Banjo shook his head in disapproval and whispered, "Tsk-tsk." Elliott leaned out and beamed triumphantly at him, and Banjo kept shaking his head and said, "How *very* disrespectful."

Dean Apperson smiled and nodded as a ball bounced off the altar and gave the freshmen a "Well played!" thumbs-up.

Now the Rebel's Rest section step-slid, step-waited across the front, communion-style, where elite student Gownsmen manned the long table draped in purple satin. Spread open in the center was a large leather book with a paragraph of ornate calligraphy across the top and columns of empty lines below. Ross, very dapper today, watched proudly from the side as first-up Caleb and Skit and Paxton and Vail dipped the quill pen in the inkwell and signed their names and shook Dean Apperson's hand.

The calligraphy paragraph, Cody knew, was the official S'wanee Honor Code, which they had sent him over the summer. It simply stated that members of the S'wanee community swore never to lie, cheat, or steal, on penalty of permanent expulsion. It was a zero-tolerance policy and the cornerstone of the S'wanee Experience. From it flowed the most important and enduring of S'wanee's traditions: doors without locks, unsupervised tests, unattended bags, purses, and computers. S'wanee was a wonderland of trust and security and openness.

Cody glanced out at The Girl from the line, but she was adjusting her maybe rhinestone/maybe diamond earring and chatting with the chick next to her, awaiting their turns to rise and sign. Banjo nudged Cody and handed him the pen. With a slight tremble, he poised it on the empty line. The calligraphy paragraph was much longer than he remembered and tiny-lettered, almost Willy Wonka–esque. He bent over and steadied his hand to make a proper signature, and nothing came out.

An upperclass Gownsman smiled and tapped the inkwell. Cody dipped the pen and stupidly dribbled a few drops across the tablecloth. As the organ music swelled—with one recurring off note from a ball stuck in the pipe—Cody felt all eyes upon him, because *this* was *his* moment. He found his line again, and, with a quick breath, signed his full legal name. And that was that.

Dean Apperson clasped his hand with both of his, and the Gownsman closed and whisked the leather book away, even though there were several lines and pages left empty, and another Gownsman (Gowns*woman*) replaced the book with a fresh one, and the Big Dog said, "Welcome, Cody. Welcome," and the line continued on, and Cody was back standing at his seat.

Now it was official: He was part of this place. And as he watched the dozens of others file past and sign and take their own place, he felt, for the first time in his life, truly part of a family. His new family was starkly different from the one he'd been forced to grow up with—his jaded Jersey friends who were simultaneously too sophisticated and too naive, who'd seen it all but lacked the wisdom to digest and understand anything, who slinked around always chatting, always prattling about nothing at all. "OMG, she, like, said that?" and "What, like, bothered me about what he said was this," and "I told her, you know, she wasn't being, like, fair about that," in endless circles, and they never shut up, and they never said anything. His new family stood tall and marched proudly with almost military posture and purpose, and when they spoke, it had a point and a direction, and they moved the ball.

The freshmen in line were kicking the Ping-Pong balls around as they waited, and some lobbed them back into the audience.

He already felt a *connection* with this family—not the Facebook/Twitter/endless texting non-connection of dead-eyed drones and idiots, but the in-person bond of those who had found this place together for a reason and would take the journey with one another, and he would be curious, just like the Big Dog demanded, and he would experiment and expand, and for the first time, he would learn, really learn things. His mind ransacked a million thoughts and feelings and pinpointed the root of his emotion: Cody belonged.

Banjo leaned over and murmured, "Why the fuck are you crying?" and Cody insisted, "I'm not," and he wasn't really, and Banjo said, "*Das Puss*!" and looked ahead.

A ball pinged Cody's forehead and ponged away. A direct hit. Cody looked up and The Girl was at the signing table, eyeing him with a mock "whoops!" She leaned over the table, shook her bracelet out of the way, and signed the book.

Dean Apperson ended the ceremony with the customary "*Ecce Quam Bonum*" and beheld the goodness as the crowd herded chaotically toward the exit. The freshmen intermingled, and Cody got separated from his section in the merry exodus, which clogged midway down the aisle. The Phantom played "Rock Lobster" on the organ, which, by this point, didn't faze anyone, and some danced to it. Cody felt a pinch on his arm and turned to The Girl next to him.

"I'm Beth," she said in a husky inside voice. "We've been flirting." She spoke without looking at him, like an old spy movie.

"I'm Cody," he said, refusing to seem flummoxed. "Flirting?"

"Well, staring," she said, inching ahead in the crowd. "Whatever you call that."

"Yeah, you look familiar. You look like someone."

"I look like Noomi Rapace," she said automatically. "So I'm told." Bingo. Marcie had taken Cody to the Swedish film after she read the book, and The Girl looked like the girl in the movie. "But I don't have those piercings," Beth continued, "or a dragon tattoo. And I'm not bisexual." Her hazel cat eyes flashed up to his. "Technically."

They were getting closer to the chapel lobby, the source of the bottleneck, as the inching crowd circled left or right, instead of straight through to the open door outside. It slowed everybody down.

"You're in Purple Haze?" she asked, still furtive, although she hardly seemed shy.

"You been following me?" he parried.

"No," she said, not taking the bait. "But I can read." She subtly nodded, and Cody saw the chapel rows were marked off with printed section names. "You were sitting with Rebel's Rest." She shot him a quick smile. "Or do you just wander around in a fog?" She pursed her glossy lips and scanned the crowd ahead.

"What section are you?" Cody asked, giving up the spar, since they were close to the lobby door. He sensed she would break it off and mingle with others once outside. She seemed hesitant to be caught with him in public.

"I'm in Tuckaway," she said, "which, funny enough, is tucked away. Out by the lake." Cody hadn't wandered that far yet. "Its nickname is the Flea Bag. Haven't figured that one out."

"I haven't figured out Purple Haze yet either," Cody said, as they inched into the lobby. "I'll come check out the Flea Bag sometime." But Beth quickly said, "No, don't bother, really," and then she took a step away from him and smiled at someone else. Across the lobby stood Ross, surrounded by freshmen girls. He smiled back at Beth and lifted his eyebrows. Were those two already hooking up? In secret?

A girl in a blue floral dress shrieked "NO!" and pointed at Cody. Everyone in the lobby turned and instinctively backed away from him toward the sandstone walls. There were a few gasps but mostly silence.

Cody was standing on top of the bronze S'wanee seal in the lobby floor. Beth looked at him and mouthed "Ruh-roh" and then slinked toward the side door and slipped out. Cody quickly jumped off the seal, but the damage was done. From the awkward silence came Banjo's racking laugh.

"Oh man," he said through laughter. "Oh man, oh man, oh man!" Now others were laughing too, but they seemed uncomfortable, and the lobby quickly cleared out. "Ole buddy, ole pal." Banjo clapped his arm sympathetically around Cody's shoulder.

"We haven't even started classes yet. You done released the curse!" Then Banjo hot-stoved and fanned his hand.

Cody, not at all superstitious, still felt clumsy and marked, in the wrong way. "Well, fuck it," he said, following Banjo and Elliott outside. At least he now knew what a "narthex" was.

Out on the Quad, the now-official freshman class mingled at their final reception, a proper tea with real china and triangle sandwiches with cut-off crusts. The word had spread, and several glanced over curiously at Cody, forever the Freshman-Who-Stepped-on-the-Seal. The stupid legend had an upside: Cody had made a name for himself and was no longer anonymous here.

"Don't worry about it." Ross laughed, slapping him on the back. "It's reversible." Caleb and Vail and Paxton and Skit also laughed and offered moral support, and Cody started to enjoy his newfound infamy. Banjo, the mastermind behind the Ping-Pong ball prank, had his own new fan club, too. Hopefully now he could put away the please-look-at-me hard hat for good. Cody scanned the crowd for Beth, but she was nowhere, apparently too cool for tea. It struck him that the most unusual girl in the freshman class had the most commonplace name.

The rest of the S'wanee all-stars were there. Pearl and Fletcher chatted by the sandwiches, and Cody overheard Pearl say, "It's so nice to have kids around again. Feels like forever." Fletcher nodded and said, "I forget how much work it is, getting ready for them. I've gotten rusty." Pearl smiled and rubbed his back. "You and me both," she said. Dean Apperson huddled with a few black-gowned professors out of earshot, and his golden retriever lay panting on the grass while several younger dogs, all mutts of various sizes, circled around playfully. One tail-wagging mutt took a tennis ball up to a professor, who tossed it across the lawn.

On the edge of the Quad, seemingly ostracized, stood Nesta. She was up to her strange antics, feverishly shaking her head and pawing at her ears. She started to retreat farther from the

Quad but stopped and shook her head again. She whined, agitated and uncomfortable. Ear mites, Cody knew, remembering Max's frequent bouts with them. A few eardrops would kill them off, and Cody, feeling sorry for the tortured dog, would suggest it to Fletcher.

"Yo! Dr. Curse!" Ross beckoned from across the Quad. "Get over here for the class photo! People are lining up to meet you!"

Chapter Five

That night, there was an air of nervous expectation at Rebel's Rest. The fanfare and hand-holding were over, and classes would start the next morning. Pearl oversaw a buffet taco supper, and everyone got an e-mailed class schedule for the week and a brief reading assignment—a Shirley Jackson short story—to kick off discussions in English class.

"Homework already?" Banjo whined into his iPad, but Cody was quietly thrilled by his new swanee.edu e-mail address and fired off a quick "Miss you and love you!" note to his mother. His Purple Haze family lounged throughout the log cabin—in the dining room, study, front living room, and back porch—settling into their reading assignment with hushed seriousness. Playtime was done. Ross had both his laptop and iPad spread out across the circular table in the living room, a model of upperclassman diligence. He clearly had more homework than the rest of them.

"Vail, I accidentally took your iPad," Skit said, returning from the kitchen with a Coke Zero and a pear. "I guess I have yours, too," Vail said, turning hers over to check the name label. "They all look alike. I can't figure the damn thing out anyway." Cody taught them how to change the screen wallpaper to personalize their iPads and then showed them a few basic tricks and shortcuts.

"Thanks, Cody," Skit said, impressed. "How the hell do you know all this?"

By ten p.m., Cody had read his assignment three times—it was a good, twisted story with a shockingly violent ending—and the log cabin had mostly emptied out. In the silence, his iPad dinged an expected-but-forgotten e-mail from the financial aid office, assigning him a campus job at DuPont Library and asking him to report tomorrow for training.

"Heh-heh." Ross smiled when Cody told him. "Working for the Widow Senex. Good times." He didn't elaborate, but as he packed up later, he muttered under his breath, "The battiest woman on campus running the goddamn library. Fucking genius." He laughed and patted Cody on the back and said, "'Night, champ," before wandering out and down the hall.

Back in his room, Cody picked and laid out his "first day" clothes—he folded his khakis to flatten out the wrinkles and shook a white oxford shirt from his box before hanging it, as the now-familiar hallway banter ping-ponged outside his lockless door. (Elliott, bathroom: "Arthur, you take my shampoo again?" Banjo, bedroom: "Mebbe. You washing your hair again? You're worse than a *fracking* chick.") Cody recharged his iPhone and set the alarm for six thirty a.m., so he could go for a run and clear his head before the first class. He was fully wired in with his iPhone, iPad, and MacBook, and he added his shiny new S'wanee e-mail address to all accounts. His mother hadn't yet responded, which was unusual, but maybe his new e-mail landed in her spam folder. He'd call tomorrow, in private, out of earshot, to alert her.

He went to add the S'wanee website to his iPad main screen, but the site was down for maintenance and simply said "Forbidden." He bookmarked it anyway and wondered who was working on the site this late at night. He wished he'd been assigned to that job.

Looking out from his window across the Quad, where a handful of students and professors still meandered about the peaceful night and ever-studious Ross disappeared behind the evergreen, doubtless on his way back to the lab, Cody felt like mayor of it all. If he had a magic wand, he'd bring back the fireflies to make the picture even more perfect. S'wanee was exciting and vibrant and fresh by day, silent and serene and comforting by night. It was a magical place at any hour, and Cody felt a sudden pang of panic that someday, before he knew it, he would graduate and have to leave here. He was, even now, dreading that awful day and tried to put it out of his mind.

A streetlight shone through his window, almost like a spotlight centered on his bed, distracting his sleep. He hadn't noticed it on his previous, passed-out-drunk nights. He got up to lower the blinds, but there were none on the wall's empty brackets. They must have forgotten to put them back up when they painted and wallpapered the room before his arrival. Across the Quad, a bright light beamed from the top arched window of Shapard Tower, like a beacon for the campus. It looked like a lighthouse, except the light was immobile and, unfortunately, hitting Rebel's Rest too squarely.

Cody thought he could rearrange his room and drag the bed to the other side, which was darker. He moved his desk and drawers and found the bed was bolted to the floor. It struck him funny that an unlocked, all-access school with bags, purses, and computers lying about would nail down a tiny, barrack-style metal bed with sagging springs.

Tomorrow he'd ask about the blinds or hang his spare flat sheet across the window at night, and hopefully the ringing in his ears, which he thought was gone but now was back because it was so quiet in here, would go away for good, and although his mind was still racing with excitement from the past few days, the sensory overload was taking its toll because even with the light shining in on him, the bed felt like a rocking crib, and suddenly he was very sleepy…

• • •

Later, Cody wouldn't recall what woke him up. It wasn't his alarm or any sound really; it was just a ransacking energy and sense of panic, like a fire, and he still felt fuzzily in a deep sleep, when in fact he was outside, walking fast, almost running, toward Abbo's Alley with Banjo leading the way and Elliott bringing up the rear. "It came from this way," Banjo said, huffing, and for once there was no sarcasm and no humor. It was still mostly dark, on the edge of dawn, and they were all barefoot and in T-shirts and underwear, having rushed right out of bed. Farther across the field, by an octopus-armed giant oak, a woman yelled, "Please! Please!" and then a string of words in Spanish.

She was standing alone, in her white food service uniform, less hysterical than desperate. On Banjo's lead, they broke into a sprint across the thick clover and tall daffodils toward her, their calves and feet wet with dew. Elliott slipped and stumbled but caught up as they neared the live oak.

"You okay, ma'am?" Banjo called out, the first to reach her. Her long black hair was pulled in a bun, hair net–ready. She clutched the straps of her big brown purse and had stopped talking, just shaking her cell phone hand at the cluster of daffodils in front of her, like a scold. Cody wondered if she might be crazy.

"Can you tell me what's wrong, ma'am?" Banjo asked, approaching her carefully, maybe thinking she was nuts, too. As if she'd been holding strong until help arrived, the servicewoman suddenly collapsed into sobs that were curiously mixed with high-pitched whines. Banjo stepped gingerly and followed her frantic pointing, Cody right behind. "Oh man," Banjo said, had he finished his thought. Fletcher lay faceup in the daffodils, his head cocked back, his throat torn out through his neck.

Cody recalled, from nowhere, a term he had learned in high school biology and never thought of since: "viscera."

"Geezus," Elliott said, and Cody said nothing because he wasn't entirely sure he was awake and had never seen a dead person before. Fletcher's eyes looked up at the oak, and they were calm, and his tongue lay from the corner of his open mouth. The skin of his face and flayed hands was a shade lighter than Cody remembered.

Nesta lay next to her master, prostrate and agitated, whining as she pawed the ground, crawling in place and getting nowhere. The black fur around her jaws and chest was shiny with dew, and there was dull terror in her eyes, and between whines she pushed her snout against the ground and made a retching hack. She hoisted her hind legs, and her stomach billowed, but the retch was unsuccessful, and she went prostrate and ground-pawing again.

Strewn about nearby were dark and glistening clumps and shreds that Cody instinctively knew used to be part of Fletcher's neck. Cody watched his step carefully.

Pearl was moving quickly toward them in silence, arms swinging, in her flowered robe and pink slippers. Her hair was coiffed as usual, but it sat crooked on her head, like an off-kilter hat. Behind her in a calm march came Dean Apperson, tied in a paisley robe over blue striped pajamas, his white hair disheveled and almost hip. The sky was turning a lighter blue, and a few birds had started singing.

"God help us," Pearl said under her breath when she saw Fletcher and then instinctively turned to shield her boys. "You don't need to see this. You don't need to see this."

"Well, now," Dean Apperson said, calmly inspecting Fletcher from above. Pearl went to console the food service woman, and Nesta followed, stooped low with her tail down. The woman yelled "No!" and Nesta backed away and circled around to Cody. She nosed his hand, and he stroked her head without thinking. He was still mesmerized by the body and Apperson's detached, analytical reaction. He might have been inspecting a flat tire.

Nesta lifted her head so Cody could stroke her jaw. His hand felt wet, and he looked down to find it coated in thin, watery blood. He yanked it back, and Nesta whined and backed away and ran in small, cowered circles.

"Nesta, Nesta, Nesta," Dean Apperson repeated in a hypnotic rhythm, as the worried dog circled farther from him. "Come, Nesta. Stay, Nesta." His voice carried a soothing command as he got closer.

Ross was running toward them across University Avenue, from the other side of campus. He had thrown on last night's clothes, and Cody wondered if he had spent the night at the lab or maybe in Tuckaway Hall, even as his own hand still glistened dewy red. "I just got your message," he called to Dean Apperson, who waved him away. He had cornered Nesta against the tree trunk. He grabbed the dog's collar and yanked him up to his side and held him there.

"Be careful, sir!" Banjo said.

"Ross, get rid of them," Dean Apperson snapped. With the dog in hand, he now seemed irritated and disgusted by the whole situation. He looked like he needed a cigarette.

"Let's go, guys." Ross herded the trio away from the tree.

"Pearl, please," Dean Apperson said more gently, nodding toward the servicewoman. "Let's take you home, child," Pearl soothed, stroking her hair bun as she led her back toward her lodging beyond the woods.

Nesta opened her throat and, with a sharp hack, regurgitated a dark, wet clump onto the ground. She lapped her tongue through her mouth to clear the taste. "Just go now," Dean Apperson ordered Elliott, who stood frozen. Banjo took him by the elbow. "C'mon, man."

Halfway through the silent, wet walk back to Rebel's Rest, Cody saw a white delivery van speeding down University Avenue. It detoured over the sidewalk and across Abbo's Alley. Two men in blue surgical scrubs sprang from the cabin and hurried toward Dean Apperson, carrying a coil of rope and what looked like a noose on the end of a long pole.

"Cody?" Ross beckoned him.

Cody turned from the front porch. The men, under Dean Apperson's direction, were carrying the bound and muzzled Nesta back to the van. She had given up thrashing, but her woeful squeals silenced the morning birds.

"Come on, Tiger." Ross motioned him inside.

"What's going on?" Sin asked in the foyer, still in her nightclothes and holding an empty coffee mug. Ross led her back down the hallway, talking in her ear.

From upstairs, Cody heard his iPhone beeping, waking him for his morning run.

Chapter Six

S'wanee canceled the first day of class, by a brief mass e-mail. The iPads dinged at 8:37 a.m.

As the university attends to an unforeseen situation, please find attached additional assignments from your professors. Classes will begin tomorrow on their normal schedule, it read. *Thank you, and have a great S'wanee Day*!

"Guys, we need to keep this quiet for now," Ross counseled the trio in Cody's room. "I mean, it's a tragedy, of course, and it's gonna get out, and everybody will be talking, but just let the university get to the bottom of it first."

"That dog killed that man," Banjo said. "That's the bottom of it."

"Banjo, just be cool. For now," Ross pleaded. He seemed exhausted. There was a knock at the door, and Caleb stuck his head in.

"Ross, is everything okay, man?" he asked, and Ross said, "Yes, Caleb. I'll talk to you about it later." "Do you need me to do anything?" Caleb persisted, and Ross paused for a breath and said, "No, Caleb. I don't need you to do anything." Caleb left, and Ross rolled his eyes.

"Tool," Elliott said quietly. "The toolest," Banjo concurred.

"The university will, I'm sure, offer counseling if...you need it," Ross continued in hushed tones. "But for now, please, just keep this under wraps. Deal?"

Fat chance. By noon, Rebel's Rest knew every detail, without embellishment or exaggeration, since the truth could hardly get more gruesome. "The dog ate his throat?" "I heard he was throwing up parts of his neck." "A worker found him dead and started screaming." "What did they do with that fucking dog? Did they kill it?" The leaks had to come from Banjo or Elliott, since Cody had not spoken a word, at all, since the night before.

"Guys, guys, guys." Ross called everyone together in the dining room. "Yes, an awful thing happened early this morning." He explained what he knew and said, "The university finds these dogs, these rescues really, and gives them homes with professors and others, and they've always done it, and it's never been a problem. This one, obviously, was a problem." He shrugged at the simplicity of it all. "It's a freak accident, and a tragedy, and it doesn't make any sense. All we can do now is get back to our work. I, for one, have a ton due tomorrow. So do you." There was really nothing else to say.

"Yeah, it woke me up," Banjo explained to Sin in the front living room. "I'm a light sleeper." "We found him together," Elliott told Houston in the hallway. Bishop and Vail, hands clutched, listened in from the dining room. Now that the word was out, Banjo and Elliott told the tale freely, repeatedly, cathartically. Cody spoke to no one.

Pearl closed herself in her room when she returned. "They were friends for years," Ross explained. The kitchen staff supervised themselves. Slowly and quietly, after an uneaten lunch, Rebel's Rest got back to work.

"*Dewd!*" Banjo moaned at his iPad. "What the frick is up with this homework?"

There were three additional short stories—Poe, O'Connor, Cheever—with a five-page writing assignment on any one, two introductory chapters from the biology textbook, an essay from ancient history, and an Econ 101 problem set with six questions that made no sense whatsoever. This was not a snow day.

"Ross," Cody said later, quietly, finding his voice dry. "Do I still go to work? To my job?"

Ross looked up from his laptop and thought. "Yeah, buddy," he said, checking his watch. "Yeah, we both should. Just, you know…what we talked about earlier."

"I won't say anything," Cody said, meaning it.

The Domain was active with Frisbees, footballs, flirting, anything but study. A boy strummed a guitar in front of a small circle of female admirers. Up on the roof of Carnegie Hall, which rimmed the Quad and connected to All Saints, a group chanted a strange, spoken song whose chorus revolved around the word "shark." Students came and went from the domed Observatory, which crowned the building and housed the school's telescopes—a must-visit, Cody thought, preferably at night, on a date, with Beth. A shaved-head kid wobbled down the sidewalk on a unicycle, his own version of the I-need-attention hard hat. The campus was laughing and carefree. Nobody knew what Cody knew.

Several groups of professors crisscrossed the lawns, in adult casual, without gowns. In the distance, Dean Apperson, dressed spiffily, walked briskly and solo past the Burwell Garden fountain, talking on his cell phone. *Not Saving S'wanee*. Cody smiled. Given the dean's position and the day's challenge, he'd give him a pass.

The DuPont Library was both serious and welcoming, a nonthreatening and manageable place for quiet study. Today, it was empty. "Are you Cody?" Mrs. Simpson, the head librarian, asked with a cocked head when he creaked the swinging front door. According to Ross, everyone called her the Widow Senex because she looked like a cartoon from a long-defunct Dick-and-Jane–esque Latin primer about a fictitious Ancient Roman family. She earned the nickname in the seventies, and subsequent generations kept passing it along. It didn't seem to matter if you called her this behind her back or to her face, as she appeared to live in her own parallel universe anyway.

The Widow Senex had the same globe hairstyle as most old women, but hers was impossibly blond. She was dressed in layers, despite the heat, in a pink cardigan sweater over a scalloped blouse and a flat khaki skirt that thwacked at the knee. Permanently attached to her hand was a wadded and dingy handkerchief, as if for chronic nasal drip. She walked with a lope that could have been old-woman stiffness or the lasting effects of polio. It was difficult to get a sense of her at all because she had a wonk eye that roamed independently in her head. Even her good eye, whichever one it was, scarcely looked where it was supposed to.

"Yes, ma'am. I wasn't sure I should come in," Cody said, and the Widow said, "Why wouldn't you?" to his shoulder/ear. Apparently, she didn't know what Cody knew either. It was equally possible she didn't know the month of the year or the state she lived in.

Her voice was a combination of a chortle, a warble, and a gargle. When she semi-trained her watery bug eyes on him, he couldn't tell if she wanted to swat him or undress him. Ross had pegged it: She was batty.

"You sit here," she said, spinning the high stool behind the front desk. "You sit here and you do this." She picked up the scanner gun wirelessly connected to the desk PC and zapped a S'wanee ID card and then zapped the bar code on the back of a library book. "That's what you do, Cody."

"I check out books, right?" he asked, to clarify.

"That's what you do, Cody." Now bored with him, she put down the gun and limp/loped back to her own desk in a separate workroom with a large glass window centered on him. She pulled off one clip earring and picked up the telephone.

The two-story atrium lobby peered into the expansive—and empty—Reading Room across from the front desk. Upstairs, lining the mezzanine, stood dozens of bookshelves that hinted at the hundreds of stacks that lay beyond. Search monitors were stationed throughout. The library was wood-paneled, oil-portraited, Persian-rugged, and S'wanee-esque.

Canopied high across the atrium was a near-invisible net from which hung thousands of multicolored origami birds, swinging independently. It was a simple and stunning art project that, like so much of the school, was weird and beautiful and hypnotic. On the front desk sat a box of rainbow-colored squares of construction paper, with step-by-step folding instructions. The art project, titled "The Fallen Flock," was an interactive memorial for US soldiers killed in the recent wars.

Cody sat on his stool and opened his laptop next to his iPad. Up on the mezzanine, several professors roamed the stacks and pulled out books and occasionally peeked down on him. Other than the hum of the air-conditioning, the place was silent. He pivoted around to the Widow Senex, chatting and laughing on the phone beyond the window. She caught him looking at her and dropped her smile and came loping to her door.

"You can study," she warbled toward his general vicinity. "You can do your homework and study." She spun her finger at him, and he pivoted back. Through the closed door, he could hear her muffled gargle-laughs on the phone. At least somebody made her smile.

On page two of his chosen paper on "The Purloined Letter"—the others were "snoozy," as Banjo would say—the front door creaked, and a gaggle of students wandered in tentatively, as if lost. Several glanced over at him before beelining for the Reading Room. They sat at the tables and quickly got down to work. Moments later, more flooded in through the creaking door and fanned out across the library, upstairs and down. Within ten minutes, the library was bustling with newly conscientious studiers. Cody wondered if it had started raining outside.

"What does it take to get service around here?" purred a familiar voice, and Cody looked up to find Beth strumming her clear nails on the desk.

"What do you need?" he shot back, swallowing a tinge of embarrassment that his desk job had outed him as scholarship. He sensed that Beth didn't judge.

"God, where to begin?" she mused. "A new roommate, for one. I mean, she's sweet when she's awake. But Geezus, I didn't sleep a wink last night. Does yours snore, too?" Instant good news: roommate + snoring + last night = no Ross hookup.

"I have a single," Cody said. "Just hall mates."

"Swanky," she said and then mimicked him exactly: "I'll have to check it out sometime."

"Do it." Cody called her bluff, and she said, "Ha!" and shrugged.

Beth was from "Minnes-OH-ta" but deflected other questions, as she was intensely curious about Cody's background and how he ended up at S'wanee. ("I'm from California," he half lied, "but my mom lives in Jersey now.") Under her bohemian surface was a poise and clearheaded intelligence that smelled like money and good breeding. They riddled one another with questions, like an icebreaker on a deadline, and she kept glancing over his shoulder as she responded curtly: "No, I've never been here either, not even to visit."; "So how did you hear about this place?"; "What kind of scholarship did they offer you?"

"So what's the deal?" she asked quietly, leaning closer over his desk. "Why'd they cancel class today? Nobody knows."

"I got the same e-mail you did." Cody shrugged, telling the truth.

"Huh." She pulled back, suspicious. "Mysteeerious, right? You didn't hear anything?"

"Nope. Nada." More truth, technically.

"Huh," she repeated. "'Cause one of the girls in Tuckaway was jogging up near you this morning and said there was some commotion up there. Some…situation."

It already seemed so long ago, a distant memory he had to reach for.

"No clue," he said, finally lying outright, while aching to tell her everything.

"Mysteeerious," she said again, reading his face, and then looked past him and said to someone else, "Okay. Okay…"

The Widow was rounding out the office door and shooed her away like a cat. "This is check-out only," she scolded, and Beth said, "Got it. Sorry. See you around." And out she slipped through the creaking door.

"This is check-out only, Cody," she repeated to Cody, and he said, "Yes, ma'am."

"Cody, my man!" Caleb startled him later, as he neared his fifth written page. "You work here, bud?"

Cody responded quietly, with the Widow on the loose.

"You check out those econ problem sets yet?" Caleb went on in his booming, fill-the-room voice. "We should do them together. It's not a test. We can crowd-source. I asked."

"Yes, you can study at the front desk together," the Widow said after Caleb tracked her down when Cody told him they weren't allowed to. "See?" Caleb turned to him. "It's not a problem. It's why we're here."

The Widow smiled at his forehead and nodded. She saved her smile for the telephone and Caleb. "Just quietly, please," she pleaded, tamping down the air. "Quietly."

Caleb pulled up a stool, and after one successful question decided they'd be study partners here at the front desk daily. Tool or not, Caleb was hard to resist.

"You figure out the lyrics yet?" Caleb asked. Their econ professor, in a clumsy stab at relevance, included a "Talking Heads" extra-credit question at the end of his problem sets. "'This ain't no party'? What's that from?"

"'Life During Wartime,'" Cody said. "I looked it up on the Internet."

The Widow let him go at six, even though the library was still full, since today was just "training." His normal schedule would be seven to ten weeknights and noon to five Saturdays, with Sundays off. It was a work-less job, just a study hall really, and it was all that was required of him for his free ride.

Halfway home, Cody realized he'd left his iPad behind. Sure enough, it was waiting safe and sound at the front desk. But now, just ten minutes later, the library was empty again, since it was dinnertime.

Chapter Seven

S'wanee put its best face forward on the take-two first day of class.

Shapard Tower—clapper intact—clanged joyfully at eight thirty a.m. as the student herds migrated across the Domain in unofficial class dress, yet another S'wanee "thing." Everyone was turned out, crisp and clean, out of respect for the teachers and the seriousness of their own academic journey, although Ross warned this would deteriorate rapidly after a few days and/or first round of laundry. "You'll all be sloppy soon," he promised. Pearl, back in mother-hen action after one day's mourning, told Cody he could wear the coat and tie "as long you like, sugar. Really."

Yesterday's tragedy, perhaps because of the intensity of their attention or the resilience of youth, seemed ancient history to Rebel's Rest today. And once the frenzy of the first week kicked in, eclipsing everything, no one mentioned it again.

Mondays and Wednesdays were literature and composition in Gailor Hall. On Fridays the section would break into smaller precepts to discuss and critique one another's essays, which would then be submitted the following week. After lunch, two alternating professors in Snowden Hall took turns on "Topics in Western Civilization"; Skit coined it "The Dick and Nancy Show," which instantly stuck.

"Which is which?" Banjo asked, loosening his tie as he lumbered toward McClurg Student Center for a pick-me-up. "Can you tell? I can't tell." The Shapard Tower Fun House riddled "Puff, the Magic Dragon" through the campus air.

Elliott manned the McClurg checkout line, his scholarship job, weekdays after class. S'wanee had an all-you-can-eat meal plan: Students and professors just swiped their ID cards, and money never changed hands. "I wouldn't let you handle money either," Banjo baited, as Elliott ignored him from his perch and waved him on. Between the sandwich station, the pizza parlor, the wok bar, vegan counter, and the home cooking line, McClurg was a bustling collegiate food court with students and professors—*lots* of professors, actually—scattered about the dining room, balcony, and outside terrace. It was an eat/study/social hub, day and night.

Early mornings before breakfast, Cody went running, sprinting, through the far reaches of the Domain. He ran down wooded Tennessee Avenue, the hilly, up-and-down stretch that branched off from the main campus; past the charming cottages where professors lived; past the smaller, modern, but matching-stoned Chapel of the Apostles and the nestled, self-contained enclave of the Graduate College. It flanked an open athletic field where, every morning, the surprisingly large, co-ed ROTC squad performed precision military drills.

Cody squinted and called out, "Hey, Huger!" but Huger was focused on his drills and didn't hear him. Cody scanned the cadets for anyone else he knew, but they had switched directions and were drilling the other way.

Overhead, Canada geese migrated south, leaving behind their fellow noisy travelers who had pit-stopped in Abbo's Alley and elsewhere on campus. One special morning, a mother deer and two fawns arched across the street in front of him and watched, quizzical and unsure, from the safety of the forest. A world apart,

Cody thought, from the strip malls, traffic snarls, and polluted haze of East Brunswick.

Tennessee Avenue dead-ended in a gravel circle that ringed the massive white memorial cross in honor of fallen S'wanee boys from the Civil War through Vietnam. S'wanee was big on memorials. Fittingly, it loomed above Morgan's Steep, the breathtaking lookout over the vast wooded eternity of the Cumberland Plateau. "Steep" was a misnomer: It was an open, jagged cliff with a straight drop down into a beautiful oblivion. A perennially muddy path to the right led downward to join the Perimeter Trail, a twenty-mile hiking loop around the Domain through its fabled caved, cliffed, and waterfalled wilderness. This was S'wanee's Yosemite, and perhaps because Cody had seen it on the DVD, it already seemed intensely, strangely familiar to him. Someday, when he wasn't late for class, he'd explore it all for real.

"I run Morgan's Steep at night," Caleb told him across the library desk. "We should run it together sometime."

Tuesdays and Fridays brought Biology and Human Affairs, with Wednesday-afternoon lab in the just-opened Spencer Hall—the newborn pride and joy of the school. From the high-tech, digital white board, a white-coated professor hammered the white-coated Purple Hazers with the basic protocols of the scientific method for "investigating phenomena"—treatment versus control groups, and single-blind versus double-blind trials, which Cody thought sounded more like a trap than an experiment, although the professor insisted they were crucial to "eliminate bias" and "achieve the highest standards of scientific rigor." The professor explained empirical and measurable evidence, formulation, testing, modification, and, most crucially, the importance of "replicating" and "reproducing" exact results on the road from "theory" to "scientific fact."

As a point of pride, according to the monotone professor, S'wanee's own research policy required twelve successful replications of any experiment before the results were published and distributed to the at-large scientific community for "peer review" and scrutiny. He called this policy the "dirty dozen rule," stressing that S'wanee took science seriously and maintained a high bar.

Skit eyeballed the labeled glass jars of pickled and floating animal innards—which the professor termed "odds and ends"—stacked in shelves at the front and turned to lab partner Buzz in suspended-animation revulsion and horror. "No fucking way," she mouthed silently. Even her silence sounded hoarse and husky.

"Science advances by accepting absurdities," the professor droned on. "The history of science is that of proving the unbelievable very much true." Banjo, to punctuate his boredom, dangled a string of drool from his slack jaw down to the lab table.

"Question everything," the professor spurred them. "It's the foundation of science, and of learning itself." Cody was tempted to snap a picture of the sea of white coats to send to his Clinique-clad mother, but he kept his iPhone in its pocket prison.

"Dude, I copped a buzz in there." Emerson laughed, waving off the formaldehyde stench as they filed out of the glass-walled lab front-and-center across from the building's main door. "When do we start cutting shit up?" Bishop yelled, and Vail playfully shushed him. They were already familiar enough to finish each other's sentences and keep each other in line, like a senior citizen couple.

One of the professors' dogs, a wide-eyed pit-bull-looking thing, had gotten loose in the building, and a female research assistant scurried past them to corral it. "Here, Puck! Come, Puck!" she called in vain. Cody stood well clear of the stocky beast and thought the school should rethink its stray dog policy. Ross waved at his charges as he hurried down the hall and through a glass door. Between his psychology major and secret, don't-jinx-it Order of the Gownsmen bid project, Ross seemed to live at Spencer Hall.

Along with their rigorous core curriculum schedule, freshmen were allowed, with advance permission, to "audit" certain upperclass elective courses like art, drawing, music appreciation, and theater. "Chick classes," Banjo dismissed them, but Cody hoped to check out a few when his schedule settled down. "The music class is really awesome," Sin told Skit at dinner one night. "They're tackling Wagner, which is pretty controversial these days."

"Did you hear me, Cody? Dude?" Caleb mock waved at him across the library desk one afternoon, on the third question of the day's problem set. He was clicking the desk stapler energetically—a nervous, annoying tick that left a needless mess for Cody to clean up. "Yeah man, I heard you." Cody nodded, although he hadn't, and he wondered if the ringing in his ears, which came and went and was initially worse in the mornings and late nights but now pestered him all day, was a result of the loud music at Wellington Lodge, where Banjo and Elliott dragged him every night after work. WebMD said it was, at best, temporary inner-ear damage from loud noises or waxy buildup and, at worst, a rare, incurable affliction called "tinnitus" or maybe some awful type of brain cancer. Cody discounted the worst-case scenarios, but his ears were clean and loud music had never bothered him before.

Banjo was angling for Wellington membership someday, and their lodge was certainly the party hub on campus, seemingly the only one. It was packed and hot every night, and the taps always flowed, and the girls flocked because the boys were there, but nobody seemed to hook up, even the upperclassmen, no matter how drunk everybody got. The girls were friendly and talked to Cody, but it was buddy-buddy, almost familylike. He hoped that once the first week's "I'm-not-a-slut" reticence wore off, they would loosen up, and college would fulfill its promise of the frenzied sexual free-for-all that MTV always told him it would be. At least Banjo and Elliott weren't faring any better.

"No thanks. I have to study tonight," Sin replied each time Banjo invited her along. "Geezus, I wanna flog the Tiger Mom that scarred *that* one," Banjo groused on the way out the door.

Sin had taken on additional electives, and Cody thought her academic zeal and discipline impressive and slightly guilt-inducing.

Beth must not have cared for the rowdy Wellingtons either, because she never showed up. Maybe the Highlanders were cooler or artsier, or maybe she was just above it all and had found her own unique social circle up on a different pinnacle somewhere.

Miss you/love you TOO, kiddo! Marcie signed her brief e-mail with a smiley heart, just back from a road trip to Bucks County, Pennsylvania, where she'd been "out of network" a couple days. Cody forgot when he had e-mailed her but was glad she was keeping busy and assumed she'd gone with her still-nameless boyfriend. A little diversion, wherever or whoever, was good for her, especially now.

Cody's lone regret was the absence of football tailgate parties, like the GAP windows at his old mall had promised. They didn't even have a homecoming. "We have reunions in the spring instead," Ross told him. "All the alums come back. Huge party weekend." S'wanee's football team had long been irrelevant, bordering on afterthought, as the school was too small to compete with once-rivals Vanderbilt and Duke, over whom ancient, black-and-white victories, rare even then, were still proudly touted in the Fowler lobby. Ross said their stadium was currently under renovation, and Cody assumed it must be on the far edge of the Domain, as he'd seen neither it nor any signs of construction. For now, the football team borrowed the stadium of a boys' prep school near Chattanooga for "home" games, and bussed—shuttle-vanned, more likely—students to and fro on Saturdays. Cody's work schedule meant he'd never go, but he could overhear the live WUTS play-by-play, albeit muffled and fuzzy, through the Widow's office, where she seemed to listen with less sporting excitement than weird, dotty-esque nostalgia.

"That Joe Scranton, there was nobody like him," she warble-mused to herself, somewhat misty, when Cody poked in for more staples. "Nobody could catch him. *Nobody*." Unwilling to share the experience, she clicked off the radio with her hanky hand and bugged her eyes to "Can-I-help-you?" challenge size. "Sorry ma'am," Cody said, backing out to leave her to her own private battiness. The game, and empty stapler, could wait.

"So, Cody, when you gonna break the curse?" Ross asked in front of everyone at dinner one night. "It only gets worse if you wait." Some of the Hazers tittered and looked to Cody expectantly. "I would do it while it's still warm out," Ross added. "It can be more…um…embarrassing in the cold." Pearl *tsk*ed and covered her ears and headed back toward the kitchen. "Oh Lord, I don't want to know about this," she said in her guttural laugh. "Don't tell me when, and *don't* get caught."

"So how do I break it?" Cody asked, game for anything, or so he thought. As Ross explained the thing, the one and only thing, that could forestall an avalanche of disaster and ruin and save Cody's college career, the titters morphed into hoots and catcalls. Skit unleashed her best "sexy" whistle, as Cody finally pieced together the taunting "S'wanee Curse/Streaker" mystery connection.

As luck had it, it rained on Thursday afternoon, and between Econ 101 and Western Civ, and while most of the campus lunched, inside and dry, Cody emerged from the men's room of Convocation Hall in a terry robe he had borrowed from Elliott. He was barefoot in the outdoor alcove, and Banjo and Elliott marched behind, holding Cody's clothes and shoes in a messy stack.

"The whole Curse Course," Ross reminded him. "If you skip even one, the curse lingers."

"Yep, yep." Cody nodded, adrenaline coursing, strangely thrilled. Shapard Tower, brushing up on the classics, for once played the kind of Count Dracula music one would expect from a college chapel.

Cody dropped the robe, and Elliott took it, and Cody went sprinting off, stark naked, into the downpour. He raced across the full expanse of the Quad, rounding the roped-off big evergreen and targeting the front door of All Saints, where the curse had begun. He tapped the door and ran down the length of the chapel and through the deserted Burwell Garden, splashing his hand in the goldfish fountain along the way. He circled around the sparkling Spencer Hall, where white-coated professors huddled by the windows and laughed and waved, as if they'd been tipped off to his arrival.

He tapped the front glass door and pivoted around toward the DuPont Library. Several of his Purple Hazers lined the sidewalk, standing in the rain, cheering him onward.

"*Day-um*!" Skit hooted and whistled, sizing him up and down.

Luckily, the Widow Senex wasn't outside to wonk-eye his naked glory as Cody tapped the front door and turned for the longest sprint, all the way across campus, whizzing behind hedges and army-green mailboxes up to the Klondyke on University Avenue. Naturally/of course/had to happen, there were several adult visitors and sightseers coming out with bags of T-shirts and hats and souvenirs, and Cody had no choice but to flap past them, tap the door, and race away. *Have a great S'wanee Day!*

Now for the gauntlet—all the way around McClurg Student Center, the hub of campus, surrounded by windows, at lunch hour rush. Students, teachers, and staff, already glued to the windows on both levels, cheered and jumped and laughed with him, not at him. Cody the Naked Gladiator fist-pumped the air triumphantly, basking in the mass adulation, as he rapped the front door. *Curse, be gone!*

The final stretch was back across the Quad, where his dripping-wet-in-solidarity Purple Hazers yelled and egged him on to the Promised Land. Banjo held a champagne bottle between his legs and mock wanked it into a frenzy. Cody raised his arms and crossed an imaginary finish line as Banjo shot his champagne wad all over him and Elliott wolf whistled with the others. Sin aimed her camera phone, but Ross covered and pushed it away.

"No pictures!" Ross laughed, but meant it. "Not cool. Not cool."

Everyone ringed around to congratulate and shield him. No run had ever been more exhilarating or mind-clearing.

Unfortunately, Proctor Bob was there to congratulate him, too. With a traffic-ticket-looking pad. "Been expecting this all week," he said, smiling, writing out a ticket, to instant boos and hisses. "Oh, c'mon!" Paxton yelled, and Sinkler yelled, "Dude, get out of here!" right in his face. "Careful now," Proctor Bob said, unsmiling. He tore off the ticket.

"Sir, please," Ross added, the voice of reason. "It's tradition. He *had* to." Elliott helped Cody back into his robe, and Proctor Bob handed him the ticket.

"Rules is rules," Proctor Bob said. "Tradition or not."

"What does this mean?" Cody asked, increasingly concerned, flipping over the funny ticket.

"Up to the dean." Proctor Bob shrugged. "Indecent exposure is typically a semester's probation." Cody's neck iced up the back.

"Sir…I'm on scholarship," he said, twice, since he swallowed halfway through the first time.

"Or maybe a fine," Proctor Bob continued. "There just has to be some sort of *restitution*, you know." Ross, looking guilty, pulled Proctor Bob over to the side for a private chat. "This frickin sucks," Banjo whispered, and Elliott said, "The dean's your adviser, right? He'll be cool. It'll be cool." None of this was fun anymore.

"Oh sure, there's *that*," Proctor Bob said, turning back from negotiations. "If he's so fond of his birthday suit, there's always *that*." He and Ross were both smiling now, coconspirators in the prank. "We can wrap this whole thing up today." Proctor Bob shrugged, as Ross explained yet another square in S'wanee's crazy quilt of customs. Shortly after, still in his robe, Cody padded past a sea of easels onto a brightly lit stage-in-the-round.

"We only have our subject for thirty minutes," the smocked art teacher told the packed room. "So sketch quickly, please."

She nodded Cody toward the stool stage center. "Thank you for volunteering." Hundreds of eyes stared passively.

On the front row sat Beth, hair clipped back, Clark Kent glasses, bright red lips, sketch pad at the ready. She didn't acknowledge him at all.

"Mr. Marko?" The teacher smiled expectantly. "You have to get to your own class soon, don't you?" She twirled her finger in the air. Cody took a breath and untied and dropped his robe. Dozens of pencils from all sides scratched on paper quickly.

Beth pursed her red lips and never glanced at his face. But she sketched very slowly.

• • •

Toward the end of the week, Cody was running out of clean clothes and had started double-dipping from his hamper, fishing out the least gamy. He was reminded of this not only by the clean-and-pressed clothes his classmates always wore, but also by the rolling racks that workers shuttled down the sidewalks between classes. The dresses and khakis and kilts were plastic-sheathed on hangers, no doubt from a professional laundry service Cody couldn't afford.

After class, Cody got change from the Klondyke and took his hamper to the Rebel's Rest basement, which was lined with gymnasium storage lockers but laundry-free, even in the back catacombs.

"Pearl, where's the laundry room?" Cody asked in the kitchen, his hand full of quarters.

Pearl stopped chopping with her big knife and looked at him blankly. "That's a good question." She seemed stumped.

"I sent the machines out for service," she said a beat later. "I need to get them back. I plumb forgot."

"I can just go use another dorm's," Cody said.

"No," Pearl said quickly. "I'll get them back fast."

And she did. That night, two brand-new high-tech machines showed up in the basement. And they were free.

• • •

"We're not going to the Lodge tonight," Banjo decreed on Friday when he and Elliott picked Cody up after work. He carried a large utility flashlight. "We're going on an expedition. Truffle-sniffing."

Twenty minutes later they stood on the edge of Morgan's Steep in the pitch-black. They'd passed night-runner Caleb in fluorescent safety armbands and heart rate monitor along the way—"*Toolissimo!*" Banjo branded.

"A Wellington told me about the S'wanee Truffles," Banjo explained, leading them down the muddy path toward the Perimeter Trail. "Watch your step," he warned, flashing back his beacon. He and Elliott were already buzzed.

"Why are we doing this tonight?" Elliott asked, slipping on a stone. The path was steep and narrow and treacherous, especially in the black. "I got a hankering for 'shrooms," Banjo replied. "You need them more than anybody, Elliott. Uptight little prick."

According to Banjo, who'd heard it from a drunk Wellington, a student in the late sixties had discovered a weird variety of wild mushrooms growing in the vast, tangled S'wanee ecosystem. The school had tested them for hallucinogenic properties and then sold the formula to the Defense Department as a potential weapon.

"The school made a killing, and the dude got his gown from it," Banjo explained.

The trio inched past a stone cave entrance with a stream running through. It was silent and still down here. Cody stepped with confidence, like his feet knew the way. He'd watched the DVD so often, he felt familiar with this path, even in the dark. More *déjà vu*, he thought.

"Atta boy. Now *that's* what I'm talking about!" Banjo said, inching closer to a massive downed tree trunk, thick enough to be a bridge across the boulders. He slowly ran the flashlight across the bark. Sprouting off the dead trunk were hundreds of dark fanlike clusters. It looked like a sculpture.

"The S'wanee Truffles are dark purple," Banjo said, inspecting them close. "The black ones are junk." He pulled out a Swiss army knife and a small ziplock bag.

"Are these purple or black?" Banjo asked, holding the scraped-off mushrooms to the light. "I can't tell."

"So black people really *are* color blind?" Elliott hectored, and Banjo said, "Shut it, white devil!"

"Whatever they are, I'm not gonna eat them," Elliott said, and Banjo said, "*Das Puss*! They're not poisonous; they're just trippy!" In the near distance, a loud rustling jolted them all.

"Dude, let's get out of here," Cody said, and Banjo agreed. "Yeah, black people are afraid of ghosts, too," he said, leading the hustle back as he tucked away his army knife and ziplocked booty.

Back at the Rebel's Rest, the trio sat staring into the empty fire pit. Cody had ignored Arianna's advice against drugs in favor of Dean Apperson's call to experiment. He'd taken a tiny, rubbery bite and swallowed with the others.

"You feel anything?" Banjo asked. "Nope," they both said.

Paxton and Sinkler stumbled past, back from their night out. "What are you losers doing?" Sinkler asked.

"Leave us alone," Banjo grumbled. "We're tripping."

"Cool," Paxton said, and Sinkler said, "Good times."

But they weren't tripping at all, and an hour later, Banjo stood up.

"Guess we got the black ones," he said, and went inside, muttering obscenities.

"Dude, let's just get drunk in my room," Elliott suggested, and soon they settled into a reliable, predictable beer buzz. S'wanee Truffles be damned.

• • •

All in all, a good week, Cody felt. He'd settled into his new academic routine, neutralized the dreaded S'wanee Curse, forged new friendships, definitely gotten noticed, upped the ante with Beth by baring it all, experimented with harmless drugs, and, most important, made a new home, his first home, for himself. It had been one long great S'wanee Day.

Each morning he greeted the day with an open window so his flower-shopping bee family could buzz harmlessly in and out of his room. Before going to bed, he shut it to drown out the workers who often did nighttime landscaping and other maintenance around the Quad, pruning and clipping and gilding the campus for the perfect day ahead. He now understood the purpose of the Shapard Tower beacon: to illuminate the grounds for the workers, and after a few nights, Cody felt familiar, even secure, in its nightly glow across his bed, and he forgot about a window covering. The clean, fresh air of the Domain mixed with the contented exhaustion from his rigorous daily schedule for a nightly, pleasant buzz that helped him ignore the constant ringing in his ears and lulled him gently into an unconscious and well-deserved bliss.

That night Cody slept soundly without dreams, which was merciful, because the next morning the piercing headaches began.

Chapter Eight

"Anybody seen Caleb?" Cody asked one night after dinner, in early October.

At first he'd been glad that booming-voiced Caleb had skipped their past few study sessions because, for the past three weeks, Cody had woken from a sound sleep each morning to an intense, jabbing pain in the front of his skull. It usually wore off after breakfast and coffee, which he drank darker now, only to return the next morning with a fresh ferocity that, at its worst, nearly immobilized him.

He thought it would pass in a few days, and when it didn't, WebMD suggested a hay-fever-type allergic reaction to any one of the million blooming things across the Domain. Cody usually kept his window open to let in the fresh S'wanee air, but he suspected the purple flowered pendulums that dangled just outside and had recently bloomed bigger and brighter might be the culprit. Google identified them as wisteria, and sometimes poisonous. His decision to close the windows for good was further prompted one morning when two of his normally docile bee visitors aggressively stung him on the neck and arm while he dressed for class. Both died in their kamikaze mission, and from the look of their comrades crawling and knocking up against his shut window, dozens more were lining up to volunteer. The maybe-poisonous wisteria might be giving Cody a headache, but it had turned his poor bees into suicidal crackheads.

WebMD's allergy page accurately pegged another of Cody's current symptoms: intense, sporadic fatigue. Luckily, Cody's fatigue mostly hit at night, which made sense, considering his hectic daily pace. But it sometimes hit so fast it overwhelmed him, and narcoleptic-like, he would fall asleep, literally, anywhere. In the past few weeks, he'd woken up on the downstairs sofa, in the laundry room, mosquito-chewed by the fire pit, and on the sticky linoleum floor of the coat closet at Wellington Lodge. He didn't choose these sleeping places, and he didn't remember how he'd gotten there. He usually felt the fatigue cloud gather around one a.m.—Wikipedia said some offending blooms were most potent at night—and until his allergies passed, he made a point of being in his room by then. That week, he woke up predawn on the stone edge of the Burwell Fountain and realized his strategy clearly wasn't working.

Soon, the headache stretched into his morning classes, then lunch and his library afternoons, and ultimately through dinner. It varied in intensity, like a wave, from a dull, focused throb all the way up to unbearable spike-through-the-forehead. He welcomed the nightly fatigue, no matter where he woke up, if only to escape the drill-bore pain for a few hours.

He stopped checking WebMD with its increasingly dire diagnoses too horrible to contemplate. Migraines? Maybe. Brain tumor? Denial. He considered, and unconsidered, a trip to Dr. Quack, whose half-assed clinic and skill set might prompt a medical evacuation to a real hospital, and then Cody would have to leave this wonderful place, perhaps for good. Instead, he drained an ever-larger amount of his Tiger Bucks stipend on over-the-counter pain-killer cocktails at the Klondyke, and, perhaps owing to his Old World Bulgarian genes, stoically kept his suffering to himself.

The headaches lessened a bit during his early-morning runs out to Morgan's Steep. The farther away he got from the wisteria, the better he seemed to feel. On Wednesday morning he had woken up with the usual throb and wondered if he should ask for a different, non-wisteria'd room. Maybe Bishop would trade with him, since a single would give him more privacy with Vail. He weighed the pros and cons of moving in with roommates in a backyard cabin as he sorted through his dirty laundry for yesterday's T-shirt to run in, and found it not only still drenched in sweat, but also ripped down the front from the neck. It was from a Guns N' Roses reunion tour at the Meadowlands; it had served its purpose, but he didn't remember it ripping when he'd peeled it off after his last run. He must have been in a rush, as usual.

Far out on Tennessee Avenue, running past the ROTC drill teams, Cody felt a relief that gave him hope his headaches were trailing off. His legs were sore today, as if he'd already been running, but he relished the tradeoff as his head throbbed less with each step farther from campus. He cranked up The Strokes on his iPod shuffle and made way for the white delivery van coming from Morgan's Steep. The two men in blue surgical scrubs nodded from the cab as they passed, and Cody made it to the end of the route, where a handful of workers did early-morning cleanup around the memorial cross.

Cody caught his breath on the edge of Morgan's Steep, as two workers climbed from below the cliff with black garbage bags, likely full of beer bottles thrown by late-night visitors. Cody gave one of the workers a hand back to solid ground and wondered how anyone could trash this beautiful place.

Cody's relief was short-lived, however, as it was most mornings. With each running step back toward Rebel's Rest, his headache intensified. The pain had become so much a part of him over the past few weeks, like a new normal, that he could scarcely remember what his daily life felt like before it.

Fortunately, Cody had been able to rise above the pain and excel in his classes. He and Caleb had gotten an A- or a B+ on their problem sets together, and another was due Friday.

"Has anybody seen Caleb?" Cody repeated in the crowded dining room Thursday night, after Caleb's second day of skipping their study sessions. Ross nodded and wiped his mouth and got up from his half-eaten dinner.

"Yeah, yeah," he said, leading Cody down the hallway into the front living room. "I meant to tell you."

According to Ross, Caleb had decided to transfer to Georgetown, to be closer to his family, for "personal reasons." "He didn't want to say anything," Ross said. "It's a family thing. His mother has, like, emotional issues." Caleb had been initially hesitant to go to school so far from her but had given it a shot. "We discussed it a lot before he decided to go back."

"I'm sorry," Cody said. "I didn't know."

"He didn't like to talk about it. You know how Caleb is," Ross said. "Sucks, 'cause he was a great get for S'wanee. We'll miss him." And then Ross said, "Keep it on the down low, cool? It's such a personal thing, but you two were friends…"

"Yeah, yeah, sure." Cody nodded. "I won't say anything." He was going to miss the tool.

"Hey, Cody." Ross stopped him as he headed to the library to finish the problem set on his own. "You doing okay, bud?"

"Yeah, man. I'm doing okay."

"I mean, you feeling all right?" Ross said more quietly. "I mean, physically?"

"Yeah, I feel all right," Cody lied.

"I'm just asking because, dude"—Ross got closer—"you're dropping a lot on pills at the Klondyke. Burning through a ton of Tiger Bucks."

"Oh. Yeah," Cody said, wondering how Ross knew he was dropping a lot on pills at the Klondyke and burning through a ton of Tiger Bucks. "Just allergies."

"We monitor that stuff, you know, through your card," Ross explained without being asked. "If you're having, you know, any kind of pain, you can tell me about it, and you should. We got a doctor here and everything, you know?"

"I think I'm allergic to the wisteria outside my room," Cody said. "It gives me a headache. Maybe if I changed rooms..."

"I don't think you need to change rooms," Ross said quickly and then laughed. "And I don't know anything about wisteria, but just let me know if your headaches get worse, okay? That's what I'm here for. Seriously."

"I will, Ross, thanks," Cody said, knowing that he wouldn't. He'd grown up nursing himself through sickness, and he'd spring back from this on his own, as well.

But a few days later, the pain took on a new, alarming dimension. The hot-poker-through-the-forehead spread across his skull and down the back of his neck with a savage fury that left him dizzy and occasionally gasping for breath. It plagued him every waking hour and started to unhinge him from his own personality and consciousness, leaving him zombielike.

"Dood! What the fuck is wrong with you?" Banjo demanded when Cody, his skull aflame, refused to hit the Lodge for the fourth night in a row. "You used to be fun." Elliott was more sympathetic, even tender. "You need anything, Cody?" he asked almost daily.

Occasionally, by the end of the day, Cody's system was so overwhelmed with the constant agony that he would dry-heave in his room with nothing to vomit up, as he hadn't been eating. Sleep was his only relief, and he dreaded, even in his dreams, waking up.

One morning, before an English quiz on Chaucer, Cody woke early and laced up his running shoes in a panic. His windowsill was littered with dead bees, and he felt untethered from his brain, and he sprinted down Tennessee Avenue, not seeing ROTC or deer or geese or trees. With each desperate stride farther from campus, he prayed for relief, but it never came, and when he reached the memorial cross and Morgan's Steep, the torture still owned him, and he fled down through the thicket onto the Perimeter Trail. Crazed, he tore past caves and waterfalls and through bushes, and he was wet and bleeding but kept sprinting as far from the torment as he could and later he would remember the high-pitched whistle he felt in his head right before everything went black.

• • •

"Well, now," was the first thing he heard before he opened his eyes. He knew the voice.

Dean Apperson perched at his bedside in the bright pastel room. Cody was hooked to an IV drip and a beeping machine.

"Well, look who's here," Dean Apperson said to Ross over his shoulder. "How you doing there, buddy?" Ross asked, drawing closer.

"I'm good, man," Cody said, knowing where he was. The headache was gone. The pain was totally gone. "What time is it?" he asked.

"Lunchtime," Dean Apperson said. "You've had a nice morning nap."

"How do you feel, Cody?" Ross asked. "How's that headache?"

"It's gone," Cody said. "I don't have a headache right now."

"And I don't think you will again," Dean Apperson soothed. "Isn't that good news?"

He explained they'd given him a shot and a drip to clear it all up. "We just had to tweak a few things," he said. From the soreness and bruises in the crook of Cody's arm, Dr. Quack must have poked around quite a bit to get it right. *Figures*, Cody thought, but he didn't care, because the pain was gone.

"It might have been those vaccines. They're live viruses, you know," Dean Apperson continued. "Or maybe allergies or some other fleeting illness; we really don't know." And Cody didn't care because he could think and breathe and the pain was gone.

"Let's do this," Dean Apperson said, standing up. "Rest as long as you like. Don't worry about class today. But come back once a week for blood tests, so the doctor can monitor and make sure you don't have any more trouble. And do tell us," he repeated, "do tell us, Cody, if you have pain or discomfort of any kind in the future. It's silly and unnecessary to keep it to yourself."

Dean Apperson went to the door and turned back. "Cody," he said, "you didn't by chance eat any of those silly things they find in the woods, did you? The mushroom-looking things? The 'truffles,' the kids call them?"

"Um." Cody paused, weighing a lie.

"I don't need to know." Dean Apperson waved it off. "But if you did, just don't do it again. They're not good for you, and they don't do what the kids think they do. We don't know really what they do, so find your fun in other ways, won't you? That's what I suggest, Cody." And he was gone.

"Dude, just chill here today," Ross said after Dean Apperson left. "Get your strength back. Just"—he got closer—"just keep this all to yourself, cool? Nobody needs to know, you know? It's like a personal medical thing, you know?"

"I'll keep it on the down low." Cody smiled at Ross's familiar phrase, which was his nature anyway.

"Yeah, keep it on the down low, Tiger." Ross laughed. "You don't want people to think there's anything wrong with you, because, you know, there's not. Just say you were helping me with a science project or something."

"Your Gownsmen project?" Cody asked.

"Sure, whatever." Ross shrugged.

"You want me to lie to them?" Cody ribbed.

"No, you don't have to lie," Ross said, getting up, and left it at that.

A nurse brought a loaded cheeseburger with fries and a chocolate-peanut butter milk shake on a tray. As Cody wolfed it down, he wondered who had found him on the deserted Perimeter Trail that morning and called for help. Someday he'd ask and thank them for saving him, on the down low.

Chapter Nine

Clearheaded and pain-free, Cody exploded back into his S'wanee life. He finished his econ problem set on time and on his own, got a weekend extension, courtesy of Dean Apperson, on his George Orwell essay—his English lit class was currently exploring political writings—and knew life was back to normal when he looked forward to the nightly hallway banter. (Banjo: "Shut it, maggot. I got my own shampoo now." Elliott: "Good. Mine doesn't work on your kind of hair anyway." Banjo: "*What?*")

"Hmm, I don't know who it was," Ross said on his way out the door when Cody asked about his Perimeter Trail Good Samaritan. "I just got a call that you were in the infirmary. Lucky you." Ross was always in a hurry these days, like the clock was ticking, and other than breakfast and late-night study sessions at Rebel's Rest, Cody would catch glimpses of him scudding through doors at Spencer Hall in his lab coat. Even more than most, Ross seemed energized and driven in his work, and Cody wanted to take him up on his semi-offer to be his research assistant on whatever psychology/Gownsmen project was keeping him so busy. It had to be more interesting than biology.

To Cody's astonishment, one night after dinner, Rebel's Rest voted him president of their section, a symbolic title with less power than glory. His job was to pass student complaints and suggestions up the S'wanee ladder. Still, it meant they liked him.

"Congrats, Tiger! I was section president myself once." Certifiable-BMOC and potential-Gownsman Ross high-fived him.

"So do I call you 'Mr. President' now?" Banjo joked in the bathroom that night.

"You call me 'Massa,'" Cody replied to Banjo and Elliott's cackles.

With his new title, however worthless, Cody instinctively grew more highly tuned to his Rebel's Rest family, almost protective. Taking a cue from psychology-major Ross, Cody observed everything. He noticed when workers moved boxes out of Caleb's old cabin—"He forgot a few things," said Pearl—and was probably the first to pick up on the trouble-in-paradise Bishop/Vail situation, as they sat together less often during meals and never held hands anymore. He didn't need his Spidey Sense to know it was Skit's period, as she proudly volunteered this information at breakfast. "What a relief!" she quacked.

As the semester moved along, hair grew longer and clothes more rumpled, just as Ross predicted. The freshmen loosened up, especially the girls. Weekends at the Lodge kicked off on Thursdays, right after Cody got off work. He saw the same faces at the library each time, diligent students committed to their study routine, but nobody ever checked out a book, and with Caleb gone, Cody was left on his own at the desk, save the occasional and often unintelligible Widow-Speak.

Like everyone else, Cody was drinking more, and not just beer, since the Wellingtons seemingly had an endless supply of Jack Daniel's, which they freely shared with members and nonmembers alike. It definitely made the girls not quite so ladylike, Cody noted, as he crushed out his third cigarette and tried to remember when exactly he'd picked up this latest—and surely temporary—experimental college habit. He'd get it out of his system soon.

One Friday night, a somewhat sloppy upperclass girl named Lucy led him by the hand upstairs to the "Crow's Nest" at the top of the Lodge by the attic. There, she dropped to her knees and blew him, all the way, before staggering back down the stairs. "I need a drink," she mumbled to no one, since Cody was still buttoning his jeans. Banjo raised his eyebrows in mock horror when Cody returned and said, "Desperate times, paleface," but Cody settled into a semi-regular routine with "Loose-y," who one time brought another friend to help out, a memorable first for Cody. He wanted to thank whoever had invented Jack Daniel's.

• • •

Having missed lunch, Cody ordered a small pepperoni and mushroom pizza and waited at a McClurg table for his number. It was nearly empty this time of day. At the next table were four grown-ups dressed in varying degrees of square and eating big salads. They had large briefcases and were talking too loudly. Cody thought tourists and intruders should lay low at his school.

They talked about the next generation of prescription drugs like Ambien and Chantix—names he recognized from his own mother's use—and others Cody hadn't heard of. They debated the pros and cons of the new "smart pills" which, according to them, contained tiny microchips that could transmit vital information back to "pharma researchers," whatever those were. They spread notebooks and laptops across the table and took up too much space. They acted like they owned the place.

"Where you staying this trip?"

"The S'wanee Inn. It's okay. My room opens up to the golf course, but I didn't bring my clubs. And it's a little far away."

"I wanted the log cabin. I stayed there in June; it's like a bed-and-breakfast right in the middle of campus."

"I wanted that, too, but they got kids staying there right now."

"They got kids everywhere right now."

Because it's our school, Cody thought, but the intruders were laughing loudly about something and didn't notice him. They looked like pudgy corporate tools on casual Friday with their geeky short-sleeve button-down shirts. Only girls and pudgy corporate tools ordered salads at McClurg. Cody checked his watch and looked back at the pizza counter.

"What time we gotta be at Spencer?" one of the intruders asked, but Cody's number was called, and he got it to go. He passed Ross on the way out, but he seemed distracted and in a hurry, and Cody walked on to Burwell Garden to eat his pizza. The goldfish in the fountain were sluggish and sucking at the surface. He fed them pieces of his crust, but apparently they weren't hungry today.

• • •

"Well, *hey* there, kiddo!" his mother answered loudly when he called from his room late one night. "I thought you'd forgotten about me!"

Cody filled her in on his S'wanee adventures, minus the debilitating headaches and tawdry Lodge hookups, and Marcie squealed, "President Marko? *That's* my boy! I like the sound of that!" In the background, Cody heard the unmistakable melody of a slot machine.

"Mom, where are you?" he asked. "At a casino?"

"Yep. I'm gaming," she said, slightly slurry. "That's what they call it here."

"Atlantic City?"

"Vegas," she said, and he heard her take a drag on her cigarette.

"Why are you in Vegas?" he quizzed.

"Because I've never been, and I always wanted to go, and it's *fantastic*!"

In the background, slot machines kept eating people's money, probably hers.

"Never you mind about that." She giggled when he asked whom she was with, and then she said, "Oh Cody, I'm with June, from the store. She dumped that deadbeat boyfriend, and we came to celebrate for a few days.

"We're at the Bellagio," Marcie continued. "The one George Clooney robbed, and Cody, it's just spectacular. The restaurants, the spa, that damn fountain! June got wet!" She giggled again and said quickly, "I mean, the fountain sprayed her, and she got wet."

She covered her mouthpiece and said to someone, "Pinot grigio, please. The Chilean one. *What?*" And then she said, "I can't use the phone in the casino, Cody. I'll call when I'm back in my room."

"I gotta crash, Mom. I got a test tomorrow."

"I miss you, kiddo! I love you, Mr. President!" she said, hanging up.

Cody went back to his iPad, listening to the rain trickle outside his window. He wondered how big that Bellagio bill was going to be.

• • •

One Sunday afternoon, Cody unlocked his iPad to find a .pdf document open on his screen. At first he thought it was one of his assigned biology lab reports, but it was full of abstract, scientific jargon that had nothing to do with his own class work. It had phrases like "Transcranial Magnetic Stimulation" and "Digitized Electro Neuron Magnesis" and "Brain-Computer Interfaces" and "Deep Brain Stimulation." It referenced "artificial hippocampus" and "involuntary implants" and "terminal experiments."

Cody flipped to the front page and saw the title "The S'wanee Call Project." It was a complicated report and started with the words "For my thesis project, I propose the following:" The proposal was seventeen pages long and counting, and there was no name on it, and when Cody hit the "home" button and saw the wallpaper, he realized it was not his iPad.

Ross's name was labeled on the back, and Cody had taken it by accident when the group downstairs watching the Army-Navy football game had made so much noise he couldn't concentrate. He had, he realized, Ross's psychology/Gownsmen thesis project in his hands. Downstairs, the crowd cheered a touchdown.

Cody had been curious about—borderline obsessed with—Ross's Gownsmen project since he'd first mentioned it on the ride to S'wanee. Ross had evaded his questions thereafter—oddly protective and borderline superstitious, claiming he didn't want to "jinx" it—but Cody was intrigued by the big, bustling Spencer Hall where Ross spent so much time and where so many researchers seemed to be doing important work far from his smelly—and frankly high-school-level—biology lab.

Now Cody had it all here in front of him, and if his curiosity was getting the better of him, well, wasn't that what Dean Apperson had demanded of them in his speech, he asked himself, as he opened Ross's mail program and attached the .pdf file. Never mind the same speech was about the Honor Code that Cody had signed, practically in blood, since it wasn't cheating to copy and paste a file that had nothing to do with his own tests or schoolwork. And it wasn't technically stealing either, he reasoned, as he typed his own e-mail address, because Ross's thesis proposal had no real monetary value, and if he simply *shared* it with his mentoree/little brother, albeit without knowing, he was only furthering his education, which was, after all, why they were here.

Downstairs, the crowd roared again with hoots and whistles, energetically invested in the Army-Navy matchup, which was understandable since S'wanee's own football team was hardly worth investing in, and Cody hit the "send" button, and the thesis proposal whooshed away toward his own iPad still down in the living room.

Cody went back to the iPad home page to find and put the thesis proposal back on the same page he had found it—not to cover his tracks, but just so Ross could easily pick up where he left off—and he was going to march it right back down to Ross and admit he had taken it by accident when he spotted in the bottom corner an app he didn't recognize but instantly leaped out at him. It was a square with a yellow dot in the middle and simply said "PURPLE HAZE."

It had a similar interface as other file-sharing and video/music streaming apps that Cody knew and had on his phone, but instead of playlists with album cover art, there was a matrix of tiny squares on the left and a Google-style aerial map of the S'wanee campus on the right. The map was dotted with dozens of purple "pins," and when Cody maximized the map and tapped on the "pin" near DuPont Library, a box popped up with a live streaming view of the sidewalks leading to the front door. The pin spearing the library itself brought up the front desk where Cody worked and which currently was vacant. After a moment, the Widow puttered into view, and the stop-motion streaming made her polio limp/lope seem even more pronounced and almost comical as she sprayed down the wooden desk with Windex and then rather doggedly picked her nose. *Your Honor, I submit into evidence proof of the Widow's battiness.*

There were live streaming views, inside and out, of McClurg Student Center, Gailor Hall, the Klondyke, the infirmary, Fowler Sport and Fitness Center, the entrance gate to campus, which was now shut and fortified with proctors. There were bird's-eyes of

Manigault Park and outside/inside Wellington Lodge, although luckily, thankfully, not up in the Crow's Nest where "Loose-y" entertained him. There were views up and down Tennessee Avenue, the memorial cross, Morgan's Steep, and several throughout the long Perimeter Trail. On this sunny day, Cody could almost make out the forbidden S'wanee Truffles growing on a log and the waterfall pool he had just fled past when his brain quit on him that not-so-distant morning.

There were no "pins" in or around Cravens Hall, where Dean Apperson lived, and no streaming views inside Spencer Science Hall, but the Quad was covered—Cody compared the stop-motion pedestrians to his own window view to confirm it was live—and Rebel's Rest was practically purpled over with pins. He saw Pearl in the kitchen stirring a vat of homemade chili for dinner; Houston coming up from the laundry basement; Vail and Skit having a tête-ê-tête on the back rocking chairs, almost like a counseling session; Sin trying to read in one living room while the crowd roared around the television in the other. Banjo was rooting from his perch on the back of an armchair, and even Elliott looked caught up in the game frenzy. Cody scanned from room to room to hallway to fire circle, but saw Ross nowhere.

One of the Rebel's Rest cluster of pins was red and blinking. On closer inspection, it wasn't a "pin" at all, but a floating red dot. Cody tapped it, and he was looking at himself looking at the iPad, through his bedroom window. He carried the iPad closer to the window, and the red blinking dot migrated with him. Cody knew these device tracking apps; he had one on his phone, in case he lost it. He peered out his window and tried to locate the camera, aimed from high and across the Quad. The phantom camera struggled to focus on Cody. The Observatory? Shapard Tower? He couldn't pinpoint it this far away, but he smiled and waved at himself anyway.

There was a single knock and then Ross said, "Hey Tiger, you in here?" as he opened the non-locked door. Cody snapped the iPad case shut.

"Hey dude, I think I took your iPad," Cody said first and Ross said, "Yeah, yours dinged an e-mail downstairs, and then I realized it wasn't mine."

"Sorry bud," Cody said, wondering if Ross had seen his thesis proposal that Cody had sent himself, and Ross said, "No biggie. They all look alike. Cool pic on your wallpaper." And then they traded out.

"Hey, what's the score?" Cody asked.

"Beats me." Ross shrugged at the top of the stairs. "I wasn't really following that game." And then he said, "Hey, you found the cameras!" His iPad was open to where Cody had shut it.

"Sorry man," Cody started, but Ross interrupted. "Yeah, that's the school's new security app. Pretty cool, right? Proctors and teachers and RA's get it."

"I won't tell anybody," Cody assured him, and Ross said, "Tell anybody you like. I'm glad we finally got one. You like the name I gave it? Gotta keep an eye on you rascals." He double-stepped down the stairs. "You coming down for chili?"

Cody checked his iPad e-mail. Ross hadn't opened it. Cody was relieved, even though, really, he had nothing to worry about even if he had been worried about it, because he hadn't, really, done anything wrong. After all, it's not like he had an iPad that *spied* on people.

• • •

For a few weeks after his headache ordeal, Cody slept normally, waking up alone in his bed. The girls at the Lodge were sleepover-averse and wanted "on site" and "no strings" only, which was fine by him. He slept like a log, unusual for him, but the air up on the Mountain was so clean and fresh, and his days so busy and tiring, that he would crash out and wake to his iPhone alarm, with the time in between a blissful, dreamless void.

Still, he increasingly found himself needing afternoon naps between class and dinner, as if his body demanded more recovery. He was drinking and smoking more heavily and often, "burning the candle at both ends," as his grandmother had warned against in a letter, albeit in her own peculiar Bulgarian phrasing, and in any event, afternoon naps seemed a normal part of college culture, which hadn't been possible, or needed, during high school.

"The air's a little thinner up here," Dr. Quack explained when Cody went in for his weekly blood drawing, which had expanded to include blood pressure and reflex testing and occasionally a vision test, like a mini exam. "It takes a while to adjust to it, like any higher elevation." He quizzed Cody about his general well-being and was glad to hear his headaches had not returned.

"And the ringing in your ears?" Dr. Quack asked one day, which Cody didn't remember revealing to anyone. "They often go hand in hand," the doctor added.

"Well, that's good news," he replied when Cody said, truthfully, that the ringing was gone, too. "Just let me know if it returns, so we can nip it in the bud." He whisked away the four vials of Cody's blood.

After drunken Lodge nights, Cody would occasionally wake up in and around Rebel's Rest, dazed and confused, but at least he was passing out closer to home.

"Who ate my cookie dough?" Pearl asked one morning at breakfast. "That was for lunch." Cody wondered why he felt a little queasy.

"Oh Lord," Pearl *tsk*ed good-naturedly when no one fessed up, as she padded back to the kitchen to start all over.

Early one morning, he woke up naked in Elliott's twin bed, with Elliott, who was also naked. He gingerly unwrapped his arms and found his clothes strewn about the floor. "Hey dude," Elliott said tentatively, and Cody said, "Hey dude," and crept out the door in his underwear. A half-asleep Banjo was shuffling back from the bathroom, scratching himself, and yawned "paleface" on his way to his room.

"Dood," Banjo said later that day, strumming on the back porch, his head cocked at Cody, who was smoking. "*Dewd*," he repeated, inspecting him.

"I'm corn-fused." Banjo finally confronted him that night in the bathroom. "Are you and Elliott dealing?"

"No," Cody answered. "I passed out in the wrong room."

"Huh," Banjo said, skeptical. "Huh." He seemed more hurt than judgmental.

Cody had never been with a guy before, although it less bothered than puzzled him. He'd certainly known gay guys in high school; that stigma was long gone among his friends, and it didn't seem to exist at S'wanee either. There had to be gays and lesbians here, but it never came up. Nobody asked, and nobody told.

Cody was more troubled that he couldn't remember any details about his Elliott night. He liked Elliott, a lot, but wasn't attracted to or curious about him, sexually, on any level. He had no clue how he'd wound up naked in his bed. He ransacked his memory for the time line of that night, but came up blank. Just another drunken blackout, he settled.

Well. Cody shrugged. *Been there, done that now*, chalking up a new, innocent college experimentation, along with the harmless mushrooms and temporary cigarette smoking, which he needed to wrap up soon. That night, he sought out Lucy at the Lodge and led her up to the Crow's Nest.

"Hey dude," Elliott said expectantly in the hallway one night, and Cody said, "Hey dude," and kept going. They never mentioned it again.

Chapter Ten

White-coated Ross hurried through Spencer Hall, past the biology lab window, and Cody decided to make his move.

Ross had a pit bull mix on a leash, and the dog was wearing a metallic collar. Whatever Ross was up to looked so much more fascinating than the stupid tapeworm they were dissecting again, that Cody had to find out.

"Where you going?" lab partner Banjo demanded. "We gotta clean this nasty shit up!"

Cody dashed through the hallways, trying to catch up to Ross, far ahead and moving fast. Down a flight of stairs and through a long corridor, through a door marked "Neuroscience," past a classroom marked "Leading Questions and False Memories," past a classroom marked "Learned Psychological Paralysis," and into an empty reception area where picked-over refreshment tables and a check-in booth with name tags and Magic Markers sat unattended. Ross must have already gone through the only door at the far end. The digital plaque next to the door read "Mind Over Matter: The Brain Atlas and Wireless Neurological Hijacking." Cody grabbed a hoagie wedge from the food table and slipped in.

It was a large semicircular lecture hall on a steep grade. Dozens of white-coated professors sat like students in the darkened room, paying rapt attention to the brightly lit stage below, where Ross, the movie star, held court.

"I apologize for running late." He grinned a little nervously, clipping on his wireless mike. "Apparently someone forgot to walk our special guest today." He laughed at himself, but the joke fell flat because no one knew what special guest he meant, except for Cody, who would have laughed in support if he hadn't been watching on the down low. The crowd seemed humorless anyway. *Rooting for you, dude!*

"Arthur C. Clarke, science fiction author and futurist"—Ross's voice filled the hall as he grew more confident in his teleprompted presentation—"once wrote that 'any sufficiently advanced technology is indistinguishable from magic.' Ladies and gentlemen, on behalf of S'wanee, I am proud to present our latest bit of magic."

Cody silently crouched behind the back row, where the adults wore name tags that said "NIH" and "CDC" and "Pfizer" and "Cisco" and "Whittemore Peterson Institute for Neuroimmune Diseases."

"Ever since Dr. Persinger invented the God Helmet," Ross continued, "scientists have struggled to use complex magnetic signals to harness the human brain. Now, thanks to the marriage of science and technology, that Holy Grail is within reach. The completion of the Human Genome Project, coupled with major advancements in wireless technology, which we all see in our everyday lives, has led us now to the precipice of the most monumental medical breakthrough since the discovery of penicillin."

On the large screen behind him whirled computerized, 3-D images of cross-sectioned, heat-scanned brains. Bannered across the top of the screen read "The Brain Atlas."

"Imagine a world without blindness," he went on, warming up. "A world without clinical depression or bipolar disorder or autism or addictions of any kind. Now imagine a world without diabetes. Without AIDS or Alzheimer's. Without cancer. Ladies and gentlemen, if you can, imagine a world without disease at all."

The scanned, whirling brains were dotted in colors that corresponded to the coded "Disease Guide" listed on the side.

The white coats sat straight. Dean Apperson, today very Gordon Gekko in a navy banker's suit, nodded and watched Ross proudly from the front row.

"A world where the brain heals the body without drugs of any kind. It's always had that latent power to cure any ailment, any disease, on its own. We just didn't have the knowledge, or technology, to tap into it. Until now."

The Pfizer man leaned back in his seat, skeptical.

"Ladies and gentleman," Ross said, raising the energy, "I present to you: Puck!"

The white-and-brown-spotted pit bull mix with metallic collar scampered happily on stage before dashing up the aisles, his excited stub tail wagging his body in half. He seemed determined to sniff and greet each white coat personally. The room laughed and responded, whipping Puck into a gleeful frenzy.

"Here, Puck! Come, boy!" Ross called from the stage, as the dog, paying no attention, scurried between legs, under seats, and occasionally pawed a startled white coat on his hind legs.

"Dog needs some obedience lessons," someone catcalled from the darkened hall, to general laughter, even though it wasn't particularly funny or clever. Ross nodded and went to a laptop on a high stool at the edge of the stage.

"We can do better than that, I think," he said. Next to the stool stood a tall, metal erector-set structure with several "branches" jutting out, treelike. Puck raced around the top level, stopping for just a second to nose a delighted Cody and get a pat on the head before bustling on across the room.

Ross typed something on the laptop, and Puck stopped running and stood still.

"We've just made the connection," Ross said. "No different from any wireless network, and yet all the difference in the world. I've just hijacked his brain."

Ross typed, and Puck slowly marched down the dark aisle stairs to the bright stage, where he stood at attention, trancelike.

"With this streaming connection, I can control what he sees or doesn't see. Hears or doesn't hear." Ross typed, and Puck started to freak out, dropping and pawing at his eyes. "I can take away his vision, and"—typing—"bring it right back." Puck stood and looked around the stage, sharp and focused.

Ross typed and placed half a hoagie on the floor, which Puck ignored. Ross typed, and Puck hungrily woofed it down.

"I can preprogram a whole series of commands, and with one keystroke, put him through a wide-ranging gamut of emotions." Ross typed, and Puck's hair stood up; he curled his lip and snarled and turned savage. Seemingly deranged and almost rabid, he viciously attacked an invisible threat stage center. Ross knelt down scarcely inches from his snapping jaws. White coats in the front row pushed back uneasily, and Dean Apperson nodded calmly.

"This isn't some Jedi mind trick, folks," Ross the Showman assured them. "This is pure, refined science."

Nesta/Fletcher flashed in Cody's mind, and then flashed out again, because that was a freak accident and tragedy, and this was a carefully controlled—and likely rehearsed—experiment. Ross didn't blink.

Yep, Cody thought. *Much cooler than tapeworms.*

Puck's mood changed, and he rolled onto his back, legs up, whining. Ross rubbed his belly. Puck cowered in terror and barked happily and went fast asleep and ran in circles over a course of seconds. Ross smiled devilishly as he typed, and Puck lifted his leg on Dean Apperson's ankle.

"Now, now, Ross." Dean Apperson laughed with the others, as he scooted from the line of fire. "Science has its limits."

"We can, if necessary," Ross continued, scratching a happy Puck behind the ears, "even override basic natural instincts. Including, but not limited to, those of self-preservation and survival."

Ross typed, and the remote-controlled Puck ran to the corner of the stage toward a tall ladder that Cody hadn't noticed. It led up to a gridlike matrix of scaffolding high above the auditorium, from which hung the spotlights. Without hesitating, Puck scaled the ladder, slipping but recovering, and walked along the rickety catwalk over the audience. Fearlessly, but carefully, Puck navigated the matrix to the back of the hall, above the darkness, to the wonderment and increasing concern of the white coats below.

Ross typed, and Puck navigated back to the front, high above the sunken stage. Without looking down, Robo-Puck leaped from the scaffolding into the bright air, as the audience gasped. Ross caught him in a large cushion he cradled in his arms, and Puck neither flinched nor flailed from the fall that could have broken his bones. Ross gingerly placed him on the stage and typed, and Puck, released from control, wagged his body and panted and scampered excitedly around the hall to thunderous applause. It was like a circus act.

"That last stunt has little practical use." Ross laughed. "But we wanted to demonstrate the degree of control that this new technology can achieve."

"Best of all," he added, "he remembers none of it. No learned fear, no psychic scars, absolutely no storage in his conscious or unconscious. Clap on/clap off, like a switch." Puck panted happily and looked around for more love.

Ross concluded his presentation, confident and masterful and with the white coats fully captive. "In a nutshell, once that connection is made, once the hijack is secure, we can replicate the therapeutic properties of any drug, any treatment, ever invented, now or in the future. Ladies and gentlemen, this is a watershed moment with unlimited upside potential. This technology can absolutely save and improve lives. Modern medicine will never be the same."

Lights came up around the hall, and assistants passed labeled glass panes that looked imprinted with pink brain silhouettes in various sizes.

"Please be careful with those," Ross cautioned, as the white coats passed and scrutinized them. "That's actual brain tissue from lab animals. Sliced paper-thin."

Ross expertly addressed the feverish scientific questions the white coats peppered him with. It was a smooth, almost hypnotic sales pitch to the abruptly less skeptical audience.

"We basically assign an IP address to the brain and plant a cookie, so to speak, so we can always tap back into it. The same technology as any mobile device."

"In Puck's case, we track him through a modified shock collar. We've also tested a tiny microchip, which you can plant in the body with a standard syringe, very noninvasive. We're still tweaking that technology."

"Yes, you can target a single individual, for specific therapy based on their disease or condition, or you can cover an entire population, without discrimination, for general therapy tailored for the common good. You could stop smoking in Boston, or even Paris. You could make a high school in Omaha crave broccoli instead of french fries. And you could, ultimately, tranquilize a mass riot anywhere in the world with a wave of digital dopamine.

"Conversely," he added, "you could also incite one."

"Yes, it's a multiuse tech with a variety of other potential applications, including military and cyberweaponry, although that's far off the horizon, and I'm not at liberty to discuss it anyway."

"Of course, dozens of research universities have been testing this tech for years, but I can confidently say we've refined it and beaten them to the finish line."

A white coat passed a glass pane labeled in large block print back to Cody, who studied the small pink brain tissue. The label said "Hrothgar." The next one said "Fuzz."

"What was considered science fiction as recently as thirty years ago is now, increasingly, very much a reality."

"Tracking and hijacking is the simple part, really. The 'money shot,' so to speak, is the actual programming: what you tell the brain to do. That's the magic we're creating, and once human trials are complete, we'll selectively start to license out the patent." He eyed the crowd. "And worth every penny…"

In the now-lit hall, Cody noticed a white coat with a "DARPA" name tag on the back row looking at him curiously. Cody smiled and nodded. The man looked familiar. Cody realized he had once mistaken him for a parent during orientation week. Evidently, he was a professor or visiting researcher from someplace Cody had never heard of.

"Why test it on dogs?" another white coat asked.

The DARPA not-a-parent white coat nodded back at Cody and started typing on his phone.

"A dog's brain is remarkably similar to a man's, which will come as no surprise to the ladies in the audience." More laughter from the hall. "But seriously," Ross continued, "thousands of years of canine domestication have synched the two, in temperament and emotional comprehension, which makes a dog a better testing subject for this particular technology than, say, a lab monkey. Although tapping into the more complex human brain requires a different frequency and, naturally, a much stronger signal."

Cody studied another brain tissue labeled "Trixie." It was a small brain. The name rang a bell from somewhere.

"Certainly, it hasn't been easy," Ross added. "Puck is the successful culmination of lots of trial and error, with more to come as we work out the inevitable kinks."

Stage-side, Dean Apperson checked his own phone and read the screen.

"So when will human trials be complete?" a woman in the audience asked.

"We wrap up phase one on January fifteenth," answered Ross, "at which point we will analyze the data and present it for peer review in due course."

"Can't you give us a midtrial update?" a white coat asked. "Since your license fees are so, shall we say, top of the market?"

Ross laughed and said, "I can probably give you a teaser." Dean Apperson leaned in to his ear and whispered, and then Ross laughed again.

"Well," he said, scanning the audience. "We seem to have an eager beaver in the house.

"Cody? What the hell are you doing here, Tiger?"

• • •

"Dude, you crack me up," Ross said, his arm around Cody's shoulder, leading him back upstairs at Spencer. "I swear, when we're ready, I'll bring you on as assistant for the final data report. Fact-checking, spell-checking, all that stuff, cool?"

Ross explained that university scientific research departments had long been the genesis for cutting-edge stuff that eventually filtered into everyday life. "Harvard made gazillions by developing the retrovirals that have saved millions worldwide," he insisted. "The University of Wisconsin derived the first human stem cell line and funded their new stadium to boot.

"S'wanee actually discovered the active ingredient in most of today's anxiety and sleeping meds," Ross continued as they strolled toward the exit. "That earned gowns for five juniors here," he added, looking around, "and paid for this whole damn building and then some.

"But it's proprietary information." Ross stopped at the glass door. "You know what that means, right?"

"Down low." Cody smiled.

"It means *down low*, Tiger." Ross nodded. "Seriously. Until we're ready to publish. My gown kinda depends on it, you know?" It was more a plea than an order.

"No clue what you're talking about."

"Good answer, Tiger. Keep it that way."

"But seriously, your radar tree thing?" Cody added. "It would never make me like broccoli." Ross laughed and said, "I'll bring you in when the time is right. Believe me, with a breakthrough this big, there are plenty of gowns to go around…"

Cody was late to work and told the Widow, truthfully, that he'd been with Ross and Dean Apperson, which befuddled her and inoculated him from scolds. He was too revved up to concentrate on his Western Civ essay due the next morning and looked around the lobby for the phantom camera, which could have been tucked into any corner or light fixture or one of the thousands of origami birds that flocked from the ceiling. Cody shot a smile and the finger into the air for good measure, just in case Ross was watching.

• • •

S'wanee threw a big bonfire party on the Quad to celebrate a rare football victory over MTSU. The Tiger Girls were too intoxicated for a coordinated stunt show, but they gamely cheered the crowd into a frenzy nonetheless. It was the biggest student crowd Ross had seen since the Signing Ceremony, because the school provided gourmet hot dogs and live music and, more important, premium kegs. S'wanee, Cody had concluded, had no qualms serving alcohol to minors, or maybe the laws were different here.

Even Beth showed up. She was on the far edge, trying to blend in but failing wonderfully. Bundled against the slight chill in a black sweater and leggings with white dabs of hat and fingerless gloves, she resembled a high-fashion cat burglar or a very sexy chimney sweep. She winked and smiled from across the Quad, but all this school spirit was too much for her. Rocking on her black boot heels, she seemed on duty, waiting to clock out and get back to whatever "mysteerious" life she led way out at Tuckaway Hall.

As he passed, Ross winked at Cody, too, and Cody nodded back, coconspirators in the scientific secret they alone shared. Ross smiled and kept going, trailed, as usual, by girls who pretended not to be trailing him.

"Dude, let's hit the Lodge," Banjo grumbled over the loud music, watching the girls migrate away. "It's kicked here."

Across the way, Vail begged off as Skit and Houston tried to drag her along for the night's adventures. Vail had been increasingly detached and withdrawn, the fallout from her now-official-and-final break up with Bishop. She'd been glum for days.

"I'll catch up with you guys there," Cody said, feeling duty bound as section president to make sure she was holding up.

"What the fuck did you just say?" Banjo asked, and Elliott said, "Dude, what was that?"

Puzzled, Cody repeated himself.

"That's not what you said, dude." Banjo guffawed. "Are you wasted already?"

"Like tongues or something," Elliott added, laughing.

Cody raised his voice over the music and his third beer. He didn't feel slurry at all.

"Oonga boonga yourself, paleface," Banjo said, as he and Elliott wandered toward Manigault Park with the others. "I want whatever *you're* on."

"I'm fine, Cody, really," Vail insisted, as the Quad cleared out and workers extinguished the bonfire. "But thanks for asking. That's sweet of you." Moments later, she was sobbing and telling him all. She sat on a bench and choked out the whole time line, as she had surely done for countless others, for anyone who asked or cared. She was heartbroken.

"But I'm fine, Cody," she repeated through tamed sniffles, wiping mascara from her lower lids. "It's not the first time I've been dumped." Then she laughed almost philosophically. "And, you know, it probably won't be the last either.

"Don't worry about me, mister," Vail said with a hug and a smile. "You're a good man. Now, go have fun. I'll see you tomorrow."

Cody was later glad he had taken the time to talk and listen to Vail, because a few hours afterward, she jumped from the Observatory and landed on her neck.

Chapter Eleven

The trees crackled orange and yellow and copper across the Cumberland Plateau, a glorious sea of fire from high atop Morgan's Steep. The air snapped, and the skies turned crisper blue, and the hydrangeas stayed green but nonblooming. Shorts and flip-flops got packed away and then brought out again, and the weather banged about, resisting the new season.

S'wanee held a low-key, sparsely populated memorial service for Vail at All Saints, two days after drunken stragglers came upon her broken, twisted body on the dark Carnegie Hall sidewalk. Ross led the service, which wasn't advertised by S'wanee e-mail. ("It's not the kind of thing a school brags about," Ross explained when Houston wondered why. "In any event, it was her parents' request.") There were hugs and tears among Rebel's Rest, but the eulogies were brief and awkward, since the well of memories to draw from was only six weeks' deep.

Vail's suicide shocked Cody. She had seemed hurt and troubled, certainly, but also grounded and resilient. He'd learned in high school the telltale signs of teenage suicide—depression, paranoia, aberrant behavior, changes in sleeping/eating habits, feeling trapped—all so vague and commonplace among Cody's peers that his whole generation could technically be at risk. Vail didn't fit the profile. She'd just been temporarily bummed out on the cusp of bouncing back.

But now, three weeks later, Rebel's Rest was back in high gear. Midterm exams were right around the corner, students were conjuring their Halloween costumes, and Cody had a sorta/maybe new girlfriend. With strange conditions.

"Meet me at the Steep," Beth quietly ordered him at McClurg one surprising Indian-summer day. "After class. Today."

She was twenty minutes late, and he thought he'd decoded her orders incorrectly. It was worth the wait.

"Give me a five-minute lead," she said without looking at him, as she stretched in gym shorts and T-shirt at the foot of the memorial cross. "I'll find you on the trail." She grimaced at his oxford and khakis and bluchers. "You dressed all stupid."

Deep down on the Perimeter Trail, Beth *psst*ed and signaled him off course, through a dense, unchartered thicket. Cody hustled to keep pace as she scaled boulders, leaped over creeks, and sandwiched through crevices. She knew her way.

"This is a weird place, Cody," she said, winding toward a narrow, jumpable bend in a brook. "Don't you find it weird?"

"S'wanee? I think it's pretty awesome," Cody said. "Where are you taking me?"

"I heard a girl from your section killed herself," Beth said, ignoring his question. "Is that true, Cody? Is that the real deal?"

Cody instantly filtered the "down-low" versus "non-down-low" information in his brain and determined this was fair game. It was sometimes hard to keep the two categories straight.

"Yeah. Vail."

"Huh. 'Cause that was just a rumor, you know. The school kept it quiet." Beth was hiking faster and not winded at all. She moved like a cat. "And didn't someone else from your section disappear?" she asked.

Filter, filter. "Caleb transferred. To Georgetown."

"Huh. And then whatever that thing was that canceled class?"

Filter overdrive. "Yeah," Cody said. "That thing."

"All the action seems to happen at Rebel's Rest." Beth pushed through a thick overgrowth that muffled water sounds just beyond. "It's sorta the Domain's Bermuda Triangle. You notice that?"

She stood at the edge of a blue, tranquil pool, surrounded by tall stone bluffs covered in moss. A waterfall poured over the top. It was a remote, private paradise. "Bridal Falls," Beth said, kicking off her shoes and pulling her T-shirt over her head. Without flinching, she waded in naked and tattoo-free. "I discovered it my first week here." Halfway in, she turned back. "Can you swim?"

"Sure," Cody said, peeling off clothes.

"I thought this was only fair," she said before she submerged. "After all, I've already seen *you* naked."

Beth was hard to figure out. Playful and flirtatious as she splashed him, elusive when he asked her questions, and positively erotic when she showered directly under the falls.

"People talk," she explained, when Cody finally asked why she was so sketchy with him. "That's how I know all this stuff about that death trap you live in. A place this small and detached and dull, word gets around. I don't want that."

"And if you tell anyone I brought you here," she added, "I'll deny it and say you're just a creeper. A stalker."

Beth grabbed his face and kissed him deep. They kept each other afloat in the center of the pool, but when Cody's hands found her breasts, she pushed him off forcefully.

"Dude, I'm not a slut," she corrected him. "Not a Wellington Lodge Crow's Nest *slut*." Word did get around.

"I just wonder," she said as they hiked back, Beth in her wet shirt and Cody squishing in his bluchers as he carried his good clothes, "what kind of fog you really live in. It's interesting to me, that's all." It got dark much earlier now.

"I'll go back first," she ordered as they neared the Perimeter Trail proper. "Wait five minutes."

"Come to Rebel's Rest for dinner," Cody said.

Beth laughed. "I don't *want* to come to Rebel's Rest for dinner."

"So invite me to Tuckaway Hall," he pressured, and she said, meaning it, "No, Cody. You can't come there."

"I do like you," she said. "You're sweet and probably clever. I'm just curious what goes on in your head."

"Can I text you?" he asked, his last chance as she peered down the trail.

"No need," she said. "You're easy to track down." And she was gone into the dusk.

• • •

Clouds brought back the cold, and it stuck this time.

The schizophrenic weather had taken its toll on the creatures of the Domain. Long gone were Cody's window bees, whose fuzzy striped carcasses had littered his sill for days before being swept away by the breeze. Gone too were the fireflies that had bedazzled the campus that first week but had been missing since. Pearl said they'd be back in the spring.

Cody had a brief flashback by Burwell Fountain one morning as a worker scooped out dozens of floating goldfish into a garbage bag. Cody had offed his share as a child through negligence and dirty water. Goldfish were a delicate bunch.

More notable were the bluebirds and mockingbirds and squirrels that increasingly lay strewn about the sidewalks and lawns and that workers picked up with long, clawlike reachers. One day Cody counted eleven workers roaming and reaching at the same time.

"Yeah, it's weird," Ross agreed when Huger brought it up at dinner. "The school's checking them for jet-stream trauma or avian virus or something. I'm sure it's harmless." Skit said, "It's totally disgusting," and Banjo said, "Sin, you didn't bring over the hen flu, did you?" "You might like them, Banjo," Sin shot back. "I hear they taste like fried chicken."

"Yeah, that happens every year," Ross explained as gloved groundskeepers paired up to hoist dead Canada geese from Abbo's Alley onto the maintenance truck flatbed. "Some are too old to migrate south, and they know it. Not a bad final resting place, I guess." The truck showed up three days in a row.

Cody had seen the arching mother deer and her growing fawns many mornings on his run down Tennessee Avenue. One day, in the shallow woods right off the road, the two fawns struggled to stay standing, as if just learning to walk again. The mother kept close and eyed Cody guardedly. Days later, the mother eyed him from the woods alone. It had now been weeks since Cody had seen any deer at all.

Cody's biology professor explained Mother Nature could be aggressively Darwinian at times.

• • •

The campus cleared out for a three-day weekend after midterms, but the Widow made Cody stay and work. "We have new books to process," she warbled. "Do you know the Dewey decimal system, Cody?"

After three days alone, Cody was happy when Purple Haze snapped back to life.

"You missed a fucking blast, paleface," Banjo said when he returned from Dollywood with Elliott. They had more lenient bosses and had hitched a ride with some upperclass Wellingtons. "Banjo got us kicked out," Elliott said. "He was drunk and kept grabbing Dolly's tits." "She was *cardboard*," Banjo insisted, showing off the photo on his phone. "Uptight hillbillies. They wanted to lynch me." He punctuated his outrage with a vibrating belch. They both took their knapsacks down to the laundry basement.

"How was shore leave?" Huger asked Emerson, and Sin said, "I got three A's and a B plus," when Buzz pried about her midterms, shaking his head at his own report.

"Please keep the back doors closed!" Pearl yelled through the log cabin. "Some critter got into the kitchen trash last night. Yuck!"

"Your grades are stable, adequate, but a bit worrying." Dean Apperson reviewed in his Cravens Hall living room over an afternoon sherry. "I think you can hunker down and apply yourself a bit more. Don't you, Cody?" "Try not to beat yourself up, Tiger," Ross sympathized later over Cody's straight B's. "Midterms are always a cold bucket of water. They try to scare you." But Cody knew better than anyone that his grades had him on the knife's edge of scholarship eligibility.

"Houston, honey, do you still have my kitchen timer?" Pearl asked that night, and Houston, her roots freshly blond, said, "Sorry I forgot to return it, Pearl." "Oh, how I *envy* hair like yours," Pearl gushed.

"You sure it's not a false alarm?" Sin asked Skit as Cody neared the front living room. "I'm never late," Skit said, and then she added, "I'm as fertile as the Mississippi." They both looked up when he walked in on them. "I'll go study in the den," he said, retrieving his iPad, and Skit said, "Thanks, bud." "It's such a fucking drag," she murmured as he went down the hall.

"She swore she was cool," Paxton stressed to Huger around the fire pit. "She swore she was all set."

"We're doing a Sonic run," Bishop said to Ross on his way out with Emerson later. "Can we borrow your wheels? You want a burger or Coney or anything?"

"Archer, is this your mess in the microwave again?" Pearl yelled from the kitchen. "Good *Lord*!"

"I didn't know you smoked," Ross remarked randomly at dinner one night, and Cody said, "I don't really," feeling the pull and wanting one.

"They're showing *The Other* at McClurg tonight." Sin canvassed for takers. "Not the Nicole Kidman, but the 1972 freaker. They have an original print!"

"Has anyone seen my big chopping knife?" Pearl called through the log cabin. "It's a Wusthof. I got a nickel for anyone who finds my big chopping knife!"

• • •

Skit disappeared next.

"A personal leave, I think," Pearl explained gingerly. "Or so I was told." "A personal *abortion*, I think," Banjo clarified later. "Or so *I* was told." He had early on nicknamed her "Sloppy Skit."

"S'wanee doesn't perform those," Houston said one late study night. "She probably went back home for it." "Guys, guys." Ross tamped down the rumor mill. "Can we just be chill about it? Geezus."

Cody had already guessed. Skit had gone on the warpath one night at the Lodge, hurling insults and unveiled threats at Paxton. It was a particularly rowdy night, and Skit was as wasted as any of them. "So what do I do now?" she yelled at the evasive Paxton. "We going *Dutch* at least?" When she threw her beer at him, dousing Cody in the collateral damage, two Kilts diplomatically ushered her out. "Fuck you! I'm fucking outta here!" she screamed hoarsely.

"Let her go," Ross said when Buzz offered to go after her. "Let her walk it off. She'll be okay." Houston added, "It just sucks." "The chick's fucking crazy," a dripping Paxton huffed.

By the next morning, as Cody walked through Burwell Garden on the way to class, he agreed with Paxton: Skit was overreacting. Cody had known girls in high school in the same situation, and none had gone that berserk or quit school. Skit was fun and rowdy, but also a prima donna, he decided, as workers scrubbed and sanitized the drained goldfish-genocide fountain with filthy rags soaked in red algae.

But on the night of Skit's outburst and exodus, Cody, beer-wet and drunker than he'd been in a while, curled up on a Lodge back-room sofa under a scratchy plaid throw, his orange backpack as pillow. He'd stumble home when the drama had passed.

• • •

A violent thunderstorm knocked out campus power one Sunday night. It was fantastic.

"Flashlights? Candles?" Pearl offered, passing them around the roaring fireplace. "Just be careful, please."

"Banjo, stop goosing me!" Sin yelled as they shared a candle down to the laundry basement. "Ruh-roh!" Banjo guffawed. "Watch out for the karate chop!" "Just shut up and *smile* so I can see the stairs!"

Cody took a candle to his room to study in silence. Salinger and Robespierre and Milton Friedman danced in his head as he resolved to course-correct his middling midterm grades. His latest econ problem set had the perfunctory Talking Heads bonus question, and Cody mined every last point he could get. *"Qu'est que c'est"* rang a bell; he could hear it in his head but couldn't pinpoint the song, and when he went to Google it on his iPad, he realized the campus Internet was down along with the power.

He switched to his laptop and plugged in the Troller, which he hadn't needed yet because the S'wanee network was so strong. Sure enough, the trusty Troller located another network named "DARPA," and the yellow wave was steady. As his password-hacking software struggled to tap in, Cody scrolled back to where he'd seen that name before—one of the white coats at the Ross/Puck show at Spencer Hall a few weeks ago. Probably one of the many academic departments at S'wanee, either immune to the power outage or, more likely, blessed with its own electric generator. They wouldn't mind—or know—if he piggybacked on them. After all, it was just for homework.

His hacking software suddenly flashed "Forbidden Attempt" and closed itself out, as if DARPA had scared it off. The Talking Heads title would have to wait, even as Cody hummed the tune.

"Cody?" Pearl called up the stairs. "We're popping corn over the fire, pioneer-style. Take a break and come get yourself some!"

"This is a fog storm," Ross was telling the captive Hazers by the fire as Cody went down. "What's a fog storm?" Emerson asked, and Ross said, "Just wait."

• • •

Cody had never seen anything like the S'wanee fog. Nobody had.

It rolled in early the next morning as the storm passed. It billowed over the Cumberland Plateau and followed Cody back on his run from Morgan's Steep. It weaved through the trees of Manigault Park and descended upon Abbo's Alley and by noon had obstructed the Domain with near whiteout conditions, as it had done for thousands of years.

"Better than snow!" Banjo cheered, and freshmen soon learned to wear raincoats and slickers as they navigated through the wet, white cotton candy. It shrouded and transformed the campus, and the flashlight basket by the front door was soon empty.

"Technically, it's not really fog," Ross explained. "It's a cloud."

"It made me cry," Sin said at dinner one night. "Seriously, I was walking through it, and I couldn't see. I was so overwhelmed by the beauty and power of it, I sat down and cried." Then she laughed at herself. "It's crazy, isn't it?" But by the second week of constant foggy gloom, Sin asked, "How long does it last?"

"It's bumming me out," Bishop said, and Elliott bought a tiny, battery-powered plastic fan from the Klondyke to clear a path as he moved around. Cody could barely see the Shapard Tower beacon from his room at night.

"It's spooky," Houston complained. "And it frizzes my hair."
"I'm over this," Paxton declared as the fog sat, owning the campus, on the fourth week.

"I love it," Beth purred when she located Cody on his way to work. She grabbed him in Burwell Garden and kissed him deep, and they met there every afternoon, in the privacy of the fog.

"You're sorta crazy; you know that?" Cody said, always on time.

"Yeah, I sorta am," she agreed, close in his ear. "Relax. Nobody can see us."

Cody's mother sent him a check for five hundred dollars. *A little pocket money, kiddo!* she scribbled on a Post-it. Cody's Tiger Bucks were dwindling, but he knew Marcie couldn't afford this. *Deposit the chick!* she texted back, ever sloppy on her iPhone. *Live a little, kiddo!* She punctuated it with a mischievous, winky-smiley face, and Cody found his way to the ATM outside the Klondyke.

"The Fog Slog is my favorite time of year," Dean Apperson declared at the surprisingly boozy Thanksgiving luncheon he hosted at Cravens Hall for select Purple Hazers who had stayed behind. "I'm always sad to see it lift, but at least Christmas comes right on its heels." Dean Apperson rang a little bell to summon the white-coated servants for the next course and soon launched an enormous conversation about art and literature and philosophy. "More oyster stuffing, Cody?" he offered.

"Dude, a Presidential Citizens Medal!" Paxton pointed to the gold eagle disc dangling from the white and blue ribbon on the wall of the dean's study. "He's got an Intelligence Star, too," Bishop added, carefully holding the leather display box. "I've heard about this," Sin said, picking up a book titled *Less Than Human* from the dean's study chair. "Dehumanization is a tough topic these days." "Hey guys, we're watching the game in the den," Ross said, herding them out for an afternoon of Thanksgiving football.

Soon, Cody couldn't remember what S'wanee was like pre-fog. It seemed a permanent fixture, and he adapted, as always, and between classes and study and work and the Wellington nights, the fog became a forgotten backdrop in everyone's new normal. As long as Beth kept meeting him "in public," he hoped it never lifted.

There were still parties and movie screenings and study breaks with pizza and buffalo wings. The Lodge still poured Jack Daniel's, and Cody still passed out here and there (but kept out of the Crow's Nest—"Fine," Lucy said, shrugging and moving on to the next one) but usually ended up in his own bed, and late one night, just as the fog was abruptly starting to thin, Bishop and Emerson and Sin and Houston were coming back from the Sonic drive-in when they lost their way and drove off the road into a tree. They were killed instantly.

Chapter Twelve

Cody wondered if All Saints Chapel was used for anything other than the Signing Ceremony and student memorials.

Today it was full, and Rebel's Rest was seated up front to mourn their lost friends. Dean Apperson led the ceremony, and the organist played appropriate music, and Cody and Elliott sat on either side of Banjo, buffering him, as he'd been particularly fond of Sin, and his humor was now gone.

Ross had delivered the tragic news at lunch two days before, and S'wanee had sent a mass e-mail canceling the afternoon's classes. Unlike Vail's hush-hush suicide, the school fessed up and embraced the catastrophe that rocked the campus.

"What the fuck?" Paxton said, more angry than sad, and Elliott said, "I can't believe this. I can't believe this."

Banjo was silent the whole day, and more than once, Pearl wrapped him in her hug and said, "I know, baby. It's so hard, baby," stroking his head. Even Ross was red-eyed, although he didn't break down like most of the others, ever the role model. By that first evening, after the initial shock and disbelief had lifted, there was a restless air of rebellion throughout the log cabin. "This is so fucked up," Banjo said finally, and said nothing more.

At the memorial, a soothing Dean Apperson waxed on about the seven stages of grief and the "providence of God" and "duty" and "greater good," and Cody found himself staring at the stained-glass window of Rebel's Rest and mushrooms and terrified students and chaos, and it no longer seemed to depict just a very wild party in the year MCMLXXI. The faces could have easily been Bishop or Emerson or Sin or Houston the instant right before they were killed in their car.

Except none of them had a car, because freshmen weren't allowed. And although Emerson had borrowed Ross's car before, he hadn't this time, because the black Jeep was still parked, safe and sound, in the Rebel's Rest driveway. Whose car had they crashed into a tree?

Cody caught Ross staring at him staring at the stained-glass window, and he turned back toward the front. He rubbed his right hand nervously, the same way his mother touched her stomach when thinking, except it wasn't nonsensical since he'd slept on it funny a few nights before and it was still cricked and sore.

He didn't remember Sin or Houston doing a Sonic run before. He'd never seen them eat junk at all. Sin, in particular, ate like a bird, and Houston usually stuck to salads, although she was less disciplined and had a sweet tooth.

The organ played, and everyone stood to sing a hymn in unison. Cody didn't know the words.

Cody had seen Bishop and Emerson at the Lodge on the night they died. They'd been drinking beer and shots with the rest of them, certainly too drunk to drive. Sin always went to bed early and would never have gotten into a car—whatever car they borrowed—with a drunk and sloppy driver late at night.

Cody glanced back and saw Beth with the Tuckaway section, standing in her assigned spot. She stared at him, mouthing the song words, and almost imperceptibly lifted her eyebrows. Banjo elbowed Cody, and he turned back to the front.

Unless, of course, Sin or Houston had been the driver. They were roommates, and Houston had been flirting off and on with

Emerson, and maybe the guys woke them up and asked for a ride, and Houston had persuaded Sin to come along. But it was a school night, and Cody couldn't imagine the überdiligent Sin going on a late-night spree. Maybe she just needed a study break or agreed to be the designated driver to keep Bishop and Emerson safe. That seemed the kind of thing Sin might do.

When the organ music stopped, the crowd filed out silently, and Cody was careful not to step on the dreaded seal again. The fog had lifted, and the campus was already Christmas-festive with wreaths and bows and garland. Cody was surprised they didn't decorate the huge evergreen, which would have made a perfect Christmas tree, but it was still roped off and untouched.

After a lunch no one ate, they resumed their normal Saturday schedule, and iPads dinged with reading and writing assignments for the upcoming week.

"Try to eat, ya'll," Pearl encouraged, before puttering back to the kitchen, where she kept decorating a cake.

"Seems inappropriate today," he overheard her say. "They should have canceled the contest."

But for a car to hit a tree so hard that it killed all four of them, even those in the backseat, the car must have been going fast, very fast, and Sin would never have done that, especially at night, in the fog. She was way too careful for that.

Cody sat at the library front desk, perched behind the big PC, looking across at the usual cast in the Reading Room. A girl at the end of his counter folded origami birds for a new string to add to the memorial flock of fallen soldiers.

That left Houston at the wheel. But wasn't the stretch between Sonic and the campus—which Cody had been on only once—a straight shot? Cody remembered that road was mostly lined with small houses, like the one the old woman was rocking in front of with the commissioner election sign out front, and most of the trees—certainly the big, hit-me-and-you're-dead trees—were way off road, behind the houses, and even if you careened off the road, in the fog, wouldn't Houston—or whoever was driving—hit the brakes, or wouldn't the car—whoever's car it was—slow down enough so that even if you did hit a tree, way back off the road, it wouldn't kill you? And didn't all these new cars have air bags? Even Cody's ten year-old Camry had air bags front and side.

In the middle of the lobby, the annual Edible Book Fair was in full swing, and housemothers nosed about, judging one another's handicraft. They had concocted elaborate book-themed cakes (a *Moby Dick* whale, a *Harry Potter* Hogwarts castle, a clever *Grapes of Wrath* angry fruit bowl), and the voting came before the eating. It was a typical S'wanee attempt at normalcy, ever-normalcy, and Pearl was right: It was inappropriate on the same day the school memorialized four dead students.

"I can't believe it's starting again," a matronly housemother whispered in the acoustically challenged lobby to another, who whispered back, "They promised it never would."

"I'm terrified to go out at night," another insisted.

"Ladies, ladies, it's nothing of the sort," hushed younger-Pearl, shaking her head at the older bitties. "The dean will never let that happen again." And then she added quietly, "Don't go scaring your kids, you hear? It's not right."

"Who made the *Princess and the Pea* cake?" the Widow warbled with a proud smile. "It's *darling*."

How late was Sonic open anyway? Cody had seen Bishop and Emerson at the Lodge around midnight, and even though he'd lost track of them, they must have gone after that. Was a fast-food restaurant, even a drive-in, in a tiny, sleepy town, open all night? Twenty-four-seven?

"Cody, I didn't see you sitting there! Come get some cake!" Pearl called out as the students clustered when the eating began. "The *Dune* chocolate mousse is heavenly." The winner, *Atlas Shrugged,* was already globe-carved and devoured.

Dinner was subdued, and there was more food to go around and more places to sit and spread out. The rumblings of anger and rebellion that flared over the past few days had quieted, and

Rebel's Rest simmered down to calm acceptance. Long gone were Caleb's booming voice and Skit's throaty cackle. Absent were Vail's sweet demeanor and Bishop's and Emerson's testosterone-fueled one-upmanship. Post-dinner study time was oddly quiet without Sin's soothing piano as Cody struggled through an essay on the main themes of *Hamlet*.

"Why are so many people dying?" Cody asked, and Banjo said, "I don't know," and Elliott said, "I don't know." They'd all wondered the same thing.

• • •

"Mrs. Simpson, does S'wanee have any archives? Like school history stuff?"

Thus, Cody learned the one utterance to bring out the Widow's smile just for him. "Why, yes, Cody." She beamed, almost coy, a wallflower asked to dance. "S'wanee has a rich, wonderful history. Are you really interested, Cody?"

"This way." She led him downstairs to a wood-paneled research room ringed with windows—a warm, clubby bunker amid the stacks. The room was a S'wanee shrine, with framed photos and shelves behind glass and drawers of primary documents. On the circular table centered on the antique rug sat a box of disposable latex gloves. "Put these on, please," she offered pleasantly.

"Do you know microfilm?" she asked, and showed him how to load the tiny reels into the boxy, archaic viewer.

"S'wanee has a rich, wonderful history," she repeated, librarian-proud. "Take all the time you want, Cody. I'll look after the front desk."

In addition to precious S'wanee artifacts—the gold pen used to sign the school's founding document, the original American flag flown and its staff made from a tree near George Washington's tomb, even the first dean's spectacles—there were framed photos of visiting dignitaries through the school's history. President Theodore Roosevelt had visited during that year's Fog Slog and, from his bully grin of delight, seemed to bask in it. President Eisenhower inspected the ROTC cadets, President Kennedy toured the school's busy labs, and a British prime minister and various other heads of state paid official visits in the mid-1960s. Apparently, S'wanee was a choice destination for notables, foreign and domestic.

The microfilm drawer was organized by academic year, and Cody quickly located and loaded 1970/1971 into the viewer. The *S'wanee Purple* was first, with weekly reports of visiting speakers, antiwar editorials, and football losses, naturally, to Vanderbilt and pretty much everyone else. There was an article about professors who commuted from other cities, the on-campus Women's Strike for Equality rally, and growing concerns about the local overpopulation of deer. Someone named Virginia Masters spoke about her discovery of "female multiple orgasms." The Wellingtons had been disciplined, again, for "drunken, disorderly conduct." Other than slightly longer hair, the students could have passed for today's.

There was a short blurb welcoming the newest housemother Pearl, girlish and glowing and thin, and Cody realized he must have undershot her age by at least a decade. In the backdrop of one picture, he spied a much younger but still spiffy Fletcher, and in another, a youthful, prewidow Widow Senex in a gingham jumpsuit and bandana headscarf, her battiness already hatching.

The *Purple*'s last paper before first semester exams was January 15, 1971.

Cody kept scrolling and came upon the *New York Times*, January 18, 1971. On page A22, in the left-hand column toward the bottom of the AP wrap-up, was a quiet headline: "Mass Suicide at Tennessee University."

According to the brief paragraph: "In a mysterious incident, twelve students at Monteagle University killed themselves in one evening after a drug-fueled rampage that inflicted considerable damage to the small liberal arts college two hours outside Nashville."

Cody scrolled ahead. The next day's *New York Times* had a stand-alone article, still short and tucked in the back, that claimed "authorities are investigating the violent deaths that are rumored to have followed an overdose of hallucinogenic drugs on the small, isolated campus." There was one black-and-white photo of a stone building engulfed in flames, set against a snow-covered ground.

Cody scrolled onto the *Chicago Tribune*, *Washington Post*, *Seattle Intelligencer*, and the *Times of London*, all of which picked up the AP feed in various incarnations with the same burning building photo. All buried the story in the back pages.

The *Nashville Banner* screamed its headline above the fold: "MASSACRE AT S'WANEE." It was top news and thoroughly investigated, day after day. The twelve students, male and female, had gone on a "violent spree" simultaneously one evening, breaking windows, torching buildings, and even carrying a professor's Volkswagen into All Saints Chapel, where they placed it, upside down, on the altar. They then fled security and scattered throughout the campus, ultimately killing themselves independently. One girl jumped from the top of Breslin Tower; a boy from Morgan's Steep. A girl slit her own throat and bled to death undiscovered in Abbo's Alley. A boy drowned himself in Lake Finney, which Cody hadn't even heard of. Another boy walked in front of a speeding truck on the main drag through Monteagle—the same street where Cody's friends died. One girl flayed her own skin from her chest and arms with an "unknown instrument." Another, according to the paper's dry prose, "removed her own eyes and tongue with a broken tree branch and was found barely conscious on one of the many trails that ring the campus." She died shortly after.

The second day's reporting shed new light, much of it based on student gossip, as the school itself was initially "tightlipped" about the tragedy. The students all lived together at Rebel's Rest, a "log cabin compound and oldest dormitory on campus." They were mostly "studious, conscientious students who exhibited signs of acute dementia immediately after dinner on the given night." Initial symptoms included speaking "nonsensical gibberish, which quickly escalated to paranoid delusions and apparent hallucinatory visions, before the prolonged, violent rampage that culminated in their tragic suicides."

The third day's reporting included portrait photos and bios of the victims, as well as candid shots of anguished students embracing one another outside All Saints after the memorial. *Been there, done that*, thought Cody. *Twice.* The victims were bright and shining, and one student was quoted, "It all happened so fast, like the flick of a switch," and another said, "It wasn't like them at all. If you knew them, you would know. It just does not make sense." A side article posed the almost comical question: "Death by Mushrooms?"

The article mined the student rumor that the victims had been poisoned that night by a "reputedly hallucinogenic mushroom indigenous to the outlying campus." The students called these S'wanee Truffles, "known and feared for their mind-altering potency." "I would never touch it," a student was quoted saying. "Everyone knows never to touch the dark purple ones." "I tried a tiny bit once," another student was quoted anonymously. "Never again. Never."

The paper interviewed the managing editor of the *S'wanee Purple*, John Crownover, a junior, whose own reporting implicated a fellow junior in the poisoning. The unnamed student, a "candidate for the Order of the Gownsmen, the school's highest honor," is suspected of testing the "mycological properties" on the unwitting victims, as part of a broader research project. According to Crownover, although the school did regular research with "outside contracts, like many universities," it would "never condone" this kind of testing, for any price or purpose.

Crownover, a fellow Gownsmen candidate whose picture could have passed for any of the current Olympians on campus, stressed this was all hearsay and "unsubstantiated," but if his reporting could confirm crimes of this "overzealous" student, he would immediately "break the story."

The *Nashville Banner* apparently stopped covering the story after the third day, and there was nothing more in any newspapers, at least on this microfilm roll. Crownover must not have broken the story after all. As far as Cody would tell, the *S'wanee Purple* didn't publish again that school year. He rewound and unspooled and reached for 1972/1973.

"There you are, Tiger!" Ross was at the door to the shrine. "I've been looking for you. Shouldn't you be at the front desk?"

He laughed as he led Cody back upstairs. "I've been trying to check out these books!" he said, although he'd never checked out a book from Cody before.

The Widow sat chastened at the front desk. "I'm sorry, Ross," she said, glowering in Cody's general vicinity. "You can go early, Cody. I don't need you any more today." The Bat was back.

Among other things, the archives had revealed the Cherokee definition of the name "S'wanee." It meant, simply, "lost."

Chapter Thirteen

"You think they all killed themselves?" Beth asked as they huddled in the Observatory overlooking the Quad, their new secret spot when Cody got off work.

It sounded ridiculous. Only Vail had committed suicide for real, but then again, the only reason they knew that was because students had found her body. Considering all the stuff that S'wanee kept on the "down low," anything was possible. After all, it had happened before, and S'wanee had stayed initially "tightlipped."

Eventually, of course, S'wanee must have fessed up about the 1971 tragedy. They even installed a stained-glass window at All Saints to commemorate it, alongside other important chapters in the school's history. At some point, the school had stopped hiding. The carnage got so much publicity, they couldn't avoid it. Too many people knew, all over the world.

But what about now? Did Sin, the most stable and balanced of their section, really go mad, so suddenly? Would she, or even Houston, have knowingly taken the same mushrooms that doomed the students decades ago? Bishop and Emerson, maybe. But Sin? No way. The strongest thing she took was coffee, and even that was decaf. Unless someone slipped it to her, against her knowledge or will.

"I mean, it's *possible*," Beth said skeptically, and Cody realized the whole thing was a stretch. Car wrecks happen, and people get killed, thousands every day. He could name at least five from his own high school. But Rebel's Rest, which had only twenty-five to start, had already lost seven, to one thing or another, in the first three months. Were other sections or dorms also losing students that he didn't know about?

"I haven't heard of any," Beth said. "And that kind of thing, you know, gets around."

Two students came into the Observatory to look through the telescope, and Beth made her usual stealthy exit. "I'll catch you later," she whispered close in his ear, squeezing his hand. "That's it? That's all?" he asked. Someday, he hoped, she'd changed her skittish ways. Until then, he'd take what he could get.

Pearl hum-sang "Silver Bells" in her Christmas-plaid apron as she oversaw the decorating of the tree in the front living room. She passed peppermint hot cocoa and laid out big, grabbing bowls of a butter/garlicky, Chex-Cheerios-pretzel-peanut mix she called "nuts and bolts." Rebel's Rest balanced Christmas revelry with the frenzied final weeks of the semester before the break.

"Dude, can I borrow your civ notes from Thursday?" Huger asked the American waif from Germany, whose name Cody had forgotten. "I'm not a 'dude,'" she dissed, "and you shouldn't have skipped class." Eventually, Cody would have to branch out and befriend this "second string" of Purple Hazers, since his initial batch of friends was so thinned out.

"We're missing you at meals," Pearl said to Cody as he rushed out before breakfast. "You already sick of my cooking?"

"I love your cooking, Pearl," he assured her. "Just been too busy to get back here lately." In truth, he'd been burning through Tiger Bucks on sandwiches at McClurg and Ramen noodles and

Red Bull from the Klondyke for afternoon pick-me-ups, which he increasingly needed.

At least he'd stopped spending Tiger Bucks on cigarettes, which he no longer craved. Maybe he could convince his mother it was easy to quit.

"Banjo, did you take my navy sweater?" asked Cody, who was also missing a T-shirt and khakis from a laundry room mix-up. "Why ask the black dude?" Banjo yelled from his room. "I got my own clothes!"

"The van's leaving in three, guys!" Ross called from the front on Sunday morning, for the Nashville field trip to see the Broadway tour of *Elf*. The school had upped its game with special events, either for Christmas cheer or to distract from the recent tragedy. It was the first time Cody had been off campus since he arrived.

"You guys go on without me," Elliott said, increasingly withdrawn and spending more time alone in his room. "*Dood*," bounce-back Banjo said, shaking his head. "What the fuck is wrong with you? It's free!"

As the van passed the stone security kiosk, its barricade arm up and back down, Cody felt an instant pierce of headache pain, just a blip really, that reminded him of his bad spell months ago, but it was gone as soon as it came, and Banjo was passing out beers from a red cooler. "Roadies all around!" he ordered.

Why didn't any information about the "S'wanee Massacre" show up on Google? Not the newspaper archives; Cody didn't expect those from so long ago. But nothing at all? No alumni postings, no commemorations or remembrances, no trace of any kind. Like it had never happened.

"Tap the ceiling, fucker!" Banjo ordered as they passed the stone gates of the Domain. "Don't forget to take your angel, dude," Ross added.

But Yahoo had auto suggested "S'wanee Massacre"—a top hit—which meant lots of people must have been searching for it through the years. And, like Cody, finding no answers. Had the school quashed it from the web, or was it so obscure and forgotten that no one bothered to write about it anymore?

"You with us, Tiger? Cody?" Ross asked as the black van with tinted windows sped through town toward the interstate. The van was packed and talkative.

"Yeah dude, just thinking," Cody said, scanning the roadside for any broken tree, any killer tree, any tree at all. The road was straight and wide and well paved and line painted, just as he remembered.

But the older woman on the plane next to him—long, long ago, it seemed—at least remembered *something* had happened there. Didn't she say it gave her a chill, or something like that? And if a random woman on a plane had heard of it, then it must have been a big story at the time, probably even on television news, maybe on Oprah or Anderson Cooper, or whoever did the news way back then.

"You remember the Batman Building, Cody?" Ross asked, as the Nashville skyline came into view.

But even the *Nashville Banner*, the pit bull on the story, dropped it after three days. Unless, of course, there was more on the next microfilm reel, which Cody would have scrolled through if Ross hadn't interrupted him to check out books for the very first time. He'd never even *seen* Ross in DuPont Library before.

"Are you boys in college?" an older man standing next to Cody in the bathroom at intermission asked.

"Yes, sir," Cody replied.

"Which school?" the older man asked, and Cody said, "We're visiting from—"

"*Vanderbilt*," Banjo interrupted. "We go to Vanderbilt. Hurry up, Cody."

"Dude, are you fucking nuts?" Banjo scolded on the way back to their seats. "A skeevy old man hitting you up at the urinal of a faggy *musical*? How clueless *are* you?"

Maybe there was nothing else to the story, no more news to break, which was why both the *Purple* and the *Banner* and every other newspaper dropped it so soon and suddenly. Maybe the kids just OD'd on drugs, which happens all the time at college and probably happened even more in the seventies. Maybe there was no "overzealous" student who poisoned them, no "crime" for that amateur-student-journalist Crownover to uncover, no villain at all.

"Don't forget to give 'er back, Tiger," Ross said, tapping the ceiling with the others as they drove back through the Domain gates. He hadn't, Cody felt, taken his eyes off him the entire trip. Come to think of it, Ross, the psychology major, hadn't really taken his eyes off him since he picked him up at the airport on that very first day.

Cody was the last to tap the ceiling.

• • •

Can't wait to see you, kiddo! Marcie texted with a Santa smiley-wink. *Got an Xmas surprise for you!*

The final two days of the semester were packed with tests, parties, and see-you-next-year goodbyes.

"Move along, please. You should know these parts cold by now," their biology professor said, as the class filed past the cut-open baby pig full of ID pins for their last weekly quiz. "So sick of this smelly pig," Banjo grumbled from the back, as they inched past the table where Vail and Bishop had once been lab partners. "I want a cat next time."

Through the window into the lobby, Cody saw a rolling rack of glass panes with brain tissue that Ross and a research assistant were picking through. Squinting, he saw Ross sort through one labeled in large block print that read "HROTHGAR," another, "FUZZ." Ross carefully put down "TRIXIE" and picked up "NESTA."

"Move along, please," the professor beckoned. "We have more to get through."

"Elliott, you sick of my cooking too?" Pearl called up the stairs that night before muttering, "Good Lord, these boys need to eat."

"Cody, I've been troubled." Dean Apperson pulled him aside after the school's Caroling-on-the-Quad. "I've been troubled by your weekly test scores since midterms. I do hope, Cody, you will hunker down for finals. Use the break to focus your mind, and…eliminate the distractions that are impeding your progress." Under his smile was a pointed concern, bordering on disappointment. "Do it for yourself, Cody. But do it."

"Merry Christmas," Beth mouthed from across the Quad, in her furry earmuffs and tiny ornament earrings. She winked and air-kissed and disappeared with her friends.

"Guys, leave your iPads here. You can access your syllabus online with your laptops," Ross told them. "Too many students lost their iPads on break last year."

"Dude, come *on!*" Banjo yelled upstairs through Elliott's open door. "It's our last night, and you're already packed! Come out with us! What's your fucking problem?"

Elliott had withdrawn further over the past week, mostly shut in his room when not in class, skipping meals, skipping the caroling, skipping parties. He'd always been a bit uptight and on edge, but this was different. He hadn't showered for days. Even his nervous tick-yawn was gone. More often than not, he was silent and still, almost zombielike.

"Come on, bud," Cody encouraged him gently. "Come to the Lodge with us. Just one drink."

The Kilts were rowdy, and most were chugging eggnog or throwing it back up, and it seemed the whole campus had descended to celebrate the end of classes. "Merry Fucking Christmas!" from the front, and "Happy Fucking Holidays!" from the back.

"Are you okay, man?" Cody asked when he found Elliott sitting alone on the back porch, in the cold, without his jacket. His eyes were red.

"It's so fucked up here," Elliott said. "I've got to get out of here."

"What's wrong, bud? Is it class, or a chick, or…someone else?"

"It's everything," Elliott said, looking ahead, not at Cody.

"They didn't tell us everything," Elliott said. "They weren't honest with us."

"*Who* wasn't honest with you?" Cody asked, but Elliot just said, "It's so wrong." And then he repeated it. "I would never have agreed to this."

"It'll be better after the break," Cody said, and Elliott said, "No, it'll be worse." He seemed increasingly deranged.

"They can't make us do this," Elliott said, shaking his head. *"Ist da bern floomel reklagracken."* Cody stared at him, and then Ross bounded out the back door. "What are you guys doing out here in the cold?"

"He'll be okay," Ross assured Cody as Elliott wandered off to finish packing for his flight out the next day. "Between you and me, his grades have gone south. Like call-the-parents south. I'm gonna tutor him over the phone and when he gets back. We'll save his scholarship. I've been there."

"When you two Nancys are done makin' love"—Banjo stuck his head out the back door—"we got Christmas shots lined up…"

• • •

"Merry Christmas!" Pearl repeated as the Hazers took off after breakfast. "Have a safe, wonderful break!"

"Elliott, the van's waiting downstairs," Cody said, bursting into his room. The bed was made, his luggage packed and ready. The room smelled freshly cleaned and mopped.

"Banjo, where's Elliott?" Cody asked in the hallway.

"He's around," Banjo, groggy and scratching, replied.

"The van's leaving for the airport."

"Well, the maggot better get on it." Banjo yawned. "He sure as hell ain't coming home with me."

"There's another van in fifteen," the driver said, engine idling. "He can catch that one."

"Elliott! Hurry up!" Cody yelled back up at Rebel's Rest, to no avail. "I can't miss my flight," a girl in the back said impatiently, and a boy said, "Me neither."

As they passed the tall stone gate, the students tapped the ceiling of the black van, and Cody did the same, to summon his S'wanee Angel to keep him safe until he returned to the Domain, where no one needed protection.

Chapter Fourteen

"Over here, kiddo!"

If it hadn't been for her red Santa hat, Cody might not have spotted his mother in the Newark Airport curbside clusterfuck. Because she was yelling out of a shiny silver BMW.

"Oh my boy!" she squealed, reaching up to throw her arms around his neck. "You've grown taller! But so skinny! Are they not feeding you down there?"

"What? *What*?" Marcie challenged the parking monitor with her threatening ticket book. "We're *loading*, missy! Bah-humbug!"

"That old car was costing too much for repairs," she explained when Cody asked about the BMW, although he remembered the Camry being pretty dependable. "It's a late-model. They all have deals this time of year, you know." She cranked up the Sirius Christmas channel, weaving through afternoon turnpike traffic.

"Where are you going?" Cody asked as she turned off a different exit, and Marcie giggled. "I told you I had a surprise," she said.

The house was two stories with yellow shingles and red shutters. The small front lawn was already hibernating in the frost and trimmed with low shrubs. There was a white picket fence.

"Your father," Marcie said, pulling into the driveway, "was really not good for much, but he did, apparently, create a college account for you. I guess he considered it his buyout." After Cody's scholarship, she had parked the funds in the house, helped by low mortgage rates. "It's safer than stocks," she insisted and then laughed. "And someday it will all be yours!"

"My Cody!" His grandmother Svetla threw her arms around him at the front door. "My grown grandson!" She took his face in her hands and inspected him carefully and said simply, "He's a man."

"Surprise number two," Marcie said, pouring a pinot grigio in the sparkling, marble-topped, professional cook's kitchen as Maisy and Max pinged about Cody's legs. "I brought her over for Christmas." Then she emphasized, "*Just* Christmas." She cuckoo-twirled her finger and rolled her eyes. "I saw that!" his grandmother barked.

Over vegan meals—a Bulgarian pre-Christmas tradition his grandmother insisted on—and tree-trimming, the henpeck questions came fast and full bore.

"Are American universities as wild as I've heard?" his grandmother asked, looking more hip and sophisticated than Cody remembered. Her black cashmere sweater had a Macy's tag hanging from the bottom, and Cody realized Marcie had supplied her with a new, chicer wardrobe. *Just add it to the bill.*

"Do you have a girlfriend yet?" his grandmother pried later over a baked apple, and Cody said, "Kinda."

"Oh Cody, don't get attached yet," Marcie insisted, and then added quickly, "You're too young. Don't make the same mistakes I did."

Cody told them about the campus and the Signing Ceremony and his library job and the bonfire and the charms of Rebel's Rest, and then mentioned the seven from his section who were already gone.

Marcie put down her fork. "What did you say?"

"Why didn't you tell me that before?" she asked, pacing with her cigarette. "Outside!" his grandmother ordered, and Marcie growled, "It's my house, old woman," cracking the back door to stream her smoke into the cold.

"I'm calling the dean tomorrow," Marcie said after Cody explained the details. "Why didn't they tell us? Why do they keep this from the *parents*?"

"Don't call the dean," Cody said, wishing he'd kept it to himself, and Marcie said, "No, Cody, I will do what I want. This is wrong."

"It was a car accident," Cody insisted. "And a suicide. That stuff happens everywhere."

And it *did* happen everywhere, Cody had Google-learned. Since September, there had been suicides at the University of Colorado, the University of Kansas, Millsaps, Wheaton, Drake, DePaul, Butler, Trinity Lutheran, and two at Bennington. A Rutgers freshman who'd jumped from the George Washington Bridge had made national news.

Since September, there had been fatal car accidents at the University of Florida, Ithaca College, Notre Dame, Duke—at practically every big school near a road, even the Citadel. There had been alcohol-related deaths at NYU and Princeton and a suspected hazing fatality at Dartmouth. Cody's professor was right: Mother Nature could be an aggressively Darwinian bitch.

"I'm still calling the dean," Marcie said. "He told me to call with any questions or concerns, and I have *both*."

Cody defended S'wanee often over the next two weeks, and there was plenty of time for shopping and dinners out and a day trip to the city to see the big tree—much bigger than the Quad tree it reminded Cody of—since Marcie had taken a leave from Macy's during the busiest shopping season. "I'll go back after Christmas," she'd said. "I guess." Cody got a Facebook alert that his high school class was meeting at the local Bowlmor Lanes, but he stayed home and couldn't get comfortable in his new bedroom, and after enough time back in New Jersey, Cody started to get homesick for Rebel's Rest.

He felt clearheaded from so much sleep and had started dreaming again at night, mostly of Beth, no doubt neck-deep in snow from the Minnesota blizzard on the news.

"Eat up!" his grandmother insisted. She'd inspected him often at first and said he looked "haunted" and made platter after platter and seemed relieved when his appetite returned, as had, apparently, Marcie's, who had filled out ever so slightly.

"Lucky me!" Marcie cheered on Christmas Eve, finding the coin in the round loaf that would bring her good fortune. "You always find the coin," said his grandmother, who had baked the bread. "Lucky me," Marcie repeated.

"Leave it till the morning!" his grandmother ordered as Cody started to clear the table. "Bad luck on Christmas Eve."

His mother gave him two cashmere sweaters and three pairs of khakis to replace the ones he'd lost at school, a tweed herringbone sport coat ("Nicer than the one they loaned you," she insisted), and a thirty-six-inch LCD, which she'd have wall-mounted in his bedroom "before your next trip back." "The PS3 was backordered," she added. "It's on the way." If there was a new man in her life bankrolling all this, she was still keeping him under wraps.

His grandmother gave him a handmade leather wallet she had brought from Sofia, with a twenty-dollar bill inside, and a gold Seiko Automatic watch for his upcoming eighteenth birthday. "Every man needs a real wristwatch," she claimed.

"So I spoke to your dean," Marcie said. "He says your concerns are 'unfounded,'" although Cody hadn't expressed any. "He talks so funny; he uses funny words."

"He said one student transferred to a different college," Marcie said, "and another girl left to deal with a 'personal situation.' I can read between the lines there."

"He said one very troubled girl did kill herself," and Cody said, "That's what I told you," and thought, "*She wasn't that troubled.*" "And that other car crashed in what he called…what words did he use? 'Inclement and treacherous driving conditions.'" Cody said, "Yep," and thought, "*The fog was lifting, the road was straight, there was no tree, and nobody knows what car they were driving.*"

"And he promises to keep the parents better informed of… oh, what did he say?… 'Campus issues.'" *Typical dean.*

"He says your grades aren't very good," Marcie added carefully. "He says you seem distracted or maybe have just been partying too much. He says your scholarship is 'in jeopardy.' Is that true?"

"Cody, do you feel in danger there?" she probed, atypically maternal. "Is anyone trying to hurt you?"

"No, Mom." He shook his head at the question. "No one's trying to hurt me."

"You know, Cody," his mother said, inspecting him, "you don't have to go back if you don't want to." And Cody said, "Why wouldn't I go back, Mom?"

Of course he was going back. S'wanee was his *home*, at least for the next three and a half magical years. He wasn't a recruit or outsider anymore. He had signed the book and was a permanent member of the S'wanee family, *his* family. And hopefully Elliott had used the break to relax and regroup and would spring back after what was, in hindsight, a rather stressful first semester. College was a transition, for everyone, and it required an adjustment before it would sail along smoothly, as Cody knew it would from now on. Cody hadn't realized how exhausted his first semester had left him—and probably all the rest of them, too, what with the drinking and hangovers and studying and late nights and constant go-go-go and sensory-overload-excitement—until he came home and got plenty of sleep and was now increasingly restless and bored and itching to get back to the Domain. *His* Domain. After all, he was president of his section.

He was ready to hunker down during the two-week Reading Period before final exams, and he would up his grades and keep his scholarship, and maybe Elliott had just been talking slurry that night on the back deck, and not gibberish, like the poisoned students way back when, right before they went crazy and killed themselves. Hadn't Cody talked slurry a few times before, according to Banjo, and he hadn't gone crazy, had he? Weren't they all sorta drunk on the last night of the semester before Christmas break, and wasn't the music loud at the Lodge, which made Cody mishear whatever Elliott had mumbled out on the back deck before he wandered into the S'wanee darkness and then missed the van the next morning?

It was stupid ("Unwise," Dean Apperson might say) to get distracted by all this other stuff—ancient-history newspaper articles, mushrooms, Ross—when he should focus on his studies. It was stupid, unwise, unproductive, he realized now, after the clarity of two weeks away, to think—*imagine*, really—that something evil and deadly was going down at S'wanee, or that Ross, his mentor, big brother, and first friend there, was somehow involved, as if following in the footsteps of whatever phantom student way back when, the one rumored to have poisoned the students with go-crazy-and-kill-yourself mushrooms as part of a research project to win his coveted gown, at least according to that journalist-wannabe editor who Cody hoped had picked a different career after graduation, he thought, as he got out curbside at Newark Airport. ("I'm so proud of you, kiddo!" Marcie said. "*Dovijdane*, Cody," his grandmother wished, hugging him tight and close.)

And it was foolish, he knew, as he sandwiched into his coach middle seat, that his brain seemed like a kaleidoscope that someone else was turning.

Winter

Chapter One

Elliott didn't return after Christmas break.

"He'll be back in the fall," Pearl said. "Or so I'm told."

Cody nodded and said, "Okay."

Reading Period was an amorphous part of the academic calendar, with students trickling back at will, and Rebel's Rest was quiet and empty when Cody arrived.

Elliott's luggage was gone from his unlocked, empty room, but in his rush to catch the next van, he had left behind his clear plastic Dopp kit in the bathroom mirror cabinet. Cody took out the toothpaste and then took out the dental floss and shaving cream and razor and nail clippers and turned the kit upside down. Out fell a tiny metal key that Cody grabbed before it fell down the drain.

It was a key for a tiny lock on an unlocked campus. It could have fit a luggage lock, but Elliott's luggage was gone. It could have fit a bike lock, but Elliott didn't have a bike, and no one locked bikes at S'wanee. It could have been for a file cabinet or small safety deposit box, like his mother kept her jewelry in, but Cody didn't find either as he searched Elliott's room, his closet, under his bed.

"Welcome back, Cody." Ross was at Elliott's bedroom door, and Cody was patting inside the closet walls for hidden panels. Ross closed the bedroom door. "We need to talk."

"Elliott's gone," Cody said, standing up straight, and Ross said, "He lost his scholarship. We're trying to reinstate it."

"That's too bad," Cody said.

"I don't want you to lose yours, too."

"Me neither, Ross."

Ross had found, while cleaning out his mail program over the break, the e-mail Cody sent to himself with the thesis proposal attached, when they accidentally swapped iPads during the Army-Navy football game. Cody had forgotten all about it. Until now.

"That's theft, Cody. That's stealing."

"I'm sorry, Ross," Cody said, not meaning it.

"It's grounds for expulsion, if I turned you in."

"I'm sorry, Ross," Cody repeated.

"I found my document on your iPad. I deleted it. From your inbox, too."

"Okay," Cody said.

"Seriously, dude, you're sorta on thin ice here anyway, you know? This would be the final nail, you know?"

"Won't happen again."

"We don't want to lose you, Cody."

"Hey Ross, do you have Elliott's cell number?" Cody asked. "Or his e-mail?"

"Because we're friends," Cody said, when Ross asked why he needed it. "I want to call and see how he's doing."

"Okay. Would you ask him for me? Or should I ask him myself?" Cody said when a hesitant Ross told him he'd need the dean's permission to release private student information.

"Because he left stuff in the bathroom," Cody said, when Ross asked what he was doing in Elliott's room in the first place. "I was checking if he left behind anything else, you know, because he left so suddenly. I was gonna send it to him. Because we're friends, Ross."

"Sure. I'm okay," Cody said as Ross descended the stairs, eyeing him carefully. "Don't worry about me, bud."

Cody went to his bedroom and popped open his laptop, where he'd stored an extra copy of Ross's forbidden thesis.

• • •

The S'wanee Call Project was a work in progress when Cody had freeze-frame/stolen it, and Ross had most certainly finished it by now. He'd divided the dense, single-spaced early draft into three sections ("Past," "Present," and "Future"—*not very original, Ross*), and the "Past" section was a brief history of university science experiments that had led to important breakthroughs.

Penicillin (University of Oxford), beta-blockers (University of Glasgow), synthetic insulin (University of Toronto, University of Pittsburgh), antiretrovirals (Harvard, MIT, UCLA). As Ross had already told him, S'wanee had a long history of successful experimentation and was instrumental in developing key ingredients in common sleeping, addiction, and antipsychotic meds. Schools worldwide raced against one another for the next breakthrough, and patent competition was fierce.

The thesis traced the history of a "highly classified" Cold War program called MKULTRA, which included university partnerships with the CIA to discover and test chemical compounds to sabotage any hypothetical enemy. These "quiet" partnerships tested LSD and a variety of "hallucinogenic botanicals" on thousands of "unwitting" subjects with "unpredictable" and "nonreplicable" results, which ultimately doomed the whole program. One particularly disastrous experiment occurred in 1951 in some French town called Pont-Saint-Esprit, in which 250 unsuspecting villagers went violently insane. These secret

CIA programs were finally exposed and shut down in the mid-1970s by something called the Kennedy Hearings, which forced new laws forbidding future experiments without test subjects' "expressed, written" consent.

Over thirty US universities had partnered with the CIA in these secret experiments. S'wanee made over seventy-five million dollars through these *down-low* government contracts in the 1960s alone, through experiments spearheaded and run by undergraduates. *Gowns all around!*

In the last paragraph of the section, Ross lauded S'wanee's "illustrious" history as a "new technology incubator." *Suck-up.*

"Soup's on, Cody!" Pearl called from downstairs. "Just a handful of us tonight!"

The "Present" included an illustrated report on a current program called HAARP (High Frequency Active Auroral Research Program), developed for the US military by several universities (Stanford, MIT, Clemson, Cornell), with the prototype built in Alaska. The pictures looked like a football-field-sized sea of antennae.

Ross's report was dense and jargony—ELF waves, GWEN networks, a magnetically sensitive material called magnetite found in mammalian brains—but the gist of the program, as far as Cody could tell, was high-powered radio transmissions that could "insert almost anything into the target brain mind systems, with such insertions processed by the biosystems as internally generated data/effects."

According to Ross, "Words, phrases, images, sensations, and emotions could be directly input and experienced in the biological targets as internal states, codes, emotions, thoughts, and ideas."

Ross used phrases like "prerecorded drugs" and "brain bombs."

Ross claimed the technology could easily transmit through any existing antenna or "digital broadcasting spectrum," including "cell towers." Ross claimed such "devices" could be tapped into and "piggybacked" on without the "owner's knowledge."

"Cody, I've saved dessert for you!" Pearl called up. "I made chocolate molten cake!"

The "Future"—Ross had just started this section, which consisted mostly of unorganized thoughts and notes. He used the phrases "double-blind study" and "terminal experiment," which Cody had heard before. He'd written "Project terminus: January 15," which was ten days away.

At the bottom of the document was a link that opened Cody's browser. The page required a password, which his software hacked easily. It was a grid of QuickTime video screens, all black, numbered one though twelve. He clicked a play button, and the screen said "Under Construction." He clicked the others; same thing.

"If you get hungry, I've left dinner in the oven." Pearl gave up. "Don't study too hard!"

The Troller, Cody had just noticed, was waving yellow from a strong wireless signal. He moved his laptop around the room, and the wave adjusted stronger and weaker. The wave was strongest at the window overlooking the Quad.

Towering above the Quad, Shapard Tower shone its nightly beacon.

Shapard Tower, which Ross had warned everyone to keep away from. "Save the Tower," he had said, and the Wellington Kilts had joined in the chant that very first week. The tallest spot on campus, aiming its spotlight squarely on Rebel's Rest every night.

Shapard Tower, which turned the yellow wave red and frantic as Cody walked across the Quad with his laptop.

All Saints was unlocked but dimly lit, and Cody moved down the aisle through the empty silence, past the pews and arches and the "S'wanee Massacre" stained-glass window that had caught his attention that first week, which had caught Ross's attention, as Cody recalled.

At the front of the chapel, to the right of the altar, was a door marked "Tower." It was unlocked, and Cody climbed the spiral staircase. At the top was another door marked "Carillon," behind which, Cody knew, sat some contraption, some transmitting device, a mini-version of the massive antennae in Ross's document.

It was a small room, almost like an office, the only light trickling from a hole in the ceiling. There was a clock on the wall and framed diploma-looking certificates. There was a sign that said "Earphones Required." Along the wall, taking up most of the room, was a monster piano thing with big wooden levers instead of keys and stacks of sheet music on the side with several pages spread out across the front. Dozens of wires strung upward from the machine through the ceiling. There was a clump of professional-looking earphones on the bench. On a desk next to the machine sat a telephone and a small laptop computer.

A sturdy, fixed ladder led up through the hole in the ceiling where the light shone down. Cody climbed into the room with its giant wheels coiling thick wires attached to dozens of bells of various sizes dangling from thick steel beams. A massive bell hung directly in the center. The spotlight, huge and blinding, aimed through the arched tower window, connected to a closed circuit box labeled "Quad Light."

Cody looked around. There was no antenna, no transmitting device, just bells and coils and wheels and a light. The Troller had dropped back to a yellow wave. Peering through the tower window, Cody saw the spotlight focused, not on Rebel's Rest, but over the whole Quad, just like it said.

There was nothing here. Just the Phantom's office, where he played his Top 40 on the mutant piano machine. Where he did his job.

The largest wheel in the tower started to turn, pulling its wire, and a cluster of bells tipped a deafening, earsplitting toll. Cody's eyes shook and his eardrums maxed out as he scurried down the ladder to flee the torturous, brain-smashing noise. He stumbled on the last rung, dropping his laptop, and fell and scrambled to his feet by the protective earphones and, clutching his laptop, fled down the spiral staircase before the chimes could lead to the massive hourly toll that would blow his head apart.

Cody burst onto the Quad just as the bell struck ten and then went silent. The Quad was well lit and empty in the cold. Cody stood shivering and ringing. *Way to go, Tiger*.

He opened his laptop, which, *Thank God*, still worked. The browser responded, a document opened, the network still connected. *Good ol' Apple*.

The Troller was red. The wave was so violent and tightly packed, it was practically a solid block.

Cody took a few steps, and the wave, still red, loosened up a bit. He reversed his steps, and the wave tightened again. He took a few more steps, and the Troller went haywire and sounded a beeping alarm. Cody looked up.

He was standing under the towering evergreen, still roped off. He backed away, and the red wave eased. He held the laptop close to a branch, and the wave alarmed and flashed. Cody got nearer to the branch, and even with the ringing in his head, he could feel a pulsing vibration in his eardrum. He stood still.

The tree made a quiet hum. From its hundreds of branches came a slight, steady buzz.

The tree wasn't a tree at all.

• • •

"Human trials," Ross had said to the white coats. "The same technology as any mobile device," he'd told the eager crowd.

Cody was running in the cold night, to clear his head. Down Tennessee Avenue, where wildlife used to roam and roamed no more.

"We can override fundamental instincts, including self-preservation and survival," Mad Scientist Ross had declared over his clip mike, demonstrating "the degree of control this new technology can achieve."

"Puck is the culmination of lots of trial and error," Ross had said. "It hasn't been easy."

Fletcher would certainly attest to that, if his throat hadn't been torn out through his neck. Didn't he get Nesta from the school? One of the many strays the school took in and "rehabilitated"? Didn't Ross experiment on Nesta as part of his "trial and error" before the poor dog went violently insane? Now Nesta's sick, hijacked brain was pressed between glass in Spencer Hall, after Ross sliced and picked it apart. *Trial and error*.

Ross had controlled Puck through an antenna that looked like a tree. Cody's Troller had zigged wild near the tree that wasn't just a tree. Hadn't Cody dreamed, or had he actually seen, Ross replacing branches on the same tree? Digging, burying electrical cables? Weren't Ross's fingers dirty that first week?

Cody caught his breath at Morgan's Steep, the treacherous dead-drop cliff, now bright in the moon. Caleb had done this run at night, too, before he disappeared. He'd even invited Cody to join. Weren't workers cleaning up below around the same time Caleb vanished? Wasn't the same white delivery van that took Nesta away speeding from Morgan's Steep on the morning that Ross claimed Caleb had "transferred"? Why were the men in blue scrubs at Morgan's Steep so early in the morning? What were they "delivering"—or "picking up"—in their van?

"'The S'wanee Call,'" Ross the Rogue had written in his thesis, "can insert almost anything into the target brain." Ross the Suck-Up had praised S'wanee as a "new technology incubator."

Ross had tracked Cody down just as he was researching the "S'wanee Massacre," right when he was finding the truth. Ross had spy cameras on his iPad and could track anybody anywhere. Ross had seen to it that the door to the archives was now locked. Ross had called the Order of the Gownsmen “a very big deal.” “Every junior is obsessed with it,” he had said. “You’re my project,” he confessed to Cody on the ride that first day. They were all his project.

Eight of Cody’s friends had mysteriously, almost magically, disappeared.

Ross called his wireless, mind-controlling science project “a bit of magic.”

At full sprint heading back down Tennessee Avenue, Cody thought, “Ross is hijacking people’s brains.” He thought, “Ross is killing off Rebel’s Rest to get his gown.”

And then he thought: “Cody, you’ve lost it.”

Chapter Two

"Dude, that's heavy stuff," Banjo said. "That's real heavy stuff."

Blowing off a study cram session, Cody had told him about Ross's 3D-Brain Atlas-Puck presentation to the white coats, his thesis proposal, the history of the "S'wanee Massacre," the non-tree tree. Cody linked them up and laid it all out.

"You sound crazy; you know that?" Banjo said, and Cody said, "Yeah, I know."

Banjo thought and said, "I never really liked Ross. I think he's creepy."

"He's watching us all the time," Cody said. "On his iPad."

"He's a creepy motherflyer. But experimenting on us? Like microwave mind control shit? Dude, you really think that?"

"Dude, it's not science fiction," Cody insisted. "It's real. I saw it myself."

"The technology's *there*, man. I've read up on it," Cody continued. "I mean, military dudes at a desk in Florida can make drones drop bombs all over the world. You can scan somebody's credit card through their pocket. You can send signals to robots and make them do anything. It's just magnetic stuff; it's in the brain, *our* brain. You can hijack it and control it. It's all in Ross's paper. I can show you."

"I don't need to see it," Banjo said. "But, dude, the fact he wrote a paper doesn't mean he's doing it. I mean, we got econ problem sets where we're selling magic rings in Middle Earth and shit like that, but it's not real. It's just homework."

"Eight of us are gone, Banjo," Cody said. "*Eight*."

"But why would he want to make people kill themselves?" Banjo asked.

"To prove he can," Cody said. "If you can make people kill themselves, you can make them do anything. *That's* his experiment. That's the selling point."

"Fuck. Me," Banjo said, shaking his head. "You know, the government experimented on my people before. With Tuscaneegee syphilis shit; you know that?"

"Dude, they did it all the time," Cody said. "LSD, mushrooms, all kinds of shit that drove people crazy. They got caught, and that's why they made it illegal."

"You think the school's in on it?" Banjo asked.

Cody shook his head. "Just Ross. He's fucking sick. Brilliant maybe, but sick."

"Yeah, you sound crazy," Banjo repeated. "You sound Cocoa Puffs, but I'm not saying you're not onto something. It's just a *crazy* something, like *Twilight Zone* shit."

"Did you see Elliott before Christmas? Did you see him leave?"

"Nope."

"Have you talked to him since? Do you even have his number?"

"Nope."

"You think Skit really quit school because of an abortion? *Skit*?"

Banjo inhaled and rocked back and forth.

"You think Vail, happy-go-lucky Vail just up and jumped to her death? Or Caleb—*Legacy* Caleb—left school in the second week?

"The school knows something's fucked up," Cody went on. "But mass suicides aren't the best recruitment tool, you know? They're covering it up, like they did last time."

"I don't know, man," Banjo resisted. "I don't know."

"Do you really think Sin drove everybody into a tree? On that road? In a car nobody can track down?"

Banjo exhaled. "Fuck. Me."

• • •

Dean Apperson looked like he needed a cigarette. He was dapper/dandy as always, but he didn't offer Cody a drink, and he spoke directly in plain words.

"Cody, do you think Ross is killing your classmates?"

"I…I don't know," Cody said, and thought, *Fuck you, Banjo*.

"Do you think he's experimenting on you? Like a science project?" Dean Apperson wasn't angry, just curious, and behind him the fire crackled and popped, like on the DVD.

"*Yes*," Cody said, the cat out of the bag. "Yes," and told him why and told him everything. The taps were open, and it felt good.

"I see," Dean Apperson said pleasantly, inspecting him. "And you think he tampered with the tree on the Quad? To make it a radar sort of thing? Is that what you think, Cody?"

"Yes, sir," Cody said. "He changed some of the branches. He ran wires, too. I saw him."

"Actually, you saw both of us." Dean Apperson nodded. "I think I understand now. Cody, that's not a tree at all. It's a cell tower.

"I picked it out myself," Apperson continued. "I didn't want an ugly eyesore marring the Domain. Would you? Cell towers that look like trees, especially evergreens, are quite common these days. Did you know that, Cody?"

Cody thought, *I did know that.* He'd just forgotten.

"And it's brand-new to us." Apperson went on slowly. "With the inevitable kinks and whatnot, but I think we've mostly sorted it out. Now we have a strong, up-to-date, cutting-edge network. It's very much an improvement."

"Did you tell your mother this?" Apperson asked. "Because she called me, you know. Over the break."

"This is my fault," Apperson said. "I should have alerted the parents immediately. Just as I ask you to be up-front with me, I owe the same courtesy and honesty. We've been shell-shocked a bit, as devastated as you've been, but that's no excuse, and I will do better in the future."

"It's happened here before," Cody said, and Dean Apperson nodded. "I remember, Cody. I was here.

"The so-called S'wanee Massacre is the darkest chapter in our history, but we don't shy away from it," he continued. "We keep records in our archives. Anyone can go read them. We created a memorial window for our chapel. We eventually commemorated the tragedy and learned from it."

"And you think what happened way back then is happening again? Now?" Dean Apperson asked. "And Ross, your mentor, is secretly behind it? Pulling the strings, if you will?

"Not merely *hypothesizing* in a paper, not simply ruminating on the *possibilities* for discussion's sake," he added, "But actually causing the deaths of his fellow students in exchange for a gown to wear around the campus?"

Cody needed a drink.

"Do you like it here, Cody?" Dean Apperson asked.

"More than anything," Cody answered, meaning it. "It's my home."

"You know, Cody," Apperson continued. "I've lived here, at this God-favored spot, most of my adult life. I grew up here and am growing old here. I've seen thousands pass through. And

I've learned that perhaps because of our isolation, or maybe even a certain loneliness, the Domain can be more prone to hysteria than one would expect."

"Do you feel in danger, Cody?" Dean Apperson asked. "Do you think someone means you harm?"

Here we go.

"Is something in your mind suggesting, or even telling you, that you're in jeopardy?"

"Do you hear voices, Cody?"

Code word for "crazy." "Going Columbine." Code word for *dangerous*.

"Do you have strange dreams, Cody?"

Cody's only dreams lately had starred Beth, but they weren't strange, and he wasn't about to share them with Dean Apperson.

"There's no shame in these symptoms," the dean soothed. "It's quite treatable, you know. It's a condition that can occur in young men your age.

"It's only when left untreated," he went on, "that problems can arise."

"Let's keep an eye on this, shall we?" He smiled as Cody left the Cravens Hall living room/examining room. Cody, the once Freshman-Who-Stepped-on-the-Seal turned Freshman-Who-Might-Be-a-Paranoid-Schizophrenic.

• • •

"I'm not afraid of you," Beth told him. "I don't care what everybody says."

"What does everybody say?" Cody asked.

"It doesn't matter."

At first Cody thought it was the stress of imminent finals that made everyone seem reserved and detached and on edge. But Rebel's Rest still held cram sessions, and everyone gathered for meals and occasional study breaks with popcorn and Pearl's pizza around the living room TV. They didn't blatantly ostracize Cody, but there was a strange hush when he was around, and he didn't feel welcome.

"I'm not apologizing, dude," tattletale-Banjo finally said in the upstairs bathroom after a few days of avoiding each other. "I did it for your own good." He and Huger now went to the Lodge together, and Cody stopped going entirely.

Ross would flash his movie star smile and say, "Waddup, Tiger?" when they'd pass in the log cabin, but it was stilted and leery.

Even Mother Hen Pearl forced an awkward, eggshell smile each time she asked, "How *are* you, Cody?"

"People think you're a loose cannon," Beth told him outside DuPont Library, where she waited for him every night after work. "Maybe that's why we get along so well."

"Come back with me," he urged her the night of the first snowfall. "Come back to my room. Please."

"I can't, Cody." She resisted for the millionth time.

"Spend the night with me," he pleaded.

"I want to, Cody," she said, "But…"

"It's my birthday."

"Oh," she gasped. "Your birthday. Happy birthday, Cody," she said, holding his face with both hands. "Happy, happy birthday." She smiled at him sadly. "But…"

"Why not? Why?" he pressed.

"It's against the…I just can't," she said, her eyes glassing.

"I'll sneak you in. Nobody's gonna think you're a slut."

"It's not that, Cody." She bit her lip, looking around. "Hell, I don't care what anybody here thinks anymore."

"You *are* afraid of me," he said. "Aren't you?"

"No, Cody," she said, eyeing him directly. "I'm not afraid of *you* at all."

"Fuck it," she said, now angry. "This is stupid. It's just so stupid."

She grabbed his hand. "Take me there, Cody."

• • •

Cody did everything he could to make Beth happy, but she wouldn't stop crying.

He even moved the yellow house with red shutters from New Jersey down to the Domain, because his mother bought it with his college fund and now he was eighteen and it was *his*. He put up the white picket fence and kept the deer family and Canada geese and squirrels in the yard, and Nesta stayed on the front porch and got along with everybody. But Beth hated the Domain and had nightmares in the house—thrashing nightmares—and eventually she talked gibberish and started to get up, and Cody feared she was going mad and would wander into personal danger. He held her tight when she gasped in her sleep and finally called for Dean Apperson, who brought the Blue Scrubs and said not to worry; they would make her better, and he'd miss her, but he knew they'd bring her back happy.

• • •

Beth slipped out before Cody woke up. She left her rhinestone earrings next to the bed, and the sheets were still rumpled where she'd lain against him all night. His room was bright from the snow that covered the campus overnight and still fell thick and silent out his window.

Cody breathed in the pillow that smelled like her hair. He'd never spent a whole night with a girl before. Eventually, soon, when she was ready and comfortable, they'd wake up together, and he'd bring her down for breakfast, and everyone would know he was normal.

Beth didn't meet him after work the next night, or the next.

"I'm not sure who that is, sugar," Pearl puzzled when Cody described her. "Do you have a picture?"

"*Who*?" the Widow asked.

"If she never even told you her last name, son," Proctor Bob said, unsmiling, "I reckon she doesn't want to be found by you. I reckon you should respect that."

"Um, she's around, I think," said a dude with a snowball in front of Tuckaway Hall. Cody had tracked it down through his own trial and error, since it wasn't on his map.

"Has anybody seen Beth?" snowball dude asked the others who had stopped their impromptu battle when Cody approached.

"Um, is she expecting you?" a girl with a purple snow hat said. "Is she even back?" another girl said.

"Is this Tuckaway Hall?" Cody asked. It was big and lifeless, with only a skeleton crew of students meandering about.

"Beth is a friend of mine," he continued, when no one answered. "Has anybody seen her?" He rubbed his hand nonsensically, massaging its kinks.

"I can give her a message," purple hat girl said. Cody felt he'd wandered onto a foreign campus.

"Where's her room?" he asked.

The skeleton crew looked at him. At the Warning-Sign-Freshman on a campus where word traveled fast.

"Should we call someone?" he heard a girl ask a boy. Cody walked away.

"Dude, you're kinda spooking people," Ross said later, pulling Cody aside. "Just chill out, dude." Cody nodded and asked everybody he saw, all the usual studiers at DuPont Library, people he'd seen every day, anybody he could find. Nobody helped.

"It's possible," Dean Apperson, who made a rare visit to Rebel's Rest, told him, "this young lady is not interested, or perhaps has lost interest, in your company. Perhaps it's best to leave it at that, Cody."

Cody nodded and went to his desk, where he kept the New Student kit S'wanee had sent him last summer. He flipped through his "S'wanee Places" book to the "Notable Alumni" section.

• • •

"*Newsweek* magazine," the receptionist answered pleasantly.

"Mr. Crownover's office," the assistant said when routed to his desk.

"May I ask who's calling?" she said.

"Cody Marko," Cody said from his bedroom. "I'm a freshman at S'wanee. He went to college here."

"Yes," the assistant said. "May I ask what it's regarding?"

"He was the newspaper editor here. The *S'wanee Purple*."

"Yes, I know," the assistant said.

"It's very important I speak to him. It's an emergency."

"I can't reach Mr. Crownover right now," the assistant said. "He's in the air. But I'm happy to take your number and pass along the message."

• • •

Dean Apperson was in on it.

Dean Apperson was there, on the front row, when Ross made his sales pitch to the white coats. Dressed Gordon Gekko, nodding proudly at his protégé.

Dean Apperson was there when Ross, under his tutelage, explained their science project and human trials that would end on January 15. "Worth every penny…"

A sales pitch that could make S'wanee millions. Millions for a new building or a new stadium. Millions for Dean Apperson.

He was there, calling the shots, when Ross and the workers fine-tuned the "evergreen," the beaming tower that popped loudly and extinguished the fireflies with its explosive, electric signal.

The signal aimed directly at Rebel's Rest that made Cody's ears ring and caused a piercing headache that made him vomit and black out on the Perimeter Trail. Where they tracked him down, unsuccessful in their initial hijacking attempt (*Good Samaritans, my ass*). "We just had to tweak a few things," Dean Apperson had said in the infirmary.

Cody was immune to the hijacking, he realized thankfully, rubbing his shoulder. His friends hadn't been so lucky. The Fallen Flock.

The dryer buzzed, and Cody folded his laundry, alone in the basement catacombs. He hadn't even started his Western Civ term paper. He'd ask Dick and Nancy for an extension.

Dean Apperson was detached and only mildly irritated that morning when Nesta tore through Fletcher's throat. He was *analytical*.

He was a junior when the S'wanee Massacre went down, Cody calculated.

He was *the* junior.

And he still wore his gown.

He'd poisoned the twelve students in 1971 and watched them go mad and kill themselves as part of his own Gownsmen science experiment. He hadn't been caught and somehow became head of the school. Dean Apperson was smooth and crafty and had outfoxed John Crownover, who now ran *Newsweek* and would get Cody's message as soon as he landed.

Apperson installed the window at All Saints, not to commemorate a tragedy, but to celebrate his crowning college achievement.

Dean Apperson was insane.

And he was Ross's mentor and role model.

He'd tried to convince Cody that *he* was crazy. He'd tried to convince the others, too.

Cody carried his laundry past the basement gym lockers and upstairs, where two dudes were taking a study break over *Call of Duty*.

But S'wanee didn't belong to Dean Apperson. Or Ross. It belonged to all the students and teachers and alumni for the past 150 years. Now it belonged to Cody, too.

Save S'wanee.

Crownover would call back soon. If not, Cody would call again. And again.

Cody was not surprised, at all, when his iPhone stopped working that day.

It was January 14.

• • •

"Mrs. Simpson, one of the dogs is loose. I think it ran downstairs."

"*Inside*?" the Widow said. "With wet paws?" She hobbled toward the library stairs, wonk-looking for prints.

As he waited on hold, crouched behind her desk phone, out of camera reach, Cody had second thoughts. His iPhone was over three years old. They broke often; he knew that. He used to check them in for Genius Bar service all the time. Maybe his had just played out. He should have bought a new one before he lost his discount.

But if Apperson and Ross could zap a human brain, then jamming a cell phone would be a cakewalk, wouldn't it?

"This is John Crownover."

The brisk manner snapped Cody to attention.

"…Hello, Mr. Crownover. I'm Cody Marko."

"The S'wanee freshman, right?" Crownover said. "How's life at the Domain?"

"It's fine, thank you," Cody answered automatically.

"It usually is. What can I do for you, Freshman Cody?"

"Actually, it's not fine, sir."

Cody laid it all out, quickly, since the Widow was bound to return soon. There was silence on the other end.

"I know it sounds crazy, sir," Cody said.

"It does sound extreme," Crownover agreed. "But extreme things have happened there before, sadly. People get very carried away."

"Ivan Apperson was the junior, wasn't he, sir? The one you suspected?"

"Appy Apperson. No one called him Ivan." Crownover chuckled. "Although we should have. Ivan the Terrible."

"Ivan the Terrible," Cody agreed, trying to pinpoint the joke. He liked the sound of it anyway.

"I think he was testing compounds, or spores really, in hopes of selling it to the military. As a weapon in Vietnam, or potentially the Soviet Union," Crownover continued. "Driving the enemy insane, making them turn on each other, has been the Holy Grail of our military for decades. But it's never been practical, or even possible. And the testing was inhumane and gruesome."

"There was lots of crazy testing back then," Crownover added. "The military-academic complex, if you will. It was a different era, the Cold War. It was quite paranoid."

"Yes, sir, I know," Cody said. "I've read about it." Cody was relieved. Crownover got it. He understood.

"But we couldn't pin it on him," Crownover went on. "And the trustees shut down the investigation. Shut down the whole paper, actually." He sighed over the phone. "Quite ironic that he runs the place now, isn't it? Oh well. It was so long ago."

"He put a window in All Saints to commemorate it," Cody said, and Crownover said, "Yes, I've seen it. I come back every spring for reunions."

"But it's happening again, sir," Cody said, and Crownover said, "Yes, that's what you said. They seem to be testing a new method. It's alarming, isn't it?"

"The experiment, the human trials end today, sir," Cody stressed. "That's what they said."

Cody exhaled. He'd passed the ball, the torpedo of truth, off to the editor of *Newsweek* magazine, who believed Cody and knew he wasn't crazy because he'd been there. He knew what Ivan the Terrible was capable of. Cody could almost hear the wheels turning over the phone.

"So you're a freshman?" Crownover asked, covering old ground, and Cody repeated, "Yes, sir," wishing they could speed things along since the Widow would return any second, and Cody needed help fast, needed to know what to do.

"You're in Rebel's Rest, you say?" Crownover asked. "I was in that section, too."

"Yes, sir. I read that in the *Purple*."

"How's Pearl doing?" he asked. "She was brand-new then. Just a young girl."

"She's good," Cody said. "She's a little older now."

"Aren't we all?" Crownover laughed.

"Is my section's picture still in the hallway?" Crownover asked. "By the stairs?"

"I…I guess so, sir," Cody answered. "There's lots of pictures in the hallway."

"Now, can I ask you something, Freshman Cody?" Crownover said.

"Yes, sir."

"What kind of stunt is this?"

"Sir?"

"There is no S'wanee."

"Sir?"

"The school closed its doors in 1972. The year after the tragedy. For good."

The Widow was in the lobby, still searching for the phantom dog.

"I was in the last graduating class. The trustees sold the campus. They let the old alums visit once a year." Crownover laughed once. "Very hospitable of them."

The Widow noticed the front desk was empty. She stopped looking for the dog and started looking for Cody.

"So, Cody, if that's your real name, I was intrigued by your call but not quite sure the purpose of it…"

The Widow saw him through the office window and limp/loped toward him.

"…unless it's gallows humor of some sort. Clearly you've done your research, which I must say has been a dark little stroll down memory lane in my busy day…"

Cody hung up.

"Your phone was ringing," he told the Widow. "They hung up."

He wandered into the lobby. He looked out over the Reading Room where sat the same diligent students he'd seen every day since he started.

He wandered outside. He looked out on students and professors crisscrossing the snow-cleared paths, the same paths they'd crisscrossed since he arrived.

He looked out on Spencer Hall, where white coats scurried as they had since the very beginning.

Cody looked out on a world that didn't exist at all.

Chapter Three

Who *were* these people?

"Dude, we're leading a snowball ambush on Gailor after dinner. You in?"

"Are those fuckers still there? Thought they'd cleared out already."

Cody eavesdropped on the Rebel's Rest dinner chatter from the front living room.

"What's up with that chick from Nevada?" Huger asked. "You gonna get on that before it's too late, or what?"

"Mebbe," Banjo said. "I'm sure she'll be skanking around the Lodge tonight."

Clueless, naive, so *distracted* with exams and parties and hookups that they had no idea what was really going on here. Some had been alarmed, briefly, by the deaths all around them, but unlike Cody, they had lapsed back into normalcy and complacency and even calm, as if they'd been drugged into forgetting. "You could, ultimately, tranquilize a mass riot with a dose of digital dopamine," Ross had told the white coats.

Sitting ducks. Forks and plates clinking.

Nobody knew what Cody knew.

"Save room for dessert, folks! I made blackberry cobbler. *Tons* of cobbler."

But Pearl knew, didn't she?

Pearl, the Widow Senex, Fletcher—still on the payroll all these years. Serving their new master, whoever it was, decade after decade. Lying to the students they pretended to care about. Cody didn't feel bad for Fletcher anymore. Nesta was the real victim. She'd been tested on and abused and now her brain sat sliced and pressed between glass for the sick freaks at Spencer Hall to pick at and study.

The same sick freaks who masqueraded as professors. No wonder the classes were so lame.

"You going to watch *Patton* at McClurg?"

"Brah, how many times we gotta sit through that? Can't they give us *Full Metal Jacket* at least?"

He had to tell them, to warn them they all had to run away. But *where*? They were high atop the Mountain, trapped by the snow and the wilderness and the fortified security gate and Proctor Bob's crew.

And even if they stormed the gate and escaped the campus—or whatever it was—they were in the middle of nowhere, in the freezing cold, and freshmen didn't have cars (*of course*). And even if they stole cars from upperclassmen, the town police must be under S'wanee's control because that one cop let Ross off without a ticket, even though he was going sixty in a forty, and he'd clearly hated Ross on sight (*good eye, Smokey*). The town cops would catch them as they fled in their upperclassmen cars.

Upperclassmen.

"How long's your furlough, Buzz?"

"Just a week. Gonna put in for two. Wish we could re-up here, actually."

S'wanee could not have tricked several hundred upperclassmen for two-three-four years.

"I wish we could keep the clothes," one girl said to another, who said, "I'm keeping my Signing dress. They won't miss it."

"*Ladies*," Pearl singsonged from the kitchen. "*Ix-nay*."

Cody had never seen several hundred. He'd seen maybe a hundred, maybe two, tops. The same ones over and over. In the chapel, at the library, on the sidewalks, at the Lodge. All the same faces, all the time.

Cody thought.

Everyone knew what Cody knew. Long before he knew it.

The freshmen, the upperclassmen, his own section, his own friends.

They weren't students at all.

"Banjo, wanna meet at midnight and hit the Lodge together?"

"Good deal, faggola."

Nobody was studying for exams. Because there were none. Today was the last day of the experiment.

Who *were* these people?

A girl came up from the laundry room. Without laundry. Up and down, all the time, but the free, high-tech machines were always empty.

Cody looked ahead.

• • •

Cody had passed the gym lockers in the basement dozens of times with his laundry basket. He had never noticed all the locks on an unlocked campus.

Now he passed with Elliott's tiny key.

Upstairs was talking and laughing and footsteps, and Cody tried lock after lock. He looked around for cameras, but there were none, since this was backstage. They hadn't thought to install them here.

The basement door swung open, and Banjo called back, "Huger, I'll come grab you when I'm done packing." He padded down the stairs. "Don't be jerking off."

Crouched behind a catacomb wall, Cody watched Banjo open his locker. Whistling a tune, he took out files and papers and his cell phone and stuffed them into his knapsack. He took out ripped jeans and a black motorcycle jacket hanging from a hook. He reached in for his wallet and flipped through it and muttered, "Need. More. Gelt." He emptied the locker and gave it one last look and carried his knapsack up the stairs.

Cody tried the key in the locker left of Banjo's. He tried the right. *Click.*

Baggy jeans and a green windbreaker hung from the hooks. Cody had never seen Elliott wear either. On the top shelf was a BlackBerry Bold. Cody powered it on and waited for it to boot.

Metal dog tags clinked against the locker door. Cody took a black nylon wallet from the top shelf and un-Velocroed the flap. Inside were thirty-seven dollars and an ATM card and a Pennsylvania driver's license with Elliott's picture and the name "Robert."

Cody scrolled through the BlackBerry and found photos of Elliott/Robert, bird's-nest hair and all, smiling with family by the Christmas tree, tuxedoed up and smiling with a so-so girl at the prom, bobbing in a life vest next to water skis, smiling and giving the thumbs-up.

There were pictures of Robert/Elliott in fatigues. Grinning from a long cafeteria table with other soldiers. Hamming it up at the karaoke mike with more soldiers as backup. Surrounded by palm trees in front of a sign that said "Fort Jackson."

Tucked in the back of the shelf, under a dog-eared and well-worn copy of "S'wanee Places," was a black three-ring notebook labeled "Elliott" on the top and "Must Not Leave Locker" on the bottom.

Inside was a dossier of "Elliott's" biographical information, some highlighted in yellow, some circled and starred in red. There was a "Mission" page with "Need to Know" across the top. There was a daily work schedule, with "Downtime" 19:00–22:00 weekdays and 15:00–17:00 Saturdays. "Mandatory Mission Update" meetings every Saturday at 12:00 with "Drills" right after and optional ones every morning. There was a scheduled "Shore Leave" in late October and a two-week Christmas break.

There was little else under "Need to Know," except "Protect Your Cover" on the bottom of the page. There was a "Classified" watermark.

Under "Test Subject" was a color photo of Cody from his Facebook page, right above his own daily class and work schedule, including locations. His hair looked redder than it really was, he thought.

The back page was a long, dense "Mission Consent" form, signed and dated by Robert.

The mission ended today.

Cody gripped the banister as he crept up the basement stairs. He listened at the door as the dinner crowd slowly migrated out the back. "When's your flight tomorrow?" someone said, and someone else said, "They should at least throw us a party."

They were all soldiers, assigned to a secret mission with very little "Need to Know." They were props, undercover extras with random code names. Blindly following orders, military-style.

"We gotta stay in touch," someone said. "I'll Facebook you when they let us," someone else said.

Cody snuck toward the foyer stairs, increasingly wobbly. He passed the framed photos in the hall. A black-and-white of the 1971 Rebel's Rest section, all smiles with the names below. There was the athletic Olympian John Crownover; the very dapper Appy Apperson. Pearl, young and thin, beamed from the side.

"Do you still have my Club Monaco blouse?" one girl asked another, who answered, "I totally forgot about that. Yes, it's *drib reflooben suitcase ankrakglob…*"

In the photo was an Arthur, an Elliott, very different boys with the same names. There was a Caleb, a Paxton, a Bishop, a Sinkler.

There was an Emerson and a Huger. There was a girl named Skit and a Vail and a Houston.

There was an Asian girl named Cynthia.

"Arn klak merofisso binflockel..."

The grandfather clock struck eight p.m.

He had to get out of here.

• • •

He would leave everything behind. He only needed his ID (his *real* one), his cash (thank you, *thank you*, Mom), the clothes on his back. He'd take his new student kit as evidence, including "The S'wanee Call" DVD. On it, he knew, were background glimpses of his "friends," including Beth, which was why she looked so familiar at first. Props, extras, liars all.

He'd take his iPhone, even though it was busted, and he definitely needed his laptop, which still worked fine. He'd send his mother an e-mail so she could call the cops in the *next* town to come rescue him, after he somehow snuck past Proctor Bob's men. There had to be more than one way out.

His hand went into spasms, and he rubbed it. *Calm down, Cody.*

He grabbed his new tweed jacket. He'd need it for warmth. He needed his wool knit cap, too, because his hair was still wet.

Why was his hair wet?

He looked in the mirror at his wet hair and red cashmere sweater.

Hadn't he been wearing his green one?

When did he take a shower? When did he change clothes?

Why did he do either?

Downstairs, the grandfather clock struck the hour.

It had just struck the hour a few minutes ago, before he came upstairs. What was wrong with the damn clock?

He checked his gold Seiko. Eleven p.m. When he'd come upstairs moments ago, it had been eight p.m. Hadn't it?

The log cabin was silent.

His green sweater was wadded on the floor. Ripped down the front.

Next to it, on top of his orange backpack, was a kitchen knife. A big, chopping knife. A Wusthof.

Pearl's missing Wusthof. The blade was red and wet and gleaming.

He checked the time on his laptop. His watch was right.

Ross's thesis proposal was still on the screen. Against his will, Cody clicked on the link at the bottom, and his Troller remembered the password to the secret page with the grid of twelve QuickTime screens. They were no longer numbered; they were named.

He clicked on "Caleb," which showed a nighttime surveillance view of a tall, blond, athletic runner with fluorescent safety armbands catching his breath on the edge of Morgan's Steep. Up behind him came a fellow runner, skinnier, with red hair and "Guns N' Roses" on the back of his T-shirt. Cody hit the stop button.

"Vail"—a girl overlooked the Quad from high atop the Observatory balcony. A scrawny kid in a sweater and khakis talked to her and comforted her. Cody hit stop.

"Skit"—by the Burwell Fountain, a visibly drunk girl approached by a tall, thin boy with an orange backpack. From his clutched right hand flashed the blade of a large kitchen knife. Stop. "Bishop." "Emerson." "Sin." "Houston." In Manigault Park. In Abbo's Alley. In a cabin. By the fire circle. All partially shrouded in fog. Stop. Stop. Stop. Stop.

"Elliott"—in his bedroom.

"Unknown"—a glowing, night-vision view. A twin bed. A naked girl with short dark hair thrashing. A naked boy trying to calm her, his hands around her neck. Stop.

"Banjo"—in his bedroom, packing, turning to his door. His cocky smile melting away. Time-stamped 10:42 p.m.

"Pearl"—slowly ascending the stairs in her floral bathrobe, calling up. 10:49 p.m.

Stop. Stop.

The last screen was still unnamed. Under construction.

Cody crept down the hallway. Banjo's door was ajar. It bumped against something on the floor, and a large pool of blood spread wider. Cody turned and left.

There was a black, globe-style wig at the top of the stairs. Toward the bottom, facedown/face-first, sprawled a large black woman, red stains saturating the floral patterns, still breathing sporadically. One hand clutched and unclutched the bottom rail.

"Just let it play out," Ross told the pair of Blue Scrubs at the bottom, standing clear of the seeping blood that pumped from her neck. "Otherwise it might not count."

"I'm sorry, Pearl," he said tenderly, touching her short, wiry hair, but she couldn't hear through her rasps and clutch/unclutch.

The floor creaked. Ross looked up.

"Oh, *hey*, Tiger!" He smiled brightly.

Cody turned and ran.

"Hey! It's *okay*, buddy!"

Cody ran to his room and pulled his chest of drawers to barricade the door.

He opened his window and slid down the snow-covered overhang. He climbed down the thick, bloomless wisteria vines and dropped to the ground on all fours, in front of Ross's black Jeep. The license plate said "US Government" across the top and "For Official Use Only" across the bottom.

"Dude, just *chill* for a sec!" Ross raced out the front door.

Cody ran.

Past the white delivery van parked out front, over the split-rail fence onto vast Abbo's Alley, sprinting through the snow toward the dense tree line at the edge leading to the dark wilderness beyond.

Ross followed in his Jeep, high beams focused and gaining as Cody zigzagged across the field. Cody darted through the trees at the edge, and the Jeep slammed the brakes and skidded across the snow and hit a towering oak.

Cody hid in the forest, shadowy-bright in the moonlight.

"Cody, listen to me," Ross, unharmed, called out, beaming his flashlight as he inched tree to tree. "You're not in danger. And you're not in trouble. You've done nothing wrong."

Cody stood still and silent, peering behind a broad trunk.

"No one is going to hurt you, dude," Ross continued. "Quite the opposite, actually." The flashlight beam scanned closer, searching.

In the snow-reflected moonlight, with the flashlight hitting his stressed-out face from below, Ross was much too old for a student. He was a researcher. A white coat. He was too old to be calling Cody "dude."

The beam got closer, and Cody took one silent step backward and tripped over a thick fallen branch. The beam found him.

"Cody, once we explain, you'll get it. You'll get it all," Ross said, moving to him. "But you can't run away, dude. Really, there's just nowhere to run up here."

Cody stood up, squinting. The beam squarely in his face.

"Please make this easy on yourself, on all of us," the beam pleaded as it got nearer and brighter. "Please come back with me now, Cody."

Cody swung the heavy branch and shattered Ross's skull with a crack-crunch. Ross fell silently backward, and Cody brought the branch down on him again, two-three-four crack-crunches. Ross lay still, his faceless red pulp steaming into the night air, spilling out onto the white snow.

Ecce Quam Bonum.

S'wanee security cars sped in all directions on the campus streets. Cody would have to escape through the wilderness. He turned back to the darkness and faced dozens of flashlight beams moving toward him from the black abyss.

"I see him!" one of the beams called out. The other beams followed and found him.

Cody ran.

Ross's Jeep was smashed and useless. Security cars blocked University Avenue at the far end near Fowler Sport and Fitness Center. Men in uniform held their post.

Cody tore across the Quad, past the evergreen and Shapard Tower, toward Spencer Hall (sciences), Gailor Hall (sciences), Snowden Hall (sciences), targeting the far side of campus where he would regroup, rethink, replan. Klieg lights burst atop every building, flooding the Domain with daylight.

"Cody!" Huger yelled, running toward him from bright Manigault Park. Archer and Buzz raced from the back of McClurg. Dozens of other soldiers closed in from all sides.

"Cut him off!"

"Cody!"

Cody pivoted and sprinted toward the main security gate. He would climb it. It could electrocute him, or they could shoot him. But if he slowed down, if he stopped, if he gave up…

"Cody, STOP!"

Instinctively, Cody stopped running and turned.

It was Marcie. It was his mother.

Chapter Four

"Mom!" he yelled, grabbing her arm. "Where's your car? *Hurry*!"

"I don't have a car, kiddo," she answered. "A nice man drove me from the airport."

"We gotta get out of here! *Now!*"

"But I just got here, Cody."

They were standing by Cravens Hall. No one was chasing him anymore.

"Cody, what's the matter?" She took his face in her hands. "You look terrified."

It was quiet again.

"Why…are you here, Mom?"

"I've come to take you home," she answered. "They asked me to come get you."

She looked immaculate in her long black coat with fur collar. It was new.

"Aren't you ready to come home, kiddo?" she added.

Proctor Bob and his men stood behind her. One held a Taser.

"Mom, they're going to kill us," he said quietly.

"Oh no, Cody. No no no," she shushed him. "Oh, Cody, is that what you think? Oh, kiddo…" She grimaced and shook her head. "I should never have let you come."

"Do you need us, ma'am?" Proctor Bob asked, stepping closer. "We're right here. Just let us know."

"*Get away from her!*" Cody yelled.

"Now, now, Cody." Dean Apperson came across the frozen lawn, tweedy and calm. "Welcome, Ms. Marko. I daresay you arrived at the right time."

"He's terrified, Mr. Apperson," Marcie accused. "What have you done to him?"

"He's just shaken up," Apperson said, smiling. "Like I warned you.

"He thinks things are happening that are not, indeed, happening at all," he added simply.

"Mom, don't believe him! Whatever he says, *don't believe him*!"

"Cody, Cody, Cody," Dean Apperson repeated hypnotically as he got closer. "There's no trouble, Cody. There's no trouble at all."

Marcie stroked his hair. "There's no trouble, Cody. We're leaving first thing in the morning."

"*Now*," Cody insisted. "We're leaving *now*."

"We can't leave now, honey," Marcie said. "It's the middle of the night."

"Let's go inside; why not?" Apperson said. "There's blackberry cobbler inside. Pearl made extra."

"I'm not going in there!" Cody screamed.

"I don't like this, Mr. Apperson," Marcie scolded. "I didn't expect this."

"Cody, where are you going to go, this late at night?" Apperson chided gently, ignoring her. "Where are you going to go?"

Proctor Bob's crew stood at the ready. Dean Apperson flicked his hand to wave them back.

"It's okay, Cody," Marcie said, rubbing his arm. "We're okay, kiddo."

"It's awfully cold out here, don't you think?" Apperson beckoned. "Cody, come in from the cold."

• • •

They were going to kill them both, Cody and his mother.

The experiment was over. They were done with him. They had lured Marcie to the Mountain to "take him home." They'd just dispose of her, but Cody's brain had empirical value. They'd slice and press it between glass, probably next to Nesta's. And nobody would know, nobody even knew about this place, except his grandmother, useless in Bulgaria.

S'wanee had done its homework.

It was a terminal experiment. It didn't stop when the test subject begged and pleaded. It stayed on its own schedule.

It was 11:45 p.m.

"Do you mind if I smoke?" Marcie asked.

"Not at all," Apperson said, signaling for an ashtray. "Not so long ago, I would have joined you."

They were sitting at the dining room table. A final, pleasant visit.

"We've put you in the Arcadian Suite for the night," Apperson said. "For our most special guests. I trust you'll find it satisfactory."

"That's very kind," Marcie said. "You've a beautiful home."

Marcie smiled and sipped white wine from a cut-crystal goblet. She was comfortable now, impressed by the lavish Cravens Hall. Marcie was easily impressed.

Don't get too comfortable, Mom.

"Palo Alto is one of my favorite towns," Apperson told her. "I've spent many weeks there over the years. Such a charming community."

Why the charade? Why not just kill them outside and avoid the mess?

A white-coated servant put blackberry cobbler with vanilla ice cream in front of Cody, who stared at it. Marcie unfolded his napkin and put it in his lap. "I *did* teach him manners, you know," she assured Apperson. Spread across the table was a white plastic cloth.

Did they think Cody had an appetite right now?

"Is Chez Zucca still open?" Apperson asked. "I've never had better paella."

Marcie shrugged and giggled and leaned closer to Apperson as he talked.

"I killed them," Cody said.

And he had. A double-blind research experiment, to eliminate bias. He was the treatment, they were the control, in a carefully crafted "down-low" environment. In his arm lived the microchip "vaccine," to track and isolate him. To tap into him.

His "classmates," these hand-picked military recruits, followed orders blindly, per their training. But their "Need to Know" was a fraction of everything Cody now knew.

They knew their false identities. They knew Cody was the Outsider. But their narrow mission didn't include the testing, the experiments, the hijacking. They didn't know twelve of them were doomed.

The Fallen Flock.

He had killed his friends, his "family," his hall mates.

His study partner and his housemother.

He had killed the only girl he'd ever love. But she hadn't loved him, had she? Not enough, at least. She'd dabbled and stepped out of bounds with him, maybe love, maybe curiosity, but she hadn't broken the rules and told him the truth. She'd protected her cover.

He'd killed twelve—against his will, without his knowledge. He remembered none.

But Ross wasn't part of the experiment. Ross was an aberration, a bonus. Cody did that purposefully, with a clear head. That was his favorite. But it didn't count.

Cody recounted and came up with eleven.

"I killed all of them," Cody repeated and started to list them.

"*No*, Cody," Apperson said firmly, and then said to Marcie, "See, this is what I was talking about…"

Nice try, dude. We're way past that now.

"Cody, please stop saying that," Marcie said, and then turned to Apperson. "Is there a way to make him stop?"

Dean Apperson rang his little bell.

"Ask Ross to bring Pearl and Banjo over, would you?" he told the servant.

"And what's the girl's name?" Apperson added. "The girl you like?"

"Beth," Cody said.

"Tell Ross to bring Beth, as well," Apperson told the servant.

"I killed Ross," Cody said.

"Kiddo, kiddo," Marcie *tsk*ed, shaking her head.

"You did?" Apperson asked, slightly alarmed. "When?"

"Just now," Cody said.

Apperson thought for a moment and then said, "Have some-one else bring them, please." The servant went to the door.

"I'll speak to Rutgers," Apperson said to Marcie. "I'm sure they'll welcome him back in the fall.

"I can also recommend specialists in New Jersey, the best in their field, to put him back on an even keel between now and then," he continued. "We'll cover the cost, of course."

"Thank you, Mr. Apperson." Marcie exhaled. "I knew you were a man of your word."

What were they talking about? Apperson wouldn't let him go back to Jersey. Cody knew too much. He could expose their crimes.

But they could expose his, too, couldn't they? After all, he was the killer. But S'wanee *made* him do it. They experimented on him without his consent.

Except he gave consent. At the Signing Ceremony. The long, rambling contract they'd whisked away for safekeeping until he turned eighteen.

S'wanee had done its homework.

"Marcie, let me refill your glass," Apperson said, pulling the bottle from the ice bucket.

"This is an *exceptional* wine," Marcie cooed. "Where did you find it?"

But when they started the experiment, Cody was a minor. He *couldn't* give consent.

Apperson said something witty, and Marcie giggled and reached over to touch his hand. She patted his hand.

"It's so nice to put a face with the voice," she said.

Marcie gave consent.

His mother had sold him.

The new house. BMW. Vegas trips. The money she sent him, out of guilt.

S'wanee had recruited, and then rejected him, because Marcie was a fierce negotiator and set the price too high. They'd called her bluff, and she'd backed down and struck a deal.

She marked him down.

His own mother had signed a contract and enrolled him in a scientific experiment. She'd had doubts and second thoughts; she'd been conflicted at times, but she'd signed him up and let them toy with his brain, control his behavior, kill his friends and loved ones. She lied to him day after day after day.

His mother who hadn't called her son on his eighteenth birthday.

Even if S'wanee hadn't told her the whole truth, the horrific extent of the experiment, she'd still farmed him out. She'd handed him over to strangers for money.

No wonder she could barely look at him now. At least she had an ounce of shame in her sick, sinister mind. Or maybe she was too busy flirting with Apperson, impressed with Cravens Hall.

His mother was a whore.

Around her neck lay a new gold necklace. Paid for by the selling of her son.

His mother was a monster.

Dean Apperson looked from Marcie to Cody and smiled slightly. His blue eyes twinkled.

His mother, this *bitch*, had been making money off him his whole life, even as a baby when she sold him to Macy's. Now she'd rented him to S'wanee for experimental testing. "You don't worry about what others think of you, and you don't look back," she'd told him. "That's how you make your fortune here." The only reason she'd had him in the first place was to stay in the US. She'd been using him even before he was born.

She'd probably smoked while pregnant, too. Greedy, self-centered bitch.

And she wanted to take him back? After what she'd done to him?

Did she think he was so stupid that he would ever, *ever* trust her again?

He would never go back to Jersey. He wouldn't cross the street with this lying bitch.

S'wanee was his home. He belonged here.

"It was a lovely drive up here," Marcie said, wanding her cigarette. "I'm sure it's even prettier in the daylight."

Shut up, bitch.

The servant went to the door. But Pearl and Banjo and Beth weren't there, because they were dead. The servant brought more sherry for Apperson.

Marcie sipped from her cut-crystal glass. Cody could smash the glass and slit her throat, right at the gold necklace.

Dean Apperson looked at him, smiling, twinkling.

It was 11:53 p.m.

The experiment wasn't over.

Cody knew what they were doing and why they were here, with sherry and wine and cobbler that no one touched. Marcie, the queen bee, was oblivious—giggly and slurry, almost *anesthetized.*

Marcie knocked her glass over. "'Pologize," she giggled, flexing her fingers. "Silly me." The servant brought her a new one and mopped up the spill, which was easy on the white plastic.

And Ross—no, not Ross, he was dead—Ross's *replacement* was somewhere typing and typing.

Cody killed eleven. The experiment needed twelve.

You don't have to go, Dean Apperson said, without talking. *We'll let you stay.*

The servant went to the door. He brought a coffee tray with spoons.

On the mantel, near the ticking clock, sat a small, wired camera, aimed at the dining table. Not hidden, just sitting there, makeshift. In plain sight.

The paintings were gone off the wall. The Persian rug had been removed, the floor bare under the dining table with the white plastic cloth.

You can stay here forever, Cody. On the Domain.

The servant placed a steak knife next to Cody. But he wasn't having steak; he was having cobbler. And it wasn't a steak knife; it was a kitchen knife. A big chopping knife.

It was a Wusthof. Clean and sharp.

"I'd love to stay few days, see the place," Marcie slurred at Apperson. "Pictures make it look so reflabben." Her smoke was disgusting. It made Cody sick.

This is your home, Cody. You belong here.

Cody clutched and unclutched the knife handle. It felt good in his hand, like it was part of him.

Cody spun the knife like a top, like a toy. He spun it again. It was fun.

Cody clutched the knife.

Your mother sold you, Cody. You can never trust her again.

"Schwizzel macglomen," his mother said numbly. *"Ach keinbennegen."*

Your mother hates you, Cody.

Dean Apperson looked at Cody and nodded slowly.

He'd watch this one live. Ringside.

Cody looked at the gold necklace around his mother's neck.

He wouldn't remember anyway.

The clock inched to 11:56. Dean Apperson nodded to the servant.

The servant went to the door. But this time, he didn't open it.

This time, using a key, he locked it.

Spring

Epilogue

A banner hung high across the Quad. "Welcome Home! Yea, S'wanee's Right!"

Magnolias and dogwoods burst with color. The thick air was hot and fragrant. Lush, emerald lawns freshly mowed.

There were dozens of round tables with purple tablecloths, bordered by a lavish lunch buffet and an open bar. A few hundred alums, nattily dressed and wearing name tags, milled about and shook hands and slapped backs. The men, those who still had hair, were mostly gray. The women were half and half. Jazz alternated with Creedence Clearwater Revival from standing speakers.

Most brought spouses, first or second or the occasional third. Some brought grown children to see the campus in full bloom. A few showed off infant grandchildren in purple jumpsuits from the Klondyke.

"That was my dorm," a man pointed out to his much younger wife.

"The whole place is magic," the young wife said. "Who stays there now?"

"Visiting Fellows, I'm sure. The dorms are usually full. They have the original housemothers, the ones still alive."

A few brought their gowns, mostly draped across the white folding chairs, because of the heat. Three men braved their old kilts and were admired for the effort.

"Have you seen the new building?" one alum asked another. "They did a tremendous job blending it in with the rest of the campus."

"I tried to go inside. It's locked."

"*Everything's* locked."

"All Saints is open."

"So is DuPont. I almost didn't recognize the Widow Senex."

They fought the adolescent urge to mimic her wonk eye, because they were old and distinguished now.

"I heard Fletcher died."

"A good man. A good life."

"Pearl passed away, too, you know."

"Too young. Too young."

"We used to play Frisbee right here on the Quad," a man told his son, who, having heard it all before, yawned and nodded.

"I don't remember this tree," he mused, and asked another alum, "Has it always been here?"

The reunion was both festive and melancholy.

"Me? I'm just having a great S'wanee Day! How the hell are *you* doing?"

"It's a pity, isn't it?" said a man watching his toddler granddaughter delight in the excitement on the Quad. "What's a pity?" his wife asked and then patted his arm. "Oh, Martin, there are *plenty* of other schools for her."

"It looks the same. Nothing has changed."

"Why tamper with perfection?"

"Hello, Appy."

Ivan Apperson turned from a cluster and smiled. "Good afternoon, John. Welcome back."

"It's kind of you to allow us back," the tall, still-athletic man said. "For one day."

"I trust all is well in New York?" Apperson asked. "Magazines have hit a bit of a rough patch, have they not?"

"Good seeing you, Crownover." A passing man patted his back. "You, too, Appy." They responded.

"Reunions get smaller every year," Crownover said.

"Well, that's basic biology, John. Biology and math."

"I wanted to show my wife your beautiful new building. But it's locked."

"Yes."

"Can you open it for us?" Crownover asked.

"Unfortunately, we're not a museum," Apperson said. "We're an active, ongoing concern."

"We still want to do an article on your active, ongoing concern. Your various projects here."

"Yes, I know," Apperson said.

"Taxpayers have a right to that information, don't you think?" Crownover asked. "Especially the DARPA projects? In the building we paid for?"

"We have plenty of private, nonmilitary contracts," Apperson said, smiling. "We're remarkably self-sustaining."

"But the Pentagon's been your main client from the first day," Crownover said. "As we both know."

"Ladies and gentlemen, we're taking section photos!" a professional photographer called from his tripod on the Quad. "We'll start with the Hoffman section. Can all classes from Hoffman assemble under the banner, please?"

"At least it would be interesting to know if your projects are legal," Crownover continued. "Especially given your personal history, Ivan."

"John, I know you do the Lord's work, up there in your glass tower," Apperson said, "scrounging for tidbits to humiliate your country. That's your life's path. I chose my own.

"But strictly off the record, without specifics," Apperson went on, "we will soon deliver a weapon that can destroy any army, any terror cell, any enemy at all, without risking a single life of our own. The penultimate asymmetrical warfare."

"Can you stand closer together?" the photographer compact-motioned the group across the lawn. "Scrunch up some, so I can fit you all in?"

"Now, I'll wager," Apperson continued, not smiling, "these taxpayers you claim to speak for would approve of my achievements. But if you expect me to divulge our secrets, our tactics, for a *scoop* you can share with the enemy…" He shook his head. "Well, John, perhaps you've been in New York a little too long. You should get out more."

"Yea, S'wanee's Right!" the group yelled as the photographer snapped away.

"Perhaps we'll follow our own leads," Crownover said. "And write about it anyway."

"Well, we can't stop you." Apperson laughed quietly, patting him on the back. "Until we do."

"Tuckaway section! Tuckaway to the Quad, please!"

"Say," Crownover turned. "I received an unusual call a few months ago. From someone claiming to be a student here. A freshman."

"Oh?" Apperson said.

"He described a very interesting research project."

"We have many of those," Apperson said. "But we don't have any students. As we both know."

"Cody Marko. Ring a bell?"

"I don't think so."

"He knew quite a bit. And sounded frantic. Terrified, actually."

"What he sounds like," Apperson said, "is a phony and a fraud who got your goat, John."

"So you don't know him?" Crownover pressed.

"We have thousands of employees," Apperson said. "I can't name them all."

"Rebel's Rest! Rebel's Rest to the Quad, please!"

"After you," Apperson offered. Crownover went ahead.

The photographer mopped sweat from his forehead as the crowd organized themselves.

"Lemonade, sir?"

The photographer turned to a tall young man in a navy blazer, purple tie, and khakis cinched about his waist.

"Thank you," he said, taking the glass. "I didn't expect it to be so hot up here."

"If I might suggest, sir," the young man said, "if you widen the angle some, you'll catch the hydrangeas on either side. They're blooming again."

The photographer looked at the young man with copper-colored hair and said, "That's a good idea, actually."

And then he said, "Are you related to someone here? Someone's son?"

"I work here," the young man said. "For the institute. The S'wanee Institute."

"Lucky you," the photographer said. "It's really quite beautiful up here."

"Yes, it is, sir." The young man smiled. "It's the greatest place in the world."

"Yea, S'wanee's Right!" a sea of gray hair cheered under the banner. Oxfords and khakis, florals and hair bands. The smiles came easily. They were happy to be home again.

The photographer framed the shot to catch the hydrangeas, some pink, some blue.

Acknowledgments

In addition to my parents, who were good-natured research assistants, I'd like to thank the following friends and family for looking over early drafts and offering constructive feedback: Beth Broderick, Debra Fish, Warren Frazier, Wyck Godfrey, Stacey and Rob Goergen, Pete Harris, Mary Kerr, Daniel King, Jacqueline Mazarella, Owen Moogan, Akiko Morison, David Reno, Jennifer Simpson, Dallas Sonnier, Chris Ward, and Chad Zimmerman. I apologize for any omissions.

Hats off to the gracious staff and students of Sewanee, the University of the South. I hope they will welcome me back someday.

Penina Lopez, my copy editor, taught me things I didn't even know I didn't know. That doesn't happen often.

Stewart Williams, my cover designer, had many wonderful ideas. I wanted to use them all. Maybe I will.

Special thanks to Ryan Rayston. I feel lucky to call her a friend.

This story would not be in your hands without the steady efforts of my book agent, the elegant and insightful Helen Breitwieser. I can't thank her enough.

About the Author

DON WINSTON grew up in Nashville and currently lives in Los Angeles.

Don Winston on Facebook

DonWinstonLA on Twitter

Don Winston on Tumblr

Don Winston on Pinterest

A first look at Don Winston's upcoming paranoid thriller "The Union Club."

College sweethearts Claire and Clay Willing are determined to start their married life independent of his rich and powerful west coast family. But the tragic murder of Clay's older brother, coupled with his own stalled career, suddenly lures them to San Francisco and into the clutches of the Willing political dynasty.

Clay's parents welcome Claire with open arms and ensconce her in their exclusive private club atop Nob Hill, where she mingles with the eccentric Bay Area elite and struggles to maintain her identity in the all-controlling Willing clan.

But her in-laws are the least of Claire's worries as she unravels the freakish mystery of their son's assassination and uncovers the shocking reason they were brought back into the fold. With no way out alive.

The Union Club. Where evil has its privileges.

November 2

Congressman-elect Dean Willing was dead before he reached the podium.

It felt different than he expected. The whole night had. He'd had plenty of time to prepare, since San Francisco was a one-party town, and his election was assured after the primary, which was also assured.

But it was difficult to prepare adequately for the moment of one's death.

Up in the Presidential Suite, where they awaited his opponent's concession, his mother had quibbled with his wife over the tie. It would be reddish, of course, but while his wife preferred the Ferragamo, his mother insisted on the less pretentious Brooks Brothers she'd bought the day before. His mother usually--and with acquired restraint--deferred to his wife, but tonight was different, because it was his Big Day and Last Night, and his mother would have the Final Say.

His wife came into the master bedroom where he dressed and flung the Brooks Brothers at him. "It's not even Golden Fleece."

In the living room, his father worked the phone wired to the wall. He wasn't checking returns, which were irrelevant, but the timing. His opponent would concede at 8:43 in the Governor's Ballroom of the four-star St. Francis on the rim of Union Square.

At 9:06 PM, he would walk onstage of the Grand Ballroom at the Fairmont on top of Nob Hill. Both rooms would be full, but the actual numbers would not be comparable.

His father hung up. “We’re on the move!”

His mother in simple navy straightened his straight tie and smoothed his smooth hair. She held his face but didn’t look him in the eye and said, “My handsome boy,” and the local reporter on TV recapped his military service and business resume for the viewers. The camera held steady on the ballroom podium, and to vamp, the reporter ran an interview she had done earlier in the day with his wife.

“Let’s do this.” His wife breezed past in her pink Chanel suit, and they followed his father into the hallway where two aides in suits and earpieces stood ready.

They rode down the service elevator in silence.

The ballroom was loud and festive, and backstage was still and quiet, and at 8:58, his parents walked on stage to cheers. His father spoke and then signaled to his mother, who resisted, and then relented, and the crowd cheered louder as she stepped up. She strained to reach the mike and growled at her husband, and the crowd laughed at her sassy pique they knew and loved.

Backstage, he felt a sudden jolt of stage fright. He took his wife’s hand at the end of her pink sleeve, and she yanked it away reflexively before collecting herself and cupping his with both of hers. She patted it in apology.

His father was back at the podium, winding the crowd up tighter, and as the teleprompter scrolled its final line, the room erupted, and it was time. An aide tapped him on the shoulder. His wife led him into the light.

Unlike the movies, you would never mistake the sound for the popping of a balloon. He went down immediately and after a confused hush heard the panic swell and spread. He felt his wife kneel next to him, and then collapse on top of him, and the ballroom got louder and more bothered.

The networks, which weren't covering this nonevent on such a busy night, would break in to cover it now. There would be live updates, and soon a hastily put-together memorial package, and possibly even an official investigation, although, from the sounds of returning gunfire, his assassin was unlikely to be of much intel use soon. Police and ambulances were most certainly already screaming up Nob Hill.

But now it was quieter, and it really didn't hurt much at all, and his wife was still but breathing. He listened to the music from the speakers and watched the white moldings darken around the ceiling. It felt too soon. He was not yet 30.

Phase One

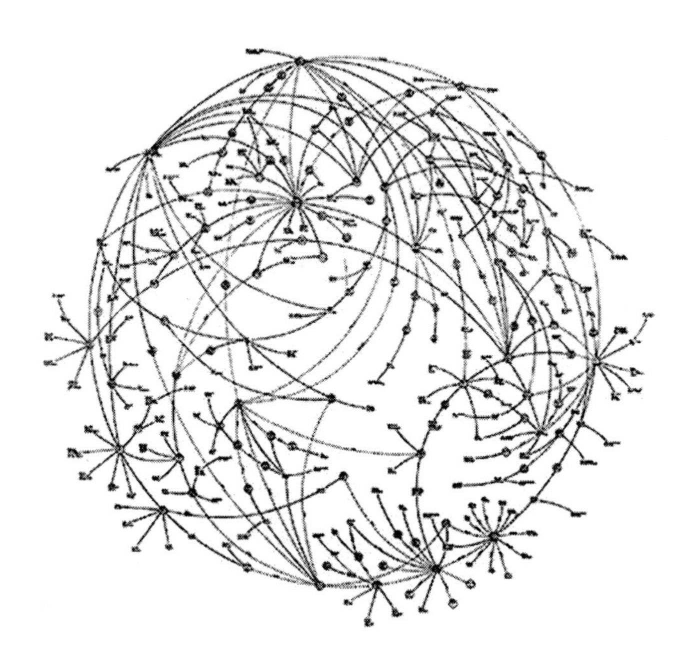

Chapter One

"Bring the left corner down an inch." Claire Willing directed her husband Clay, both twenty-six. "A little more. That's better. I think."

"Best is out back in the dumpster," Clay in paint-marked overalls said as he surveyed the enormous, maybe-straight canvas. "Nonsense," Claire said. "Never." It was a perfectly proficient sunset and fit just right over their raw hide sofa. Even cockeyed.

"It makes the room," she insisted, tilting up at the 20-ft high loft ceiling. Plus, she'd spent hours packing and unpacking it for the move along with the rest of his landscapes. There was plenty of wall here for all of them. Even the orangish adobe which was not her favorite, being a bit too on-the-nose, although she'd never admit that, because it was one of Clay's first. Fortunately, it was small and would fit best in their bedroom. "Between the windows!"

Claire and Clay had arrived earlier in the day in his 1983 purple Mustang. Amazingly, it survived the trip from Santa Fe, thanks in part to her insistence on a last-minute full tune-up, as the heretofore undiagnosed leaky radiator would have stranded them in the desert. Claire had quickly unloaded her hybrid Accord on a fellow teacher, but Clay refused to leave his shiny toy behind, in spite of California's out-of-state car penalties. It was wholly unsuitable for their new city life, and he promised to park it at his parents' once they settled in. In her mind, Claire had already circled a blue/grey Ford Escape that would fit in the single parking space that came with their lease. "No minivans!" Clay had decreed to Claire's taunting giggles.

A Grand Canyon detour added a day to their journey—neither had seen it before—and Clay insisted on a "soul-cleansing" pit stop at Joshua Tree, another half day's out-of-the-way adventure. He seemed in little hurry to get to San Francisco, and Claire didn't mind their leisurely pace, after the rather frantic rush of their packing. Clay's relocation allowance afforded full-service pros, although she'd spent an exhausting week editing—3 1/2 years' worth!—before they arrived. Nonetheless, her visit to the Hearst Castle would have to wait, since the movers were right on schedule, and the still-under-renovation Townsend Lofts lacked the proper staff to let them in.

"Where you want your Hitler Youth?" Clay held up Claire's homeroom class photos—rows of seated children, mostly brown, in white polos and navy pants or skirts, Claire proudly to the left. Clay's stale joke aside, Hitler would have approved the uniforms; the brown wearers, not so much. She herself had long been conflicted about public school uniform policy, especially at that young age. San Francisco, she'd learned, had the same policy. They probably invented it.

Claire took another look at little detached Marisa on the front row and felt a prick of concern, then pushed it away. She'd make it to fourth grade on her own. Hopefully.

"Probably the upstairs hall," she said. "Just lean them against the wall for now."

The three-bedroom duplex apartment was freshly painted white, gallery-like, although they thankfully kept the exposed brick on the outward walls. She'd found it online and signed up from the slideshow alone, with Clay's bemused approval. In addition to the airy spaciousness, she liked the hardwood floors for their Navajo rugs, the Neutra-esque slat staircase, and the Miele/Viking/Silestone kitchen. The stainless Sub Zero still had its protective plastic film.

Most importantly, the SOMA Warehouse District—technically Mission Bay, if you looked closely at the map—was far removed from the Pacific Heights/Presidio Heights/Seacliffs of Clay's youth. It didn't feel so obviously like coming home.

The master bedroom looked out over the China Basin toward the Bay, cinematic in the early February gloom. The guest bedroom would double as Clay's studio, although it fronted Townsend and would provide less inspiration. The third bedroom sat empty, for now.

The whole place was offensively expensive—part of Claire's San Francisco acclimation. She considered downsizing to a cramped two-bedroom in the same building, or even the less-offensive Castro, but Clay vetoed both. "Stop pinching," he encouraged her.

They repositioned their Aztec cane chairs with green serape cushions three times before giving up. They didn't work anywhere. Neither did the pine and cowhide. At least the rugs fit, Claire tried to convince herself.

"Stop scowling!" Clay laughed, pulling her onto the cowhide, and Claire mock-pouted, "They look so *podunk* here." "My parents are renovating," Clay said. "We'll get their cast-offs."

"Oh Goody," Claire mocked on, and Clay retaliated with an octopus-tickle. "Stop! Stop!" Claire shrieked, fighting back. "*Careful*."

"Not now," she resisted when his hands stopped tickling and got serious. "She'll be here any minute." "For good luck," Clay pressed, quietly in her ear. "In our new home..."

The door bell rang.

"She hasn't lost her Sixth Sense," Clay growled, and Claire giggled, pushing him off.

• • •

"My God, you could dock the Space Shuttle in here," Martha announced instantly, before hugs—quick to Clay, tight to Claire. She put the chilled Veuve on the kitchen counter and paced, inspector-like. She wore blue scrubs and had dark circles and needed a root touchup. She'd put on weight. Medical residency was a shock to the system, and Martha was still adjusting. She smelled and sounded like she'd just had a cigarette.

"Lotta room for *two people*," she declared, making a point of peering upward and side-to-side. "You keeping the wigwam furniture?"

"It's southwestern," Claire said, relishing Martha's digs. Thank God she hadn't changed.

Martha sized up Claire's chambray shirt and turquoise necklace and said, "Well, Tigerlily, you could've sent up smoke signals. I cannot believe I had to read about Clay's new job in the *Chronicle*. Is that our new normal?"

Claire made hurried excuses/explanations—"It happened so quickly," "I was going to call earlier,"—while Clay's hospitality morphed into familiar tolerance. His and Martha's uneasy co-presence had held static since freshman year at Yale. She'd never quite excused him for snapping up her roommate so quickly.

Martha nodded—"Uh huh," "Yeah yeah OK," "Glad you got here safely,"—and commented on the neighborhood and then pivoted the conversation craftily. "You know, they tow on Townsend at four."

"Hurry!" Claire said, and Clay, *released*, said, "Gotta do a drugstore run anyway. Where's your list?" He pushed into his clogs and raced out.

"Pull that main door behind you!" Martha ordered. "I waltzed right in off the street." She turned back, unsmiling.

"What the Hell is going on here?"

• • •

Claire was cornered. Hoisted on her own petards.

Yes, she'd shrugged off Corporate America, even before it was fashionable, or necessary. *Guilty*—after the latest financial collapse, when GoldmanMorganCitiBankofAmerica descended on Yale to skim the best/brightest—of championing, quietly at first, then louder, a bolder, more socially responsible path. Not-for-profits, Peace Corps, volunteerism, even startups were preferable to being a tool—*gear*, really—in the Wall Street Brain-Drain Machine. She was hardly alone.

Teach for America sent her to Lansing for two years––"*Where?*" Clay had griped—after which they settled in Clay's choice (she preferred Jackson Hole but didn't push it). She taught, he painted, they made friends and stayed thrifty.

That was then.

"Dean's death changed a lot," Claire explained. "Well, everything." Abruptly. Clay talked to his parents in a flurry of calls, even went on a never-before-happened father/son getaway for a long, post-Christmas weekend, and came back to announce—and shock—that he was joining his father's firm.

Welcome to San Francisco.

"Welcome to the New World Order," Martha quipped.

And goodbye to her third graders, midyear. Devilish Teresa, Nose-Bleed Ernesto, and fingers-crossed-godspeed to Marisa, whose mother never did come to a parent-teacher meeting.

Claire didn't get to say goodbye, so jerked was her departure.

"You hear me?" Martha said. "Ignoring you," Claire said.

Martha's ribbing had started gently enough. Just email links to the Forbes 400 after Claire/Clay first met in college. Then, as they became inseparable, news articles about Clay's father on White House economic councils, international corporate boards, sightings to/fro the Council on Foreign Relations "headquarters" ("Yep. Holding the door for Kissinger. Yep, yep."). By the time they were very much in love, Martha's obsession with Mr. Willing had turned almost stalker-like: a Sun Valley Retreat ("Gates, Buffett, *Oprah.*"), The Bohemian Grove ("Camping with Cheney!"), and a super-secret—i.e. "shadowy"—conference called The Bilderberg Group ("God *knows* who else is there.") outside Bilbao, Spain. Martha had his annual itinerary down cold.

She crossed the line a bit, an ill-advised Hail Mary, as their marriage became inevitable. She'd discovered some crackpot New World Order conspiracy theorist—Claire forgot his no-name—on the internet who accused The Willings and their *ilk* of ruinous financial crimes, gross human rights violations, and a wild parade of horribles that would have been funny at a distance. But Claire was no longer at a distance.

Not that she was close to Clay's parents. They'd only met a couple times, back at Yale: Homecoming her sophomore year and then again at Graduation, both over dinner at Mory's. They never spent holidays together, much less vacations or quick visits. They weren't at the wedding. Claire herself didn't go—wasn't asked—to Dean's memorial, although she did send flowers and received a thank-you note, signed by both.

Clay's father, once a lowly gear, *had* amassed an unconscionable fortune on his way up to running The Machine. Such wealth in one lifetime rarely came clean. That he came from nothing—in *Texas*, of all places—only fueled his critics more. Without taking sides, Claire hoped they had the decency for a time-out with their barbs after the tragedy last November.

But she wouldn't know, since she and Clay lived a removed, independent life. Until now.

"That's a tricky family you're getting sucked into," Martha had warned for years, but she didn't today, because she'd been proved right. She refilled her own glass and let Claire convince herself.

"Clay was ready for a change," Claire said. "And I...have to support him. We're a team, you know?" Martha nodded.

"It *is* the first time his parents have paid much attention to him," she mused. "But that never bothered him before."

"At some point, we all grow up a little," Claire continued. Martha shrug-nodded.

"And let's face it," she said, "it's not like his art career was really taking off." Martha glanced about the walls without comment.

"Oh, shut up, Martha!"

Martha cackled.

"Relax, Bitch! I'm psyched you're here," she said. "Relieved, actually."

"And who am I to talk?" she added. "I wouldn't turn down Charles Manson at this point. You know, I joined the fucking DAR just for its Singles Night?"

"Don't transfer to Chicago," Claire begged. "I just got here. I *need* you."

"I've already dated the five straight men in this town," Martha said. "And I have doubts about two of them."

"Don't you have a blind date tonight?"

"If that were *literally* true, I might stand a chance." Martha inspected her bags in the microwave door. *Harumph.*

"Hey!" she said, turning back. "You two should join us!"

"Tonight?"

"Double-date," Martha insisted. "We're good like that."

"We have plans," Claire said.

"What? Where?"

"The Union Club," Claire said simply.

Martha collapsed to the floor, flailed with drama.

"Oh my God," she said, her eyes frozen upward. "You've already joined the Union Club."

"No no no...," Claire protested.

Martha sprang up. "You don't understand. *Nobody* gets in the Union. Half its *members* can't get in!"

"We're not members," Claire said. "Clay's parents are taking us."

"I see," Martha sucked her front teeth once. "In-law night. Is *that* why you're not drinking?"

Claire looked at her full champagne. Back at Martha. She took a breath and held it.

"Well..." she exhaled.

Martha squealed first.

• • •

"Let's wait, Clay. Please. It's too early."

"Relax. When did you get superstitious?"

"Can you slow down?" Claire said. "Or at least send a Sherpa to help me?"

The steep incline up Nob Hill was murder in her heels. Clay had offered to drop her off, but she didn't want to wait alone while he looked for a street spot. Apparently his muscle car wasn't suitable for the club's private lot. God save their cranky parking brake on the hill.

"We're late," Clay said, normally a non-concern. And normally Claire didn't change outfits three times, the root of their lateness. They were both a-wonk tonight.

"I just don't want a big deal until we're absolutely....Ack!"

Claire stood on one foot, her broken heel clinging by one nail.

"Clay, we have to go back. I have to change."

"They're waiting," he said.

"How am I going to explain this?" She hobbled up/down in a circle.

"Polio?" he suggested.

"That's not funny," Claire said, and Clay said, "Yes it is. And so are you."

The piggyback ride both embarrassed and relieved her. They'd been pecking at each other more the past couple weeks—rushed, disorienting weeks with Big Change on the other side. It had zapped their humor. Clay's gallumping carriage was playful and helpful, traits that typically came easy to him. Claire held on tight.

"Good evening," she nodded at an older couple heading into the Masonic Auditorium on the corner, for a touring performance of "Henry IV." They smiled and "Good evening"-ed back.

"You cool from here?" Clay asked at the summit, as the sidewalk leveled out.

Claire looked ahead.

"Good God," she said. "Is that it?" A pointless question.

The Union Club stood sentry on top of the hill, a Beaux Arts dark mansion on the border of a grassy space. It hugged the edge, away from the public playground, separated by an ornate, round, alive fountain. It was lit from within by dozens of windows, each glowing through shrouding sheers.

"Yes'm," Clay said, Dickens-like. "Where I spent much of me youth."

"Well, that explains a lot," she replied in earnest, instantly wishing she'd made it a quip.

Ringing the square stood taller residential buildings, a massive church, the familiar and very grand Fairmont Hotel, its bank of international flags snapping in unison above the porte-cochere.

The Union Club was the smallest building on Nob Hill, and it dwarfed the rest.

"Not yet," Claire said, still clinging. "Closer."

He waited for the cable car to clang past, tourists pressed against the far side, and carried her across California Street.

"You gonna sit on my lap during dinner, too?" he asked, and she said, "Just to the front door," and giddy-upped him. They passed the surrounding low stone wall with swirling, bronze railing—fishes or dragons or sea monsters, hard to tell at night. The stone wall matched the manor walls, which matched the portico, the window moldings, the roof railing, the two flanking wings, the four streaming chimneys—all reddish-brown, serious and stately. A lavish monolith.

Neoclassical, Claire recalled from her one architecture class in college. Palladian windows. The square columns either Doric or Ionic, she could never keep them straight. Definitely not the leafy Corinthian. There were neither sign, awning, nor welcome mat. Other than the light-shrouding windows, a burnished lantern above the portico cast the only glow, dim-watted at that. The mansion stood silent, hiding its life within. Or not.

"You sure it's open tonight?" she asked, as he mounted the reddish-brown stone stairs, two at a time. She looked up at the dark, silent door. "Is Lurch gonna answer?"

Clay unshouldered her, and she scanned the hedge lining the stairs. "What are you looking for?" he said. "Doesn't Cousin Itt hide in the bushes?" she asked.

"You're awfully breezy tonight," he joked. "Did Martha get you tipsy?" Claire tee-hee'd and opened the bronze mailbox and peered inside. "Why, good *evening*, Thing! Thank you for your kind invitation." She shook the imaginary hand.

"You rang?" a man asked from the front door. Claire shut the mailbox and stood upright on one foot.

"Allen!" Clay said, handshaking/shoulder-clasping the smiling man with doorman hat and doorman coat. "Welcome back, Clay," Allen said. "Your parents asked me to keep a lookout."

"A pleasure, Claire," he said, taking her hand, tipping his hat at their introduction. "I was joking about the Lurch thing," Claire apologized. "Not at all," he smiled. "I *have* felt a bit ooky today."

Claire laughed and clarified quickly, "And Clay was joking about the tipsy." Allen nodded, blank, and Claire added, "I'm totally sober." Allen, still blank, said, "That's good!"

"I don't think he heard me," Clay said *sotto voce*, and Claire said, "Oh!", and Allen held open the glass-windowed wooden door into the vestibule. "Let's get you inside, why not?"

A low, beeping alarm sounded as they crossed the threshold.

"We check our...cell phone?" Claire asked, when sent to the coat room just inside. A powerful black man outfitted like Allen, but without hat, sat behind the counter and smiled warmly, expecting her.

"The club discourages business." He nodded in agreement, almost in apology, at her confusion. He wore a wedding ring and had the kind, knowing face of a father. Claire wondered how many, how young, and how unfortunate their father worked night hours. "We'll take good care of it."

He took her coat and phone, both of which Clay had left at home. She held out her hand for the claim ticket, and when none came, she pulled back and wrapped her pashmina around her shoulder, an involuntary correction. The man grinned and placed her phone in a cubbyhole along the wall. "Safe and sound." he assured her. "Oh, I know," Claire said quickly. She nodded and turned to go and collapsed on her broken heel, catching on the counter.

"Sorry," she said, smiling, but freshly concerned. "That hill..." The man held out his own hand. "May I?"

He surgically superglued the heel with an at-the-ready tube and held it tight to set. "You aren't the first lady to limp in here," he chuckled. She strapped her shoe back on, and he added, "Just go easy until after dinner. Then tear up the dance floor."

"Claire honey," Clay called from the vestibule. "This evening?"

"Thank you," she said, glance-checking her savior's name tag, "Jess." She slid a folded five-dollar tip across the counter.

"My pleasure, Claire," Jess replied, politely sliding it back.

She turned and laughed. "How...do you know my name?" Jess laughed, too, and said, "Welcome to the Union."

Allen held open the door of solid oak. Claire and Clay walked through it.

CPSIA information can be obtained at www.ICGtesting.com
Printed in the USA
LVOW13s1328120713

342645LV00001B/14/P

9 780615 770574